Critical Acclaim for Ross E. Lockhart's

"The enduring allure of H. P. Lovecraft's (century old, is evident in this representati most of which were written in the last deca(
—*Publishers Weekly* (Starred Review)

"Gathering Cthulhu-inspired stories from both 20th and 21st-century authors, this collection provides such a huge scope of styles and takes on the mythology that there are sure to be a handful that surprise and inspire horror in even the most jaded reader."
—Josh Vogt, *Examiner.com*

"There are no weak stories here—every single one of the 27 entries is a potential standout reading experience. *The Book of Cthulhu* is nothing short of pure Lovecraftian gold. If fans of H. P. Lovecraft's Cthulhu mythos don't seek out and read this anthology, they're not really fans—it's that simple."
—Paul Goat Allen, *BN.com*

"*The Book of Cthulhu* is one hell of a tome."
—Brian Sammons, *HorrorWorld.org*

"…a stunning collection of Lovecraft inspired tales all centered around the infamous Cthulhu myth."
—Drake Llywelyn, *Dark Shadows Book Reviews*

"…thanks to the wide variety of contributing authors, as well as Lockhart's keen understanding of horror fiction and Lovecraft in particular, [*The Book of Cthulhu*] is the best of such anthologies out there."
—Alan Cranis, *Bookgasm.com*

"As he did for his previous anthology, Lockhart has cast his net far and wide to haul in outstanding stories from publications both well-known and obscure, none sampled more than once. He has also commissioned four new stories, several so good that they are likely to be selected for reprint anthologies in the future."
—Stefan Dziemianowicz, *Locus*

"The second volume of *The Book of Cthulhu* exemplifies the richness of Lovecraft's legacy: gloomy terror, mystery, thrills, vivid action, chilling visions, satire, science fiction, humor—all of that, and then some, is crammed into more than 400 pages awaiting readers eager for some apocalyptic horror."
—Dejan Ognjanovic, *Rue Morgue*

"…any fan of Lovecraft can't afford to miss out on this one."
—Justin Steele, *The Arkham Digest*

TALES OF
JACK THE
RIPPER

Other books by Ross E. Lockhart

Anthologies:

The Book of Cthulhu
The Book of Cthulhu II

Novels:

Chick Bassist

TALES OF

JACK THE RIPPER

EDITED BY
ROSS E. LOCKHART

WORD HORDE
PETALUMA, CA

Table of Contents

This volume is dedicated to…

Mary Ann Nichols
Annie Chapman
Elizabeth Stride
Catherine Eddowes
Mary Jane Kelly

…and others unknown.

Introduction

Ross E. Lockhart

You can say a lot of things about humans. One is certain: We are exceedingly good at killing one another.

So much so that one of our formative myths, the story of Cain and Abel, is one of fratricide—brother killing brother. The cycle repeats throughout history. Man kills man. Over power. Over property. Over money. Over gods. Over lovers.

And just as frequently, man kills woman.

What are we to make of brother killing sister?

Well, that's where Jack comes in.

The killer known as Jack the Ripper wasn't history's first murderer. He wasn't even history's first murderer of women. But in the canon of vicious killers populating humanity's collective nightmares, Jack the Ripper was the first rock star.

For Jack's crimes captured the public's attention in a way unlike any previous murderer. The public was rabid for news of the Whitechapel slayings, and the press was happy to oblige. In October 1888, just a few short weeks after the discovery of Jack's first victim, John Francis Brewer's *The Curse Upon Mitre Square,* the first novelization of the murders, appeared. Other books followed, as did short stories, plays, radio dramas, films, and television episodes (including one of my all-time favorite classic *Star Trek* episodes, Robert Bloch's "Wolf in the Fold").

Which begs the question: Why does a killer of women garner so much attention?

Because Jack the Ripper is a cipher. A mystery.

Jack the Ripper only killed five women—that we know of—Mary Ann Nichols, Annie Chapman, Elizabeth Stride, Catherine Eddowes, and Mary Jane Kelly. We know more about these victims than we do about their killer, including such details as how they lived, what they wore, even the contents of their pockets (a detail that formed the backbone of Alan M. Clark's excellent novel *Of Thimble and Threat*).

But we don't know jack about Jack, so he has become a quintessential boogyman.

Which leads us to wonder, to ponder, to imagine. Because we are narrative-driven creatures, we make up stories to fill in the blank spaces. And many of our greatest storytellers have added their own voices to the chorus recanting the tale of, and warning future generations about, Jack the Ripper. Marie Belloc Lowndes, Robert Bloch, Harlan Ellison, Patricia Cornwell, Roger Zelazny, Maureen Johnson, and Alan Moore are just a few of the master storytellers to have spilled ink in examination of Jack and his bloody craft.

This year, we arrive at the 125th anniversary of the Whitechapel Murders. Jack's quasquicentennial, if you will. In commemoration of this sanguine anniversary, I have asked an assembly of my favorite authors to share with you their own tales of Jack the Ripper: seventeen stories and two poems. Most are brand new, a handful are classics that you may have missed. All provide a unique glimpse at Jack the Ripper and his legacy, filtered through the authors' lives and locales, visions and voices. Some will horrify you, others will terrify you, still others will entertain and amuse. It's best you not know which is which going in.

So light a lamp and pour yourself a drink, then sit back in a comfortable chair and settle in for a good read. And I sincerely hope you enjoy these *Tales of Jack the Ripper*.

Whitechapel Autumn, 1888

Ann K. Schwader

No changing leaves lament the season here,
for nothing grows but woe in Mitre Square.
The belles of Ten Bells, numbed on gin & beer,
have small appreciation for this air
refreshed at last by dawn mists drifting cold
around the corners of St. Botolph's Church
where twilight draws the desperate & bold,
parading past on mankind's oldest search.

Yet summer dies in Buck's Row—not alone—
& Annie follows Polly down to dust
as cries of wholly simulated lust
are silenced by steel whispering on bone.
Their secret reaper rides a sharpened wind,
signing himself *your own light-hearted friend.*

A Host of Shadows

Alan M. Clark and Gary A. Braunbeck

"Every man has a host of shadows, all of which resemble him
and for the moment have an equal claim to authenticity."
—Kierkegaard

Jack the Ripper was dying.

How strange to think of himself that way after so many years.
But for that short period in 1888, he had always been Howard
Faber, celebrated academic physician, member of the American
Association of Anatomists, the American Neurological Society,
the Association for the Treatment of Mental Disorders, as well as
countless others. His credits and accomplishments would fill several pages of any textbook. Howard Faber was a pioneer in neuro-
physiological research and had even been the subject of an article
in *Time* magazine in November of 1937. His was—had been—a
life filled with glories and triumphs and he would not allow his
conscience to take those pleasures and prides away from him.

Now, in his eighty-second year, lying on his death bed at his
home in Knoxville, Tennessee, he could all but forget the angry
young man who murdered right before his wondering eyes. Never
could he forget, however, the faces of the women, captured in swift
moments like photographic images and twisted over the years into
caricatures of disbelief, terror, and the grim resolve of death—

—except for the last one, sad, doomed Mary Kelly. He tried not to think about her final words to him, lest the guilt come snarling to the surface.

I'm not the same man I was then, he would scream within to his conscience. *It wasn't really me.*

The malignant tumor in his brain had grown rapidly. His right side was now completely paralyzed, severely limiting his mobility, and aphasia had all but eliminated his ability to communicate. He was confined to his bed and dependent upon his doctor and best friend, Wilson Springer, who had come to stay at the house, and a nurse, whose name he could never remember. He was alone with his thoughts even in the presence of others.

"It's getting dark so early," said the silhouette of Faber's sister-in-law, Estell. She had been talking for some time, but he had not heard much of it, preferring instead to watch the warm yellow and orange of the trees blowing in the icy blue of the sky outside his bedroom window.

Dr. Springer flipped on the light switch. "Winter is coming on quickly."

Still holding Faber's lifeless hand, Estell rose from the chair beside his bed and faced Dr. Springer.

"Let this be a lesson to you," the doctor said, gesturing toward his patient. "Don't take chances with your health. If you're feeling poorly—whatever it is—see your doctor."

"It's hard to believe he was allowed to work for so long, and no one noticed his illness."

Dr. Springer turned and glared at his friend, still very angry with Faber. "He has never been a very good liar, but it wasn't until he began to hobble about the laboratory that we knew something was wrong."

"For all his knowledge of medicine," said Estell, at times he seems to have little faith in it."

"And he won't ever listen to anyone. I have never seen such a fuss over a few simple tests. You know, it wasn't until after the Dean had a talk with him that he finally gave it up. And I've had to take a leave of absence to come here and take care of the sissy."

Faber knew Dr. Springer was right to be angry. Six months ago, when he was just beginning to have difficulty controlling his right side, diagnostic studies could have confirmed or denied Faber's suspicions. There was the slim possibility that surgery at that early stage in his illness might have remedied the problem. But the thought of going under the knife caused him to quickly put this out of his mind. Although he had used the scalpel for nothing but good for over fifty years, he had a fear of putting himself in a position in which poetic justice might lend a hand.

"Try not to be too hard on him," Estell said, squeezing Faber's hand and placing it beside him. She looked him in the eyes. "Well, I'll be leaving in the morning. The bus should get me back to Nashville by mid-afternoon. I want to be home in time to fix supper for Danny and the boys. But I will be back to see you soon."

Better hurry, then, Faber thought, although he didn't much care. He knew she had come only out of a sense of obligation.

"Thank you for coming, Estell," Dr. Springer said as she left the room. He sat down beside Faber and, while taking his pulse, turned to speak to the nurse in the hall. "He can have one more visitor today."

Faber heard the murmuring of those waiting in the dining room as they rose to depart. They seemed to number six or eight. When there were that many, all conversing at once, their words overlapped so that he couldn't understand what was being said. He was amazed that after nearly a month of being bedridden, he still had so many daily visitors.

Miss Lumbly entered the room. "He was such a saint," she told Dr. Springer. "I always tell people about the case of that little Simmons girl—you remember, don't you? All those headaches and the sickness, and every doctor her father took her to diagnosed simple migraine."

"I remember," said Springer.

"When Dr. Faber heard about it, he said it sounded like brain abscesses and told the man to take her to Baltimore to see that specialist." She shook her head. "How could he have known. He just had an intuition about such things, and that little girl is alive and well today, all because of him."

She was wearing maroon, a color which had always irritated Faber. It was the color of irritation, the color of a bruise. He remembered that first drunken prostitute, Polly Nichols, as wearing maroon. And she—not the whore, but Miss Lumbly—was wearing a shapeless black straw hat with fake flowers sticking out all over. Come to think of it though, he could remember Polly as wearing one like that too.

Faber's wife, Carolyn, had known Miss Lumbly through her involvement with the Daughters of the American Revolution.

"She's a haughty socialite," he remembered Carolyn saying, "who prides herself on knowing everyone of *substance* in Knoxville."

He didn't get to know the woman until after his wife's death. Since then from time to time, Miss Lumbly had come to call on Dr. Faber. No doubt she thought that since he was a widower, he might easily be persuaded to relieve her of her spinsterhood.

A saint, she had said. If only she knew. The cow—he would like to show her....

Over the years the memories had bled together into one chilling corpse, an experience devoid of spiritual beauty or revelation. As if awakening from a blackout, he would be in the midst of his work before he knew what was happening.

He knelt beside the woman, savagely piercing her, dividing and violating her hot, wet tissues, his knife penetrating to her most secret flesh.

He took the woman, her mind, her body, and her life—the feeling had never been the same with a cadaver.

To prove his knowledge of her, he carefully separated the organs. And though he was privy to the smells of her living blood, her vagina, even her bowels, she suffered the shame of it without protest, remaining lifeless on the damp flagstones.

What else could she do? He could see that he had cut her throat, no doubt to quiet that horrible mouth. If she struggled, he would overpower her again. And after all, if they were caught, her shame would be that much greater.

He had almost had his fill when a staggering drunkard entered the road. Faber automatically thought to use his cloak as a curtain for the exposed woman. No, he decided, let her suffer the man's disapproving stare. The fellow seemed not to notice them, however, as he reeled away into the night.

Faber looked at his watch. He was still too drunk to see it well. It looked to be about two o'clock in the morning.

No one else was about. But at any moment, a policeman might see them from his beat along an adjoining road. The woman was the one who had shamefully allowed herself to be exposed in public, however Faber might be detained and questioned about his involvement. That would never do.

He put away his knife, gathered his cloak about him, and started walking. When, several blocks away, he encountered a policeman, he tried not to stagger and draw attention to himself. He didn't want the man to see he was in his cups.

Faber shook off the memory.

Miss Lumbly was still going on about him. How did she speak of him behind his back?

Just like your mother, Jack—all sweetness and light, singing the praises of the lord of the manor when in his presence, but damning him when he could not hear her. Faber could think of nothing worse than having to listen to his mother's mouth—the damned whore.

But that was an ugly way to think of poor, lonely Miss Lumbly. She had never done him any wrong. She obviously did the best she could with what life had offered her.

"Why do you talk about him as if he were not here?" asked Dr. Springer. "He *can* hear you. He can also respond, although it is often too frustrating for him to try and find his words."

Ignoring Dr. Springer, she looked down at Faber with a smile and took his right hand. He watched it being lifted, but couldn't feel it. "Such a wonderful man."

Dear God, was that genuine *sadness* in her voice? Her expression darkened. "Oh, but that son of his, Wayne."

"Miss Lumbly," Dr. Springer said, "I think it's time for Dr. Faber to rest."

"But sir, I have *just arrived.*"

"Nevertheless." He ushered her from the room.

"Well I never," Miss Lumbly exclaimed, her voice receding down the hall. "I'll come back soon, Dr. Faber."

"She doesn't mean to be so insensitive," Dr. Springer said when he returned. "Then again, perhaps she does."

He chuckled and Faber did his best to laugh with his eyes, as his paralyzed face formed a half smile.

There wasn't much more in life that Faber wanted for himself and he would have accepted death as reasonable at this time if it weren't for the loose ends he was leaving behind. There was his research; that would go on without him. Most of all, there was Wayne. He had always been a very troubled soul, and now, at the age of twenty-one, the young man already had a reputation about town as a drunk.

Faber knew and understood the problem. With great patience and sympathy, he had talked with his son many times about his drinking, suggesting that he attend the Thursday night AA meetings at the Methodist Church on Hyde Street.

"You do know, don't you," Dr. Springer said looking him squarely in the eyes, "that I'll make sure Wayne gets along all right? He's going settle down with time." He placed one of his hands on Faber's shoulder. "He's had a good father and a good upbringing and you know that's got to go a long way toward building his character. I think he never got over the loss of his mother—he was so young and they loved each other so much. "Faber turned his eyes away.

"I know what you think—even the death of that little girl didn't change him. We both know it was an accident and he wasn't charged because he was your son—everyone does. I'm just glad no one thinks the less of you for it."

Everything his friend said was true, but none of it suggested the cause of his son's drinking. He remembered the times when whiskey burned in his own belly and rage burned in his head. *"No, sir, please!" she cried. She had actually called me "Sir," as I raised the knife to slash at her throat.*

Wayne had never known about that part of Faber's life, had never known his father was an alcoholic. But if it were not hereditary, and Faber believed it wasn't, then what was the cause?

Faber had gone over the possibilities endlessly. He was sixty years old when Wayne was born and had always been concerned that he might not relate to his son easily. But he had always been nothing if not a good example to the boy. He had not had a drink, smoked, cursed, or otherwise demonstrated anything but temperance in manner or lifestyle since long before the boy was born.

His own father, a stable master by trade, died when Faber was a very young boy, kicked in the head by one of the Earl's prize horses. His Lordship allowed the boy and his mother to stay on, eventually moving them into one of the servants' quarters in the big house. Faber's mother took care of the charring and he worked in the stables as his father before him. The Earl became something of a father to him and lavished special attention on the Fabers. He brought in a tutor and the boy received a good education. Faber thought this was because the Earl loved him and, perhaps, because the man felt somewhat responsible for his father's death.

He remembered the wind was hard biting that day and he had returned for his cap and gloves. Just outside their apartment door, he heard his mother's urgent voice, whispering. "Not here, sir. Please—not now!"

"The boy will be busy for some time," His Lordship said. "He'll be repairing the tumbled-down wall near the front gate until early evening. "Faber returned to his work. He knew now how he and his mother earned special favors from the Earl. This was how he had gained an education and a surrogate father, and how, eventually, he was afforded the opportunity to go into medicine.

Wayne as a seven-year-old child came into his mind. "Come on, Father, take me to work with you today."

The boy had been asking for over a week. Faber was reluctant—there was a lot a boy could get into at the laboratory. But his mother, poor Carolyn, had been dead only two months and he needed to spend time with his father.

"If you promise to stay out from under foot."

Wayne promised, they made sandwiches for their lunch, and headed for the university in the Ford. As they moved through the streets of Knoxville, Faber allowed his son to control the gear shift.

"First gear, co-pilot," Faber would say, pressing in the clutch. Wayne would push the stick into position. "First gear, Sir," he would say.

On the campus lawn, Faber introduced him to the friendly squirrels. They sat in the cool grass for a moment and fed the animals the crusts from their sandwiches. Wayne told a bad joke, and as they laughed together he put his hand on his father's shoulder. In a rare fit of affection, Faber reached out and hugged his son.

"Today, will you do an experiment just for me?" Wayne asked, hugging him back.

"Of course I will."

In the Epley Building, Wayne was introduced to those who shared Faber's work and laboratory, Dr. Walker and Dr. Bennett. He was more interested, however, in the strange equipment that filled the lab, and as he explored, he discovered the animals with the metal and glass electrodes implanted in their brains. At first, he wandered silently up and down the rows of cages, almost tiptoeing past the pitiful monkeys, cats, and dogs. "You stuck pieces of metal in their heads!" he said quietly, turning to his father with eyes wide. Tears rolled down his cheeks. "Frankenstein—you're just like Dr. Frankenstein!"

Dammit—Faber was engaged in serious research and would not have his son think poorly of him! He, too, hated what he had to do to the animals.

"Now, son," he said, not knowing what else to say. "They aren't in any pain."

But Wayne wasn't listening. He was crying and the animals added their voices to his.

Dammit all to hell, he was doing the best he could to make amends for what he'd done. It just had to be enough!

Through the din, Walker and Bennett looked helplessly to Faber. "Come to me, Wayne, this instant!"

Sniveling, the boy crawled behind a stack of empty cages in a corner and Faber had to wrestle with Wayne to get him out.

He should never have let his son see that horrible movie. Although the film contained much that was pure fantasy, the story attached a great deal of emotion to what were essentially simple medical processes. He shouldn't have been surprised at the effect on his son. Jack was accustomed to atrocities of the flesh. But the boy….

Faber was not proud of the way he handled that incident. He had punished Wayne in front of the others and made him sit in a corner and read a book for the rest of the day.

He always wondered if this had contributed to his son's problem.

"I'm going to let you rest, now," Dr. Springer said. "If Wayne comes at a decent hour and isn't too intoxicated, I'll send him in to see you."

White Chapel District, London: Aug. 31st 1888, Sept. 8th, Sept. 30th and Nov. 9th; four were women in their 40s, the fifth victim 24, three months pregnant. The first two looked much older than their years. 3rd & 4th within the space of an hour. All occurred outdoors accept the last. Mutilation increased with each—

—but you must remember, Faber reminded himself, *the penance you have paid since then, all you've done to balance the scales. Advisor*

to the National Pediatrics Foundation, member of the American Can-
cer Society and the Multiple Sclerosis Society, served on the National
Board of Medical Examiners; all of it, so much good, so much to wipe
away the sins of youth when you were so angry and had no idea how
to channel that fury, that lust and energy—

—he opened his eyes and saw standing at the foot of his bed a figure wearing a dark hat and cloak, a physician's black bag held in its left hand. There was not enough light in the room for Faber to see the figure's face, so he opened his mouth and tried to beckon the figure to come forward, but all that emerged from his throat was a pitiful, thick gurgling sound, not even remotely human.

"Shhh," said the figure, opening the bag and reaching inside. "I only mean to worship your body, dearie, worship and enjoy it in a way few of us ever know."

No! Faber screamed inside himself.

"No need to be afraid, dearie," said the figure, raising the scalpel into the light and admiring its gleaming. "It will bring you such bliss."

Not any more, screamed/thought Faber. *I'm not you any more. I left you behind, I was never you, never, and you've no part of my life now!*

"What life is that, sir?" whispered the figure. "This world of four walls and a bed, is that the life to which you refer? Think about it, Jack, my friend, my creator; bit by bit, little by little, the boundaries of your world have shrunk; first it was the hospital, then this house, then only a few rooms of this house, and now your world, your life, is this bed." The figure leaned in closer, but the darkness covering its face only grew deeper.

"Soon, dear Jack, your world will shrink until all that is left for you is the central core of Dr. Howard Faber, and do you know what you're going to find waiting there for you?

"Me, dear sir. It's been a long time, and I've missed you." The figure dropped the scalpel back into the bag. "So, until then."

And Howard Faber fell back into the darkness of disease to find its familiarity broken by an immense, organ-crumpling pressure that he feared would crush his bones down to the very marrow.

Tubes.

He was aware of the plastic tubes in his body; a Foley catheter in his bladder, a nasogastric tube through which he was provided sustenance, and a nasopharyngeal tube pumping extra oxygen into his lungs from the bottles by his bedside.

"Just like Frankenstein!" he heard seven-year-old Wayne cry.

Uncomfortable, he tried to reach with his left hand to pull out the tubes, but found he was unable to move anything but his eyes.

He had a vague memory of Springer saying something about "'Locked-In' Syndrome," and "...a stroke."

If he had been able to, Howard Faber would have laughed.

What he had done to Catherine Eddowes, Polly Nichols, Alice Mackenzie, and all the others, that was not undignified death; no, they had died in such a way that everyone would remember their names and the unique manner in which he'd worshipped their flesh. It had been quick—brutal, perhaps, but quick nonetheless, much more than those whores deserved. They weren't conscious for most of the so-called "indignities"; they didn't have to depend on people to turn them over in bed, to daub the perspiration from their brows or wipe their asses when they could no longer control their bowels; they didn't have to listen to the *tsk-tsk-ings* and the *isn't-it-sads* and—the worst of them all, the most infuriating and degrading—those horrible, terrible, disgraceful *Well-at-least-his-suffering's-almost-at-an-ends.* Bloody idiots, all of them. Talking about him as if he weren't even in the room, as if he had no grasp of the language any longer. At least Springer, the tough old bastard, at least he had the nerve to address Faber directly, to look him in the eye and speak his mind.

"You look me in the eye, guv'ner," said the one in the tattered blue velvet, the one who must have been... what was her name again? Polly Nichols—yes, that must have been her. *"You're going to do that*

to me, you at least look me in the eye so's you remembers what was in m'heart before you took ever'thin' away from me."

A brave one, that Polly Nichols. Almost too bad about that one. Almost.

From outside his bedroom door he again heard the seemingly perpetual cacophony of whispering voices: Springer, and the nameless nurse, and of course Miss Lumbly... but today there was an additional voice, slurred, pained, but still recognizable.

"He's my *father*, dammit! I've a right to see him if I want."

"Not in your condition, Wayne," replied Springer curtly. "I'll not stand for your upsetting him."

"You should be ashamed of yourself," said Miss Lumbly. "Your father lying in there on his death-bed and you show up here in a drunken state. Have you no respect for him? The man was—"

"—such a saint," snapped Wayne. "Yes, yes, I know—*believe me, I know.* All my life I've had to listen to everyone tell me what a fine, wonderful, upstanding man my father is. 'You've quite a large shadow to step out from behind, Wayne,' you say to me. Well, I've tried! I did everything I could. It wasn't my fault the Army wouldn't take me for duty in Korea—"

"—that was because of the condition of your liver, Wayne," said Springer. "The drinking has taken a toll on your system. You weren't fit for active duty. Couple that with your history of emotional instability and—"

"All right!" snarled Wayne, nearly shouting. "All right, maybe I have brought a lot of my problems on myself, but you have no idea what it's like to be... to be the offspring of a *saint*. Compared to a miracle worker like my father, I'll always be a failure."

"I find your behavior extremely distasteful," said Miss Lumbly.

"My behavior? Oh, that's rich. Let's talk about your behavior for a moment, shall we, Miss Lumbly? Which of us is worse, I ask you—the one who shows up in his cups to see his dying father, or the one who arrives day after day in her finest dresses and gloves in the hopes that a dying man might take her as his wife before he

shuffles off his mortal coil—leaving her with not only a respected name but all his worldly goods, as well? Answer me that, will you, Miss Lumbly? All I want from him is… is forgiveness for not measuring up to his perfection. I don't give a *tinker's damn* about the money or the house or any of it. All I'm looking for is some trace of the father I worshipped when I was six. So here we stand, Miss Lumbly, the drunkard and the decaying debutante, and I want you tell me which of us is worse!"

"Enough," said Springer. Then the sound of the front door opening. "I think you'd better be on your way now, Wayne. If and when you can come back here sober, you can see your father."

The sound of shuffling footsteps, then Wayne's voice, empty, defeated, disgraced: "It's a terrible thing, never knowing if you're your own man or simply the sum of your family's parts. Try living with that for a while and see how you'd react. I figure I can either drink or I can weep, and drinking is so much more subtle." The door closed.

Faber opened his eyes again to see the dark-cloaked figure standing at the foot of the bed.

"That was quite a show Wayne put on for the others, don't you think?" it said. "Oh, don't bother trying to say anything; I'll already know what it is before it's out of your mouth and you'll need your strength for later, anyway.

"It seems to me, dear Jack—oh, all right, have it your way— *Howard*—it seems to me that you've only now begun to realize what your son has been going through all these years. The boy *does* make a strong case, does he not?

"You've made your 'contributions,' Howard. You've pioneered your research, you've helped ease the suffering of others, all the things one would expect of a fine, upstanding saint such as yourself. But the one thing you've not bothered to ask yourself, *Jack*—and Jack you are, as you have always been and shall always be—the one thing you've never asked yourself is: Does it make any difference?"

The figure walked around the side of the bed and seated itself on what Faber had come to think of as Springer's chair.

"Guess what, Jack—it doesn't. Everything you've done, the great strides you've made in your medical research, the pain you've prevented, the diseases you've helped to fight, none of it means a thing because it will never erase what you did, what we did.

"Have you ever heard the expression 'Kill two birds with one stone'? I've a way for us to do that. It's very simple.

"Confess. You're dying anyway, so you needn't worry about the authorities doing anything to you. It will not take away from the medical accomplishments, so the advancements you've made will go on helping others, and—and this is the most important one, Jack, so pay close attention—it will destroy this aura of sainthood that has protected you lo these sixty-two years, and that destruction will free your son to become the man he was meant to be. No more will others look at him and say, 'What a waste, why couldn't he be more like his father?' No, from now on they'll look at his accomplishments, however grand or meager they may be, and rejoice in them, for at least he won't *be a thing like his father!*

"A name and reputation only serve you when you're alive, Jack, and you don't have all that much longer left, dear fellow. So my suggestion is that you confess to your son what you really are— what we really are. 'The truth will set you free,' and all that rubbish. It's time. You have the ability to speak—it's going to take everything you have to do it, but you *can* do it. Have him open the safe behind the Botticelli print on the wall of the study.

"Ha! Can you imagine the looks on the faces of Springer and Estell and that puffed-up Miss Lumbly when they read your journals and see the photographs you took? When they compare your handwriting to that of the letters published in the papers and find them to be the same? And let's not forget the little trinkets and trophies we took each time—though, looking back on it, I think that pancreas was overdoing it a bit. Ah, the *details!* Dear God, the details you'll fill in for the world after all these years. How I wish

I could be here to see it all happen, but..."

It stood up, adjusted its cloak and hat, then paused for a moment, considering something, and set its black medical bag on Faber's bedside table. "Well then, I have to dash. Fare thee well, Jack. Confess to your son and set him free. Set us all free."

Faber was awakened by the sound of the bedroom door opening. He looked toward the clock on the fireplace mantel.

1:45. *Morning or afternoon?* he wondered.

The nurse came forward and said, "I'm sorry to disturb you, Dr. Faber, but your son is here to see you. He said it was important."

Wayne came in behind her, and Faber nearly gasped at the sight of his son.

Pale, sweaty, and shaking, with dark circles under his eyes. He looked like he hadn't slept in days, but that couldn't be because he was here only a few hours ago, wasn't he?

"I'll leave the two of you alone now," said the nurse, closing the door behind her.

"I'm guessing she'll give us about ten minutes before she wakes Springer," said Wayne. "She actually smelled my breath before letting me come in! My God!" He looked down at his father. "I'm glad you're awake, Father. I've... I've got something to tell you." He sat down in Springer's chair.

This close, Wayne looked even worse than Faber had first thought. There was a hollowness in his cheeks that reminded him of pictures he'd seen of Jews rescued from Nazi concentration camps. He looked so bad that Faber actually felt frightened for his son.

"I, uh, I finally took your advice, Father. I went down to the Methodist Church on Hyde Street Thursday night. I joined AA. I..." He pulled a handkerchief from the breast pocket of his jacket and wiped the sweat from his face. "I haven't had a drink in three days."

Three days? thought Faber. He'd been unconscious for three days?

"It's horrible," said Wayne. "I mean, I feel like everything inside of me is going to implode for want of a drink, but I haven't even looked at a bottle or a bar. God, it's so hard."

My boy, whispered Faber within himself. *My good son.*

Wayne rose from the chair and began pacing back and forth. The light from the bedside table cast his shadow large upon the wall, changing its shape, expanding it, contracting it, twisting it into other shapes: a cowering whore, a splatter of blood over flagstones, a stack of warm innards, a figure cloaked in black.

"The oddest thing crossed my mind when I was asked to stand up in front of the group and speak, and I tried to tell them about it but for some reason it wouldn't come out the way I wanted it to, and then it occurred to me that I had to ask you about it first.

"Do you remember the day of Mother's funeral? I was in my room getting dressed, and you came in and looked at me and said, 'Don't wear the green tie, wear the blue one—and your other good shoes.' I didn't think anything of it at the time, but later on—hell, for years now—it's kept... *gnawing* at me. The blue tie and my *other* good shoes?" He stared at Faber with eyes of anguish. "We were burying my mother, *your wife!* What the hell difference did it make what color my tie was or what shoes I wore? Someone we both loved dearly was *dead,* but instead of sharing your grief with me, instead of allowing me to share my grief with you, we wasted that time on a tie and a pair of shoes!

"Why, Father? Can you tell me that?"

Unable to move his head, Faber could only stare at his son, feeling the tears form in his eyes.

He had no memory of that incident; no memory at all.

Wayne continued to pace as his shadow continued its metamorphosis: a torn section of a skirt, a crushed hat, a pair of blood-soaked white gloves. *Confess,* said the figure in the dark cloak as Wayne walked right through it. *Set him free. Set us all free.*

"It doesn't really matter, I suppose," said Wayne. "It's just bothered me for all these years and I wanted you to know that. I... I do love you, Father, and I have nothing in my heart but the deepest admiration for all you've accomplished in your life.

"But I don't possess your genius, your skills and abilities, your... virtue.

"Goddamn it, Father, where is your human side, your fallibility? Not once have I ever seen you... *stumble*... I mean stub your toe and have to let out with an impropriety!

"And just once in my life I would have liked to hear you utter the words, 'I don't know.' Wayne lowered his eyes and turned away.

"A man's worth shouldn't be measured simply by his accomplishments, it should also be measured by the intentions in his heart, and I know that my intentions have almost always been good. That's what makes the failures all the more disgraceful. But if nothing else, I can at least be glad that they haven't tainted your good name."

Tell him, said the dark-cloaked figure as Wayne once again passed through it, only this time Wayne paused, then shivered as if he'd felt another presence in the room.

Who's there?" said Mary Kelly from behind her door at 13 Miller's Court.

"An admirer," Jack/Faber replied.

She opened the door just a crack and looked him over. "Well, now, ain't'cha a fine one?" Her voice was oddly pleasant, almost musical. "A real gentleman what's come to call on me?"

"I saw you earlier this evening at the pub, but I... well..."

"No need to explain, luv," she said, placing a surprisingly delicate hand on his arm. "You're what's we call the shy type, am I right?"

"Yes, of course."

"Well, what says you come on in and I'll get out the snifter I keeps for my special gentlemen friends?"

"Sounds wonderful."

She smiled. Her teeth, though yellowed, seemed in good condition.

"Come on in, then, 'fore you catch yourself a death of cold."

Faber/Jack removed his hat and stepped in, locking the door behind him.

"Damned drafty house," said Wayne, locking the bedroom door, then stumbling back toward Faber's bed. "Sorry about that, Father. My legs seem to be a little unstable these days." He sat in Springer's chair and removed the black medical bag from the table.

"I was thinking about that day in the lab, when I caused such a scene about the animals and you put me in the corner with a book for the rest of the day. Do you remember what the book was?"

No, said Faber with his eyes. Wayne reached over and wiped away some of his father's tears.

"It was a collection of quotes from various literary works, and the one I remembered best—in fact, it's the only one I remember *at all*—was from Thoreau: 'One true selfless act on the part of a man can erase a thousand small hurts.'"

He opened the bag and reached inside, removing a vial of morphine and a syringe.

The cloaked figure stood behind him. *Speak to him, Jack; speak to him now, before it's too late.*

"I've never been and will never be Wayne Faber, I'll always be *your son,* understand? And that's not how I want to be remembered. I want to be remembered as having erased a thousand small hurts. All of them yours."

Faber's eyes widened with realization.

Wayne looked down at him. "I can see the pain in your eyes, Father. I can't even begin to imagine the agony you're in."

There's nothing, son, not a thing, no pain, I'm beyond that, dear God there's no pain, no suffering!

Wayne tried to fill the syringe but his hands were shaking too violently and he dropped the morphine vial, which shattered as it struck the wood floor.

"Dammit!" He looked at Faber. "I'm sorry, Father."

Sorry the place ain't what the likes of you is accustomed to," said

Mary Kelly, brushing the dust off the small, ugly wooden table in the center of her cramped room. "But I suppose we don't really need to have ourselves a palace for what we's got in mind, eh?"

"Turn down the light," he said, removing his cloak.

"Don't'cha want a bit of a drink first?"

He smiled his most charming smile at her. "Afterward."

"Oh, I got a feeling about you, luv. You ain't like all them others, is you?"

"Not at all." He slipped his hand into his pocket and grasped the scalpel. "I don't want to just use your body, I want to worship it."

"Worship, is it? My, my," she said, beginning to unbutton the front of her pathetic dress. "I thinks maybe I'll make some noise for you."

"I hope so," he said, moving toward her.

The shadows on the wall of Faber's bedroom were changing shape again, bleeding together, dancing and writhing.

"I don't want you to hurt any longer, Father," said Wayne, reaching into the bag again and removing the scalpel—

—which glided smoothly into Mary Kelly's flesh, opening her skin like the petals of a blossoming flower, her blood so purely red and sacred, and she never made a sound, simply lay there on her sad bed in her pathetic room as Faber took her apart, slowly, savagely, arranging her breasts and liver on the table beside her bed, and just as he was moving up to work on her face, he saw the glistening viscera in his hands, the blood staining the walls and sheets, and for the first time he became aware of the magnificence of the human body, the organic wonder of its intricacies, and he saw Mary Kelly's face, was stunned into reverential silence by the expression of bliss she wore—bliss, where the others had been grimacing in agony, and he knew, then, that these whores had been giving him a gift, the gift of wonder and knowledge, their gutted bodies offering up the treasures with which he had been seeking communion, saying, "This is holy, this blood, this tissue, these veins and organs, and you are right to worship them, to hold them steaming in your hands and shape them into altars where you might kneel before the miracle of the flesh," and Faber was both grateful for *and angered by this gift; grateful because his life now had a purpose, angered because the look on Mary Kelly's face conveyed such peace, such acceptance, as if she too were receiving a gift beyond articulation, something so wondrous and fulfilling that he would never know it's like until the day he lay on his own death-bed, and in a last burst of anger he decided to savage her face so none but he would ever know the look of ecstasy that she wore at the moment of her death, and as he touched the scalpel to her face she opened her mouth and said—*

—"Open this door at once, Wayne!" screamed Springer from outside Faber's bedroom, then pounded against the heavy wood with his fists. The shadows danced around Faber's bed, trailing dark viscera.

"I love you, Father," said Wayne, as he lowered the scalpel toward Faber's throat—

He knows! thought Faber. *He's known all along, why else would he cut my throat?*

Wayne did not cut Faber's throat; instead he turned his father's head and sliced across an artery at the base of Faber's skull, then gently rolled his head back into place so they might look at one another.

"Your suffering's at an end, Father," whispered Wayne, nearly gagging on his snot and tears. "Don't you see? *This* is how I erase a thousand hurts, all the failures, all the times I disappointed everyone. I'll always be the one who took away your suffering. You're free of your pain, and I am my own man."

The shadows danced, becoming children in a circle, singing at the tops of their lungs, their voices echoing through the East End London streets: *"Jack the Ripper's dead/And lying on his bed/He cut his throat/With Sunlight Soap/Jack the Ripper's dead!"*

"The police are on their way, Wayne," screamed Springer, still pounding on the door.

"It doesn't matter now," said Wayne, his face filling with bliss, with peace and wonder. "It's all over."

"Jack the Ripper's dead…"

"Confess," said the dark-cloaked figure. "Else your son has damned himself for you."

Drawing on his last reserves of strength, Faber tried to speak, tried to say something, anything at all, to let his son know what must be done, where the evidence could be found, but nothing emerged from his throat, nothing at all.

"...and lying on his bed..."

The scalpel, once gleaming, now bloodied... was it *the* scalpel? Faber couldn't tell.

"...he cut his throat/With Sunlight soap..."

"I forgive you," said Mary Kelly.

"Forgive me," said Wayne.

My son, thought Faber; *my poor, fine, damned boy.*

"...Jack the Ripper's dead...."

Jack's Little Friend
Ramsey Campbell

It's afternoon when you find the box. You're in the marshes on the verge of the Thames below London. Perhaps you live in the area, perhaps you're visiting, on business or on holiday. You've been walking. You've passed a power station and its expressionless metallic chord, you've skirted a flat placid field of cows above which black smoke pumps from factory chimneys. Now reeds smear your legs with mud, and you might be proposing to turn back when you see a corner of metal protruding from the bearded mud.

You make your way towards it, squelching. It looks chewed by time, and you wonder how long it's been there. Perhaps it was dumped here recently; perhaps it was thrown out by the river; possibly the Thames, belabouring and dragging the mud, uncovered the box. As the water has built the box a niche of mud so it has washed the lid, and you can make out dates scratched on the metal. They are almost a century old. It's the dates that provoke your curiosity, and perhaps also a gesture against the dull landscape. You stoop and pick up the box, which frees itself with a gasp of mud.

Although it's only a foot square the box is heavier than you anticipated. You skid and regain your balance. You wouldn't be surprised if the box were made of lead. If anyone had thrown it in the river they would certainly have expected it to stay sunk. You

27

wonder why they would have bothered to carry it to the river or to the marshes for disposal. It isn't distinguished, except by the dates carved on the lid by an illiterate or clumsy hand—just a plain box of heavy grey metal. You read the dates:

31 / 8 / 1888

8 / 9 / 1888

30 / 9 / 1888

9 / 11 / 1888

There seems to be no pattern. It's as if someone had been trying to work one out. But what kind of calculation would be resolved by throwing away a metal box? Bewildered though you are, that's how you read the clues. What was happening in 1888? You think you read somewhere that expeditions were returning from Egypt around that date. Have you discovered an abandoned archaeological find? There's one way to know. But your fingers slip off the box, which in any case is no doubt locked beneath its coat of mud, and the marsh is seeping into your shoes; so you leave off your attempts to open the lid and stumble away, carrying the box.

By the time you reach the road your excitement has drained somewhat. After all, someone could have scratched the dates on the lid last week; it could even be an understated practical joke. You don't want to take a heavy box all the way home only to prise from its depths a piece of paper saying APRIL FOOL. So you leave the box in the grass at the side of the road and search until you find a metal bar. Sorry if I'm aborting the future of archaeology, you think, and begin to lever at the box.

But even now it's not as easy as you thought. You've wedged the box and can devote all your energy to shifting the lid, but it's fighting you. Once it yields an inch or two and then snaps shut again. It's as if it were being held shut, like the shell of a clam. A car passes on the other side of the road and you begin to give in to a sense of absurdity, to the sight of yourself struggling to jemmy open an old box. You begin to feel like a tourist's glimpse. Another car, on your side this time, and dust sweeps into your face. You blink and weep and cough violently, for the dust seems to have been scooped into your mouth. Then the sensation of dry crawling in your mouth recedes, and only the skin beneath your tongue feels rough. You wipe your eyes and return to the box. And then you drop the bar, for the box is wide open.

And it's empty. The interior is as dull as the exterior. There's nothing, except on the bottom a thin glistening coat of what looks like saliva but must be marsh water. You slam the lid. You memorize the dates and walk away, rolling your tongue around the floor of your mouth, which still feels thick, and grinning wryly. Perhaps the hitch-hiker or whoever finds the box will conceive a use for it.

That night you're walking along a long dim street towards a woman. She seems to be backing away, and you can't see her face. Suddenly, as you rush towards her, her body opens like an anemone. You plunge deep into the wet red fronds.

The dream hoods your brain for days. Perhaps it's the pressure of work or of worry, but you find yourself becoming obsessive. In crowds you halt, thinking of the dates on the box. You've consulted such books as you have access to, but they didn't help. You stare at the asymmetrical faces of the crowd. Smoke rises from their mouths or their jaws work as they drive forward, pulled along by their set eyes. Imagine asking them to help. They wouldn't have touched the box, they would have shuffled on by, scattering their waste paper and condoms. You shake your head to dislodge the crawling thoughts. You aren't usually so misanthropic. You'll have to find out what those dates mean. Obviously your brain won't give you much peace until you do.

So you ask your friend, the one who knows something about history. And your friend says, "That's easy. They're the dates of Jack the Ripper," and tells you that the five murders everyone accepts as the Ripper's work were committed on those dates. You can't help smiling, because you've just had a flash of clarity: of course you must have recognized the dates subconsciously from having read them somewhere; and the recognition was the source of your dream. Then your friend says, "Why are you interested?"

You're about to answer, but your tongue sticks to the floor of your mouth for a moment, like the lid of the box. In that moment you think: why should your friend want to know anyway? They've no right to know, they aren't entitled to a fee for the consultation. You found the box, you'll conduct the inquiry. "I must have read the dates somewhere," you say. "They've been going round in my head and I couldn't remember why."

On the way home you play a game with yourself. No, that bus shelter's no good, too open. Yes, he could hide in that alley, there would be hardly any light where it bends in the middle. You stop, because the skin beneath your tongue is rough and sore, and hinders your thoughts. You explore the softness beneath your tongue with your finger, and as you do so the inflammation seems to draw into itself and spare you.

Later you ponder Jack the Ripper. You've read about him, but when you leaf through your knowledge you realise you're not so well informed. How did he become the Ripper? Why did he stop? But you know that these questions are only your speculations about the box, disguised.

It's inconvenient to go back to find the box, but you manage to clear yourself the time. When you do you think at first you've missed the place where you left the box. Eventually you find the bar, but the box has gone. Perhaps someone kicked it into the hedges. You search among the cramped roots and trapped crisp-bags until your mouth feels scraped dry. You could tell the local police, but then you would have to explain your interest, and they would take the credit for themselves. You don't need the box. To-morrow you'll begin to research.

And so you do, though it's not as easy as you expected. Everyone's fascinated by the Ripper these days, and the library books are popular. You even have to buy a paperback of one of them, glancing sideways as you do so at the people browsing through the book. The sunlight glares in the cracks and pores and fleshy bags of their faces, giving them a sheen like wet wax: wax animated by simple morbid fascination. You shudder and hurry away. At least you have a reason, but these others haven't risen above the level of the mob that gloated squirming over reports of the Ripper's latest killing. You know how the police of the time must have felt.

You read the books. You spread them across the table, comparing accounts. You're not to be trapped into taking the first one you read as definitive. Your friends, and perhaps your spouse or lover as well, joke and gently rebuke you about your singlemindedness. No doubt they talk about it when you're not there. Let them. Most people seem content to relive, or elaborate, the second-hand. Not you.

You read. 31/8/1888: throat cut twice, head nearly severed, disembowelled twice. 8/9/1888: handkerchief wrapped around almost severed neck, womb missing, intestines cast over shoulder, relatively little blood in the yard where the corpse was found. 30/9/1888: two women, one with windpipe severed; the other, less than an hour later, with right eye damaged, earlobe cut off, intestines over shoulder, kidney and entrails missing. 9/11/1888: throat cut, ears and nose missing, also liver, and a mass of flesh and organs on the bedside table. There's a photograph of her in one book. You stare at it for a moment, then you slam the book and stare at your hands.

But your hands are less real than your thoughts. You think of the Ripper, cutting and feeling his way through the corpses, taking more time and going into more detail with each murder. The last one took two hours, the books tell you. A question is beginning to insist on an answer. What was he looking for?

You aren't sleeping well. You stare at the lights that prick your eyeballs behind your lids and theorize until you topple wakefully into sleep. Sometimes you seem almost to have found a pattern, and you gasp in crowds or with friends. They glance at you and you meet their gaze coldly. They wouldn't be capable of your thoughts, and you certainly don't intend to let them hinder you.

But even as their dull gaze falls away you realise that you've lost the inspiration, if indeed it were one.

So you confine yourself to your home. You're glad to have an excuse to do so, for recently you've been growing hypersensitive. When you're outside and the sunlight intensifies it's as though someone were pumping up an already white-hot furnace, and the night settles around you like water about a gasping fish. So you draw the curtains and read the books again.

The more you read the stranger it seems. You feel you could understand the man if a missing crucial detail were supplied. What can you make of his macabre tenderness in wrapping a handkerchief around the sliced throat of Annie Chapman, his second victim? A numbed denial of his authorship of the crime, perhaps? If there were relatively little blood in the yard then surely the blood must have soaked into the Ripper's clothes, but in that case how could he have walked home in broad daylight? Did he cut the windpipe of Elizabeth Stride because he was interrupted before he was able to do more, or because she had seen too much for him simply to leave her and seek a victim elsewhere? An hour later, was it his frustration that led him to mutilate Catherine Eddowes more extensively and inventively than her predecessors? And why did he wait almost twice as long as hitherto before committing his final murder, that of Mary Kelly, and the most detailed? Was this the exercise of a powerful will, and did the frustration build up to an unprecedented climax? But what frustration? What was he looking for?

You turn to the photograph of Mary Kelly again, and this time you're able to examine it dispassionately. Not that the Victorian camera was able to be particularly explicit. In fact, the picture looks like a piece of early adolescent pornography on a wall, an amateur blob for a face and a gaping darkness between the legs. You suck your tongue, whose underside feels rough and dry.

You read the Ripper's letters. The adolescent wit of the rhymes often gives way to the childish illiteracy of some of the letters. You can understand his feelings of superiority to the victims and to the police; they were undoubtedly at least as contemptible as the people you know. But that doesn't explain the regression of the letters, as if his mind were flinching back as far as possible from his actions. That's probably a common trait of psychopaths, you think: an attempt to reject the part of them that commits the crimes.

Your mind is still frowning. You read through the murders again. First murder, nothing removed. Second, the womb stolen. Third, kidney and entrails stolen. A portion of kidney which had been preserved in spirits was sent to the police, with a note saying that the writer had eaten the rest. Fourth, the liver removed and the ears and nose, but the womb and a three-month-old foetus untouched. Why? To state the hunger which motivated the killings, presumably, but what hunger was that? If cannibalism, surely he would never have controlled himself sufficiently to preserve a portion of his food with which to taunt the police? If not, what worse reality was he disguising from the police, and perhaps from himself, as cannibalism?

You swallow the saliva that's pooling under your tongue and try to grasp your theories. It's as if the hunger spat out the kidney. Not literally, of course. But it certainly seems as if the Ripper had been trying to sate his hunger by varying the delicacies, as if it were a temperamental pet. Surely the death of Mary Kelly couldn't have satisfied it for good, though.

Then you remember the box. If he had externalized the hunger as something other than himself, could his mind have persuaded him that the hunger was alive independent of him and might be trapped? Could he have used one of the portions of Mary Kelly as a lure? Would that have seemed a solution in the grotesque algebra of his mind? Might he have convinced himself that he had locked away his hunger in time, and having scratched the dates on the box to confirm his calculations have thrown it in the river? Perhaps the kidney had been the first attempted lure, insufficiently tempting. And then—well, he could hardly have returned to a normal life, if indeed he had left one, but he might have turned to the socially acceptable destruction of alcoholism and died unknown.

The more you consider your theory the more impressive it becomes. Perhaps you can write it up as an article and sell it somewhere. Of course you'll need to pursue your research first. You feel happy in a detached unreal way, and you even go to your companion willingly for the first time in, now you think about it, a long while. But you feel apart from the moist dilation of flesh and the hard dagger thrust, and are glad when it's over. There's something at the back of your mind you need to coax forward. When you've dealt with that you'll be able to concentrate on other things.

You walk towards her. The light is flickering and the walls wobble like a fairground corridor. As you approach her, her dress peels apart and her body splits open. From within the gap trails a web towards which you're drawn. At the centre of the web hangs a piece of raw meat.

Your cry wakes you but not your companion. Her body feels like burning rubber against you, and you flinch away. After a minute you get out of bed. You can't stand the sensation, and you want to shake off the dream. You stare from the window; the darkness is paling, and a bird sings tentatively. Suddenly you gasp. You'll write that article now, because you've realised what you need. You can't hope to describe the Ripper or even to meet a psychopath for background. But there's one piece of first-hand research you can do that will help you to understand the Ripper. You don't know why you didn't read your dream that way at once.

Next day you begin searching. You read all the cards you can find in shop windows. They aren't as numerous or as obvious as you expected. You don't want to find yourself actually applying for a course of French lessons. You suppose there are magazines that would help you but you're not sure where to find them. At last, as the streets become grimmer, you notice a group of young men reading cards in a shop window. They nudge each other and point to several of the cards, then they confer and hurry towards a phone box. You're sure this time.

You choose one called Marie, because that was what Mary Kelly used to call herself. No particular reason, but the parallel seems promising. When you telephone her she sounds dubious. She asks what you want and you say "Nothing special. Just the usual." Your voice may be disturbing her, because your tongue is sticking somehow, to the floor of your mouth, which feels swollen and obstructive. She's silent for a moment, then she says "All right. Come up in twenty minutes," and tells you where she is.

You hadn't realised it would be as swift as that. Probably it's a good thing, because if you had to wait much longer your unease might find you excuses for staying away. You emerge from the phone box and the sunlight thuds against your head. Your mouth is dry, and the flesh beneath your tongue is twitching as if an insect has lodged there. It must be the heat and the tension. You walk slowly towards your rendezvous, which is only a few streets away. You walk through a maze of alleys to keep in the shade. On either side of you empty clothes flap, children shout and barks run along a chain of dogs.

You reach your destination on time. It's in a street of drab shops: a boarded betting shop, a window full of cardigans and wool, a Chinese take-away. The room you want is above the latter. You skid on trodden chips and shielding your face from the eyes of the queue next door, ring the bell.

As you stare at the new orange paint on the door you wonder what you're going to say. You have some idea and surely enough money, but will she respond to that? You understand some prostitutes refuse to talk rather than act. You can hardly explain your interest in the Ripper. You're still wondering when she opens the door.

She must be in her thirties, but her face has aged like an orange and she's tried to fill in the wrinkles, probably while waiting for you. Her eyelashes are like unwashed black paintbrushes. But she smiles slightly, as if unsure whether you want her to, and then sticks out her tongue at a head craning from next door. "You rang before," she says, and you nod.

The door slams behind you. Your hand reaches blindly for the latch; you can still leave, she'll never be able to pursue you. Beneath your tongue a pulse is going wild. If you don't go through with this now it will be more difficult next time, and you'll never be rid of the Ripper or of your dreams. You follow her upstairs.

Seeing her from below you find it easy to forget her smile. Her red dress pulls up and her knickers, covered with whorls of colour like the eye of a peacock's tail, alternately bulge and crease. The hint of guilt you were beginning to feel retreats: her job is to be on show, an object, you need have no compunction. Then you're at the top of the stairs and in her room.

There are thick red curtains, mauve walls, a crimson bed and telephone, a colour TV, a card from Ibiza and one from Rhyl. Behind a partition you can see pans and knives hanging on hooks in the kitchen area. Then your gaze is wrenched back to her as she says "Go on then, tell me your name, you know mine."

Of course you don't. You're not so stupid as to suppose she would display her real name in the window. You shake your head and try to smile. But the garish thick colours of the room are beginning to weigh on you, and the trapped heat makes your mouth feel dry, so that the smile comes out soured.

"Never mind, you don't have to," she says. "What do you want? Want me to wear anything?"

Now you have to speak or the encounter will turn into a grotesque misunderstanding. But your tongue feels as if it's glued down, while beneath it the flesh is throbbing painfully. You can feel your face prickling and reddening, and rooted in the discomfort behind your teeth a frustrated disgust with the whole situation is growing.

"Are you shy? There's no need to be," she says. "If you were really shy you wouldn't have come at all, would you?" She stares into the mute struggle within your eyes and smiling tentatively again, says

"Can't you talk?"

Yes, you can talk, it's only a temporary obstruction. And when you shift it you'll tell her that you've come to use her, because that's what she's for. An object, that's what she's made herself. Inside that crust of makeup there's nothing. No wonder the Ripper sought them out. You don't need compassion in a slaughterhouse. You try to control your raw tongue, but only the throbbing beneath it moves.

"I'm sorry, I'm only upsetting you. Never mind, love," she says. "Nerves are terrible, I know. You sit down and I'll get you a drink."

And that's when you have to act, because your mouth is filling with saliva as if a dam had burst, and your tongue's still straining to raise itself, and the turgid colours have insinuated themselves into your head like migraine, and tendrils of uneasiness are streaming up from your clogged mouth and matting your brain, and at the core of all this there's a writhing disgust and fury that this woman should presume to patronize you. You don't care if you never understand the Ripper so long as you can smash your way out of this trap. You move towards the door, but at the same time your hand is beckoning her, it seems quite independent of you. You haven't reached the door when she's in front of you, her mouth open and saying "What?" And you do the only thing that seems, in your blind violent frustration, available to you.

You spit into her open mouth.

For a moment you feel free: Your mouth is clean and your tongue can move as you want it to. The colours have retreated, and she's just a well-meaning rather sad woman using her talents as best she can. Then you realise what you've done. Now your tongue's free you don't know what to say. You think perhaps you could explain that you sneezed. Perhaps she'll accept that, if you apologize. But by this time she's already begun to scream.

You were so nearly right most of the time. You realised that the stolen portions of Mary Kelly might have been placed in the box as a lure. If only you'd appreciated the implications of this: that the other mutilations were by no means the act of a maniac, but the attempts of a gradually less sane man to conceal the atrocities of what possessed him. Who knows, perhaps it had come from Egypt. He couldn't have been sure of its existence even when he lured it into the box. Perhaps you'll be luckier, if that's luck, although now you can only stand paralysed as the woman screams and screams and falls inertly to the floor, and blood begins to seep from her abdomen. Perhaps you'll be able to catch it as it emerges, or at least to see your little friend.

Abandon All Flesh

Silvia Moreno-Garcia

The chamber of horrors. The cobwebs and the torture instruments and the lights. And Jack. She loves Jack most of all. He stands in a corner, past the mummies and the witches, in his cape and stylish top hat. Black satin. Gloves. Right hand raised, knife gleaming. He sports a wicked smile.

If you stand in front of Jack all you can see is the smile. The angle of the hat wraps the rest of his face in rich shadows. However, if you move to the side and step a bit forward, against the velvet ropes, you can look at him up close.

The quality of the wax sculptures varies. The older ones are good and the newer ones are less detailed. But Jack. Jack is not good, he is *great*. The one who crafted him did so with exquisite detail, labouring over the eyes and the skin, striving to approximate life as much as one can within the confines of a wax mold. The result is a face that seems alert, capable of speech, of drawing a breath. The fingers curl around the knife with true strength, the body tenses, ready to leap down from its dais.

Even the background of this exhibit is flawless. Behind Jack there is a bed, unmade, the sheets splattered with blood. The subdued lighting reveals a brick wall and a shuttered window.

Julia stands in front of Jack and touches the sleeve of his jacket. She is fourteen. During class she draws skulls and dragons in the

margins of her notebooks. In the afternoons, she does her homework with more haste than effort. Twice a week she walks the wax
museum, pausing before Jack and admiring him.

Her father works for the museum. He spends his days in a
cramped, windowless office. Julia brings him his dinner on Mon-
days and Thursdays. Sometimes she also visits on Fridays, if mother is too preoccupied with the twins. Julia suspects Father does not
take his meals at home in an effort to avoid his six children, not
because he is too busy to depart from his post.

Julia sets down the tin containers filled with food and goes behind the ropes, standing on her tiptoes to look at Jack. It's Monday and the museum is closed but Father still goes to the office. It's
Monday and it means there is no one to interrupt her. She removes
Jack's hat. She sets it on her head.

She tilts her head and stares at him. She brushes the knot of his
necktie.

Finally, she sets the hat back on his head, jumps down and continues on to Father's office.

The teacher speaks of the Aztecs. Speaks of sacrifice. Of the
tonacayotl, the spiritual flesh-hood. We only exist thanks to the
sacrifice of the gods. There is a constant cycle of death and re-
birth. The Aztecs pierced their body with maguey thorns, drawing blood from their tongues, their ear lobes, their feet, their
genitals. Offerings written in blood.

Julia draws a snake. It curls on the page of her notebook, growing in size. She adds details: tiny little crosshatches for the skin,
a forked tongue.

The teacher assigns partners for a project. Julia will work with
David.

David lives four blocks from Julia's house. His father owns
a small convenience store. Julia has seen the boy there, with a
green apron tied around his waist, assembling pyramids made
out of soup cans.

David proposes that they consult his leather-bound encyclopedia for the project and Julia agrees. Julia sits on the floor of his living room while he turns the pages. An image of a sacrifice taken from a codex catches her attention and she places her palm upon the page, staring at it.

David turns on the radio. He pours her a glass of soda.

He has no siblings. The music echoes through his apartment without the wailing of a baby punctuating it in the background. She finds that odd.

While she looks at the picture, David's hand falls upon her knee, brushing the hem of her skirt.

He should not touch her and she should remind him of this. She makes no effort to move the hand away. The touch irritates her, but she is also curious. She wonders whether he will attempt to move his hand higher. The hand remains at her knee and eventually she stands up, tossing the remains of her soda in the kitchen sink.

David walks Julia home a few times. She does nothing to encourage him or to refuse him. They walk together but she feels as though he was at a great distance. Curiosity and indifference mix together.

Twice a week David's father has him come in to the store to work the cash register. One afternoon, David gives her a grand tour of the premises. He takes her to the storage room and they sit behind a pile of cardboard boxes. He runs a sweaty palm across her knees, touches her. Julia stares at a box filled with tuna cans. She leaves half an hour later, after purchasing milk and coffee for her mother.

In her bed that night she thinks about the tonacayotl. Everything is but one flesh. The world is but an illusion. Omeyocan. The dual space, the dual time. Everything is immaterial, innate, eternal, without beginning or end. We are but the manifestation of the gods, a fleck in the double pupil of Ometeötl. Everything dies, everything is abandoned, everything exists again and remains.

If time and flesh are an illusion…well, then…

Julia lays still upon the bed and relaxes her limbs. She breaths slowly, until her body feels very light. Until her body seems to drip onto the bed, through the bed, down. It sinks. The sounds of the city morph into sounds of carriages and horses. An unusual cold drifts into the room. She hears the patter of the rain upon cobblestones. Her bedroom window seems narrower and fog whirls outside, hiding the buildings and the sky.

A shadow drifts across the room, towards her. He stands in the ghostly light that filters through the yellowed curtains.

She knows his face. She knows his smile.

He lowers the knife, plunging it deep into her stomach.

She screams.

In the morning she wakes to find blood on her thighs. Her period has arrived.

She showers and when she emerges the bathroom is filled with steam. The mirror has clouded. She traces a serpent upon its surface, then wipes it off with the palm of her hand. She observes her reflection.

The bodies of war captives were carefully handled. The locks to the captor, the heart to the Sun, the head skewered onto a skull rack. David's encyclopedia provides facts, words, pictures, but no knowledge.

Julia sits cross-legged, turning the pages. She asks David for the J volume, asks him if he's heard about Jack Ripper. David turns the volume of the stereo higher, making the walls of the apartment reverberate.

He rubs her legs and touches her arms. She feels like a doll that is being maneuvered into different poses. Her body feels like it is made of rubber or wax.

She asks David if he believes that all flesh is but an illusion but the music is loud and he isn't listening.

Julia sinks into the sheets, drowns upon the bed. Her whole body dissolves, ceases to be, is assembled again. She resurfaces in the room she's seen before—his room—to the scent of incense, the sound of rain upon the streets.

He comes into focus, a blurry figure at first, his face growing clearer. Jack's eyes narrow when he sees her.

She breaths slowly.

Her mouth is dry.

He nicks her with his knife. He cuts her arm. Tiny, sharp, little cuts.

But she doesn't mind. This is the art of sacrifice. Thorns and bones and blades to make the body sing.

There's an anatomical illustration of a man and a woman, their skin removed, that she enjoys looking at. The illustration consists of several layers of acetate that you can flip on or off. Flip and you reveal the muscles. Flip again and see the veins. Flip to see the naked skeleton.

Peeling layers of reality. This is exactly what the Aztecs understood.

David looks at her with a bored expression as she spreads his books on the floor. He has no use for books. Those are his parents' things, tomes that contain no useful lessons for him.

Julia agrees. The pages cannot hold knowledge. Only the body—fragile, immaterial as it is—can hope to transmit a hint of truths.

David understands only the body. She does not fault him for it. The language of hands, nails, tongue is as honest as any saga upon the printed page.

But David only understands the first layer. The skin and the flesh. He cannot peel the acetate to reveal the muscle and blood. He does not see the shape of her skull beneath her face.

Perhaps she should be content with this one layer of truth, this slim understanding.

She can't. She just can't.

She takes David to the museum, to see Jack. David acts like he is not impressed by the chamber of horrors. He laughs at the mummies and snorts at the witches. When they reach Jack, Julia tells him about the crimes.

David has been all laughter and bluster, but as they stand in front of this wax figure, he seems to shrink a bit. *What are we doing here when we could be at the movies?* he asks. Beneath the irritation there is a hint of dread.

Julia says nothing. The feeling of distance, of disinterest, invades her once more.

He runs his hands down her arm. He wants to do something fun. He wants to make out. Sex. It's all David understands.

David understands *nothing*.

"Not now," she says, her eyes upon Jack.

David kisses her, wraps his arms around her. His insistent hand palms her breast, as if he were kneading dough.

She bites down on his lip. She bites down until it bleeds. David yelps like a puppy.

He shoves her away and rushes out of the chamber of horrors with an angry curse.

Julia stumbles and falls in front of Jack, bruising her knees. She wipes her mouth with the back of her hand.

David walks another girl home. Julia watches them with the same vague indifference as before. Her mother sends her to buy eggs at the little store and when she comes in, David ignores her, busy rearranging some cans.

When she returns home, her mother tells her to cook some eggs. Mother is busy with the twins and the other children are hungry. Julia cracks an egg. It is bloody in the centre. She stirs it with a wooden spoon, as though she were scrying. The egg burns.

She touches the tiny points on her arm were Jack nicked her with his knife.

Julia pictures the universe like an infinite, incessant assembly of fractals branching out into forever. She sinks into them. *Cahuitl*, the Aztec word for space, derives from the word for abandon. To abandon oneself. And so she abandons herself upon her bed— which is no longer her bed. She opens her eyes to a room that is not her room.

But in the currents of time and being, here can be there.

The light from an oil lamp washes the room in warm yellows and browns. A sweet, pungent scent clouds the room. A man rises from a chair and gazes at her with familiar eyes.

She peels off her nightgown and prepares for the knife to nick her stomach. He spreads open her legs instead, digs his finger into her flesh until he draws bruises.

The scent in the room is the memory of altars and incense.

The rains have arrived. Julia watches the water swirl into the sewer grate. She waits under an umbrella until David walks by. He hasn't spoken to her in several weeks, but he turns his head when she calls his name, like a charm.

It's Monday. The museum is closed, but she always has access to its wax figures and its hallways.

She asks him if he'd like to go with her.

He looks reluctant only for a second. She knows, by the way he smiles, that he's been expecting this. In some corner of his mind he's thought she'd pursue him, grovel, beg for his renewed attentions.

She takes him to the chamber of horrors. She goes behind the velvet rope, behind Jack, and sits on the bed. David's eagerness has subsided.

Yes it's dark here, she says. *No one comes here. No one can see us.*

He hesitates. She casts off her sweater and her shirt and David follows her to the bed. He pinches her nipple, tries to get on top of her.

Julia reaches beneath her and firmly clutches the knife, making a firm cut. Warm blood splutters upon her chest. She strikes again. Again. Again. And David slides down, wriggling, twisting.

Julia holds up her hand. It's stained crimson. She rubs her hand against her lips and heads towards Jack. She stands on her tiptoes and kisses him. She can feel the acetate film of the here and now peeling off, like a dead skin.

His waxen flesh grows warm.

His mouth tastes of incense.

God of the Razor

Joe R. Lansdale

Richards arrived at the house about eight.

The moon was full and it was a very bright night, in spite of occasional cloud cover; bright enough that he could get a good look at the place. It was just as the owner had described it. Run down. Old. And very ugly.

The style was sort of gothic, sort of plantation, sort of cracker box. Like maybe the architect had been unable to decide on a game plan, or had been drunkenly in love with impossible angles.

Digging the key loaned him from his pocket, he hoped this would turn out worth the trip. More than once his search for antiques had turned into a wild goose chase. And this time, it was really a long shot. The owner, a sick old man named Klein, hadn't been inside the house in twenty years. A lot of things could happen to antiques in that time, even if the place was locked and boarded up. Theft. Insects. Rats. Leaks. Any one of those, or a combination of, could turn the finest of furniture into rubble and sawdust in no time. But it was worth the gamble. On occasion, his luck had been phenomenal.

As a thick, dark cloud rolled across the moon, Richards, guided by his flashlight, mounted the rickety porch, squeaked the screen and groaned the door open.

Inside, he flashed the light around. Dust and darkness seemed to crawl in there until the cloud passed and the lunar light fell through the boarded windows in a speckled and slatted design akin to camouflaged netting. In places, Richards could see that the wallpaper had fallen from the wall in big sheets that dangled halfway down to the floor like the drooping branches of weeping willows.

To his left was a wide, spiraling staircase, and following its ascent with his light, he could see there were places where the railing hung brokenly askew.

Directly across from this was a door. A narrow, recessed one. As there was nothing in the present room to command his attention, he decided to begin his investigation there. It was as good a place as any.

Using his flashlight to bat his way through a skin of cobwebs, he went over to the door and opened it. Cold air embraced him, brought with it a sour smell, like a freezer full of ruined meat. It was almost enough to turn Richards' stomach, and for a moment he started to close the door and forget it. But an image of wall-to-wall antiques clustered in the shadows came to mind, and he pushed forward, determined. If he were going to go to all the trouble to get the key and drive way out here in search of old furniture to buy, then he ought to make sure he had a good look, smell or no smell.

Using his flash, and helped by the moonlight, he could tell that he had discovered a basement. The steps leading down into it looked aged and precarious, and the floor appeared oddly glasslike in the beam of his light.

So he could examine every nook and cranny of the basement, Richards decided to descend the stairs. He put one foot carefully on the first step, and slowly settled his weight on it. Nothing collapsed. He went down three more steps, cautiously, and though they moaned and squeaked, they held.

When Richards reached the sixth step, for some reason he could not define, he felt oddly uncomfortable, had a chill. It was as if someone with ice-cold water in their kidneys had taken a piss down the back of his coat collar.

Now he could see that the floor was not glassy at all. In fact, the floor was not visible. The reason it had looked glassy from above was because it was flooded with water. From the overall size of the basement, Richards determined that the water was most likely six or seven feet deep. Maybe more.

There was movement at the edge of Richards' flashlight beam, and he followed it. A huge rat was swimming away from him, pushing something before it; an old partially deflated volleyball perhaps. He could not tell for sure. Nor could he decide if the rat was trying to mount the object or bite it.

And he didn't care. Two things that gave him the willies were rats and water, and here were both. To make it worse, the rats were the biggest he'd ever seen, and the water was the dirtiest imaginable. It looked to have a lot of oil and sludge mixed in with it, as well as being stagnant.

It grew darker, and Richards realized the moon had been hazed by a cloud again. He let that be his signal. There was nothing more to see here, so he turned and started up. Stopped. The very large shape of a man filled the doorway. Richards jerked the light up, saw that the shadows had been playing tricks on him. The man was not as large as he'd first thought. And he wasn't wearing a hat. He had been certain before that he was, but he could see now that he was mistaken. The fellow was bareheaded, and his features, though youthful, were undistinguished; any character he might have had seemed to retreat into the flesh of his face or find sanctuary within the dark folds of his shaggy hair. As he lowered the light, Richards thought he saw the wink of braces on the young man's teeth.

"Basements aren't worth a damn in this part of the country," the young man said. "Must have been some Yankees come down here and built this. Someone who didn't know about the water table, the weather and all."

"I didn't know anyone else was here," Richards said. "Klein send you?"

"Don't know a Klein."

"He owns the place. Loaned me a key."

The young man was silent a moment. "Did you know the moon is behind a cloud? A cloud across the moon can change the entire face of the night. Change it the way some people change their clothes, their moods, their expressions."

Richards shifted uncomfortably.

"You know," the young man said. "I couldn't shave this morning."

"Beg pardon?"

"When I tried to put a blade in my razor, I saw that it had an eye on it, and it was blinking at me, very fast. Like this... oh, you can't see from down there, can you? Well, it was very fast. I dropped it and it slid along the sink, dove off on the floor, crawled up the side of the bathtub and got in the soap dish. It closed its eye then, but it started mewing like a kitten wanting milk. Oooowwwwaaa, Oooowwwaa, was more the way it sounded really, but it reminded me of a kitten. I knew what it wanted, of course. What it always wants. What all the sharp things want.

"Knowing what it wanted made me sick and I threw up in the toilet. Vomited up a razor blade. It was so fat it might have been pregnant. Its eye was blinking at me as I flushed it. When it was gone the blade in the soap dish started to sing high and silly-like.

"The blade I vomited, I know how it got inside of me." The young man raised his fingers to his throat. "There was a little red mark right here this morning, and it was starting to scab over. One or two of them always find a way in. Sometimes it's nails that get in me. They used to come in through the soles of my feet while I slept, but I stopped that pretty good by wearing my shoes to bed."

In spite of the cool of the basement, Richards had started to sweat. He considered the possibility of rushing the guy or just trying to push past him, but dismissed it. The stairs might be too weak for sudden movement, and maybe the fruitcake might just have his say and go on his way.

"It really doesn't matter how hard I try to trick them," the young man continued, "they always win out in the end. Always."

"I think I'll come up now," Richards said, trying very hard to sound casual.

The young man flexed his legs. The stairs shook and squealed in protest. Richards nearly toppled backward into the water.

"Hey!" Richards yelled.

"Bad shape," the young man said. "Need a lot of work. Rebuilt entirely would be the ticket."

Richards regained both his balance and his composure. He couldn't decide if he was angry or scared, but he wasn't about to move. Going up he had rotten stairs and Mr. Looney Tunes. Behind him he had the rats and water. The proverbial rock and a hard place.

"Maybe it's going to cloud up and rain," the young man said. "What do you think? Will it rain tonight?"

"I don't know," Richards managed.

"Lot of dark clouds floating about. Maybe they're rain clouds. Did I tell you about the God of the Razor? I really meant to. He rules the sharp things. He's the god of those who live by the blade. He was my friend Donny's god. Did you know he was Jack the Ripper's god?"

The young man dipped his hand into his coat pocket, pulled it out quickly and whipped his arm across his body twice, very fast. Richards caught a glimpse of something long and metal in his hand. Even the cloud-veiled moonlight managed to give it a dull, silver spark.

Richards put the light on him again. The young man was holding the object in front of him, as if he wished it to be examined. It was an impossibly large straight razor.

"I got this from Donny," the young man said. "He got it in an old shop somewhere. Gladewater, I think. It comes from a barber kit, and the kit originally came from England. Says so in the case. You should see the handle on this baby. Ivory. With a lot of little designs and symbols carved into it. Donny looked the symbols up. They're geometric patterns used for calling up a demon. Know what else? Jack the Ripper was no surgeon. He was a barber. I know, because Donny got the razor and started having these visions where Jack the Ripper and the God of the Razor came to talk to him. They explained what the razor was for. Donny said the reason they could talk to him was because he tried to shave with the razor and cut himself. The blood on the blade, and those symbols on the handle, they opened the gate. Opened it so the God of the Razor could come and live inside Donny's head. The Ripper told him that the metal in the blade goes all the way back to a sacrificial altar the Druids used."

The young man stopped talking, dropped the blade to his side. He looked over his shoulder. "That cloud is very dark... slow moving. I sort of bet on rain." He turned back to Richards. "Did I ask you if you thought it would rain tonight?"

Richards found he couldn't say a word. It was as if his tongue had turned to cork in his mouth. The young man didn't seem to notice or care.

"After Donny had the visions, he just talked and talked about this house. We used to play here when we were kids. Had the boards on the back window rigged so they'd slide like a trap door. They're still that way... Donny used to say this house had angles that sharpened the dull edges of your mind. I know what he means now. It is comfortable, don't you think?"

Richards, who was anything but comfortable, said nothing. Just stood very still, sweating, fearing, listening, aiming the light.

"Donny said the angles were honed best during the full moon. I didn't know what he was talking about then. I didn't understand about the sacrifices. Maybe you know about them? Been all over the papers and on the TV. The Decapitator they called him.

"It was Donny doing it, and from the way he started acting, talking about the God of the Razor, Jack the Ripper, this old house and its angles, I got suspicious. He got so he wouldn't even come around near or during a full moon, and when the moon started waning, he was different. Peaceful. I followed him a few times, but didn't have any luck. He drove to the Safeway, left his car there and walked. He was as quick and sneaky as a cat. He'd lose me right off. But then I got to figuring… him talking about this old house and all… and one full moon I came here and waited for him, and he showed up. You know what he was doing? He was bringing the heads here, tossing them down there in the water like those South American Indians used to toss bodies and stuff in sacrificial pools… It's the angles in the house, you see."

Richards had that sensation like ice-cold piss down his collar again, and suddenly he knew what that swimming rat had been pursuing, and what it was trying to do.

"He threw all seven heads down there, I figure," the young man said. "I saw him toss one." He pointed with the razor. "He was standing about where you are now when he did it. When he turned and saw me, he ran up after me. I froze, couldn't move a muscle. Every step he took, closer he got to me, the stranger he looked… he slashed me with the razor, across the chest, real deep. I fell down and he stood over me, the razor cocked," the young man cocked the razor to show Richards. "I think I screamed. But he didn't cut me again. It was like the rest of him was warring with the razor in his hand. He stood up, and walking stiff as one of those wind-up toy soldiers, he went back down the stairs, stood about where you are now, looked up at me, and drew that razor straight across his throat so hard and deep he damn near cut his head off. He fell back in the water there, sunk like an anvil. The razor landed on the last step.

"Wasn't any use; I tried to get him out of there, but he was gone, like he'd never been. I couldn't see a ripple. But the razor was lying there and I could hear it. Hear it sucking up Donny's blood like a kid sucking the sweet out of a sucker. Pretty soon there wasn't a drop of blood on it… I picked it up… so shiny, so damned shiny. I came upstairs, passed out on the floor from the loss of blood.

"At first I thought I was dreaming, or maybe delirious, because I was lying at the end of this dark alley between these trashcans with my back against the wall. There were legs sticking out of the trashcans, like tossed mannikins. Only they weren't mannikins. There were razor blades and nails sticking out of the soles of the feet and blood was running down the ankles and legs, swirling so that they looked like giant peppermint sticks. Then I heard a noise like someone trying to dribble a medicine ball across a hardwood floor. *Plop, plop, plop.* And then I saw the God of the Razor.

"First there's nothing in front of me but stewing shadows, and the next instant he's there. Tall and black... not Negro... but black like obsidian rock. Had eyes like smashed windshield glass and teeth like polished stickpins. Was wearing a top hat with this shiny band made out of chrome razor blades. His coat and pants looked like they were made out of human flesh, and sticking out of the pockets of his coat were gnawed fingers, like after-dinner treats. And he had this big old turnip pocket watch dangling out of his pants pocket on a strand of gut. The watch swung between his legs as he walked. And that plopping sound, know what that was? His shoes. He had these tiny, tiny feet and they were fitted right into the mouths of these human heads. One of the heads was a woman's and it dragged long black hair behind it when the God walked.

"Kept telling myself to wake up. But I couldn't. The God pulled this chair out of nowhere—it was made out of leg bones and the seat looked like scraps of flesh and hunks of hair—and he sat down, crossed his legs and dangled one of those ragged-head shoes in my face. Next thing he does is whip this ventriloquist dummy out of the air, and it looked like Donny, and was dressed like Donny had been last time I'd seen him, down there on the stair. The God put the dummy on his knee and Donny opened his eyes and spoke. 'Hey, buddy boy,' he said, 'how goes it? What do you think of the razor's bite? You see, pal, if you don't die from it, it's like a vampire's bite. Get my drift? You got to keep passing it on.

The sharp things will tell you when, and if you don't want to do it, they'll bother you until you do, or you slice yourself bad enough to come over here on the Darkside with me and Jack and the others. Well, got to go back now, join the gang. Be talking with you real soon, moving into your head.'

"Then he just sort of went limp on the God's knee, and the God took off his hat and he had this zipper running along the middle of his bald head. A goddamned zipper! He pulled it open. Smoke and fire and noises like screaming and car wrecks happening came out of there. He picked up the Donny dummy, which was real small now, and tossed him into the hole in his head the way you'd toss a treat into a Great Dane's mouth. Then he zipped up again and put on his hat. Never said a word. But he leaned forward and held his turnip watch so I could see it. The watch hands were skeleton fingers, and there was a face in there, pressing its nose in little smudged circles against the glass, and though I couldn't hear it, the face had its mouth open and it was screaming, and *that face was mine*. Then the God and the alley and the legs in the trashcans were gone. And so was the cut on my chest. Healed completely. Not even a mark.

"I left out of there and didn't tell a soul. And Donny, just like he said, came to live in my head, and the razor started singing to me nights, probably a song sort of like those sirens sang for that Ulysses fellow. And come near and on the full moon, the blades act up, mew and get inside of me. Then I know what I need to do… I did it tonight. Maybe if it had rained I wouldn't have had to do it… but it was clear enough for me to be busy."

The young man stopped talking, turned, stepped inside the house, out of sight. Richards sighed, but his relief was short-lived. The young man returned and came down a couple of steps. In one hand, by the long blond hair, he was holding a teenaged girl's head. The other clutched the razor.

The cloud veil fell away from the moon, and it became quite bright.

The young man, with a flick of his wrist, tossed the head at Richards, striking him in the chest, causing him to drop the light. The head bounced between Richards' legs and into the water with a flat splash.

"Listen..." Richards started, but anything he might have said aged, died and turned to dust in his mouth.

Fully outlined in the moonlight, the young man started down the steps, holding the razor before him like a battle flag.

Richards blinked. For a moment it looked as if the guy were wearing a... He was wearing a hat. A tall, black one with a shiny, metal band. And he was much larger now, and between his lips was a shimmer of wet, silver teeth like thirty-two polished stickpins.

Plop, plop came the sound of his feet on the steps, and in the lower and deeper shadows of the stairs, it looked as if the young man had not only grown in size and found a hat, but had darkened his face and stomped his feet into pumpkins... But one of the pumpkins streamed long, dark hair.

Plop, plop... Richards screamed and the sound of it rebounded against the basement walls like a superball.

Shattered starlight eyes beneath the hat. A Cheshire smile of argentine needles in a carbon face. A big, dark hand holding the razor, whipping it back and forth like a lion's talon snatching at warm, soft prey.

Swish, swish, swish.

Richards' scream was dying in his throat, if not in the echoing basement, when the razor flashed for him. He avoided it by stepping briskly backward. His foot went underwater, but found a step there. Momentarily. The rotting wood gave way, twisted his ankle, sent him plunging into the cold, foul wetness.

Just before his eyes, like portholes on a sinking ship, were covered by the liquid darkness, he saw the God of the Razor—now manifest in all his horrid form—lift a splitting head shoe and step into the water after him.

Richards torqued his body, swam long, hard strokes, coasted to the bottom; his hand touched something cold and clammy down there and a piece of it came away in his fingers.

Flipping it from him with a fan of his hand, he fought his way to the surface and broke water as the blond girl's head bobbed in front of him, two rat passengers aboard, gnawing viciously at the eye sockets.

Suddenly, the girl's head rose, perched on the crown of the tall hat of the God of the Razor, then it tumbled off, rats and all, into the greasy water.

Now there was the jet face of the God of the Razor and his mouth was open and the teeth blinked briefly before the lips drew tight, and the other hand, like an eggplant sprouting fingers, clutched Richards' coat collar and plucked him forward and Richards—the charnel breath of the God in his face, the sight of the lips slashing wide to once again reveal brilliant dental grill work—went limp as a pelt. And the God raised the razor to strike.

And the moon tumbled behind a thick, dark cloud. White face, shaggy hair, no hat, a fading glint of silver teeth... the young man holding the razor, clutching Richards' coat collar.

The juice back in his heart, Richards knocked the man's hand free, and the guy went under. Came up thrashing. Went under again. And when he rose this time, the razor was frantically flaying the air.

"Can't swim," he bellowed, "can't—" Under he went, and this time he did not come up. But Richards felt something touch his foot from below. He kicked out savagely, dog paddling wildly all the while. Then the touch was gone and the sloshing water went immediately calm.

Richards swam toward the broken stairway, tried to ignore the blond head that lurched by, now manned by a four-rat crew. He got hold of the loose, dangling stair rail and began to pull himself up. The old board screeched on its loosening nail, but held until Richards gained a hand on the door ledge, then it gave way with a groan and went to join the rest of the rotting lumber, the heads, the bodies, the faded stigmata of the God of the Razor.

Pulling himself up, Richards crawled into the room on his hands and knees, rolled over on his back... and something flashed between his legs... It was the razor. It was stuck to the bottom of his shoe... That had been the touch he had felt from below; the young guy still trying to cut him, or perhaps accidentally striking him during his desperate thrashings to regain the surface.

Sitting up, Richards took hold of the ivory handle and freed the blade. He got to his feet and stumbled toward the door. His ankle and foot hurt like hell where the step had given way beneath him, hurt him so badly he could hardly walk.

Then he felt the sticky, warm wetness oozing out of his foot to join the cold water in his shoe, and he knew that he had been cut by the razor.

But then he wasn't thinking anymore. He wasn't hurting anymore. The moon rolled out from behind a cloud like a colorless eye and he just stood there looking at his shadow on the lawn. The shadow of an impossibly large man wearing a top hat and balls on his feet, holding a monstrous razor in his hand.

The Butcher, The Baker, The Candlestick-Maker

Ennis Drake

"There floats a phantom on the slum's foul air,
Shaping, to eyes which have the gift of seeing,
Into the Spectre of that loathly air.
Face it—for vain is fleeing!
Red-handed, ruthless, furtive, unerect,
'Tis murderous Crime—the Nemesis of Neglect!"
—John Tenniel, *The Nemesis of Neglect*

Hey…
  Hey, Boss…

I could be anyone. Anyone at all. The butcher, the baker, the candlestick-maker. I could be you…

…you need to rip them. The whores. The sluts. The slags strutting round Whitechapel thicker than the garbage crusted round the mouths of the streets. Strutting round thicker than the Arabs and the Asians—who at least have the social conscience to cover their women.
  You know what I mean.

You can't *not* see them. And once you see them, you can't look away. You can't look away and you can't forgive them.

You see them all day long. Whores in their skinny jeans and fuck-me boots. With their clever hair. With their face paint. Plunge-cut tanks showing the soft, seeping fat of their tits. Everything about them begs LOOK AT ME!

Everything about them begs... rip me.

You want to oblige the filthy little pigs. It's a need growing in your guts, in your mind; a misplaced fetus with a mouth full of teeth. And you know, as the anniversary of Sickert's first "event" approaches...

...you *will* oblige them.

You have (them) one *allllllllll* picked out. Ha. Ha. And you're going to give it to her. You want to keep the ritual—29 thrusts—but you don't know if you'll be able to. Your chest's a kettle and your blood is whistling. The wad of flesh God cursed you with (cursed him, Sickert, with too) is hot in your pants. A straining, pulsing lump that sickens you.

But the blade...

(draw it from its sheath; the scrape of steel on leather)

...the blade is perfect.

Harder than hard.

Eight inches.

Beveled.

(the fine, fine rasp of flesh as your finger moves along the razored edge; Papa always said a knife wasn't sharp till you could run your finger along it and bring it away wet and sticky as fresh pussy)

You pull the greasy satin panel back from the window. Dusk. Street still teeming. You look down on them.

The blade, ever-hard, in your hand. Gleaming like purest silver in the un-whole light.

You look down on them.

It's August 4th.

Two more days.

Only two.

2:00 A.M. August 6th. The Day of the First Event.

You call this THE WILL TO KILL.

You're ready.

Clothes dark and tight out of necessity. To hide staining blood. To minimize the whore's purchase. Naughty whores will grab, you bet. Fight for their miserable whore lives. Wouldn't you? Even if you were the filthiest of filthy animals? Even if you sucked dicks for pounds? Wouldn't you fight for your life? For your survival?

Even the most trusted dog will bite if you kick it hard enough, long enough.

And there isn't a whore in all the world as good as a good dog.

High Street is intermittently dark. You imagine it by gaslight. The smell of the coal-gas. You imagine the stench of East London, East End, a hundred twenty-five years and however-many-tens-of-thousands of bodies less foul. You imagine what it must have been like: a Jewish ghetto in the midst of the Second Industrial Revolution; God's chosen children, the sons of Abraham, Isaac, and Jacob crowding the storefronts, the flats, the streets, forever seeking Salvation from the Oppressor; forever in Exodus. You stop on the south end of Whitechapel High Street, step back into the doorway of a Pakistani-owned grocery store. The red Perso-Arabic script against the white of the store sign stands out like blood runes in the window. You wipe sweat from your forehead with the sleeve of your shirt. The fabric's synthetic. It doesn't do much good. You turn your attention across the street. The White Swan isn't the White Swan anymore. It's a private pub, now. The Visage.

2:08 A.M.

She'll be coming soon.

Your Martha.

A Martha Tabram for the post-millennials.

The street is empty. Empty of eyes that care. The Rule of Law is as blind as Justice here. Both are impotent. The Metro only sees aftermath. Reports it. Catalogues it.

The unseasonable heat is the breath of an angry God; an Old Testament God; a God of the desert.

Your sweat doesn't cool, it just saturates your shirt. Slides down your temples, down your neck, into your collar, beads on the fabric (but finally takes, wet on wet). The knife is on your belt, hid in its black leather sheath, handle wrapped in electrical tape. Slung round your neck by its cord is the gender-neutral plastic mask you formed yourself in your kitchen. It's translucent. Almost pearlescent—something bad in the mix—but it's plenty serviceable. Across the mask's forehead you have written CRIME in Sharpie, mimicking Tenniel's famous cartoon, *The Nemesis of Neglect* (There floats a phantom on the slum's foul air).

She's coming. She's here.

Martha.

Her name's not Martha, of course. Which is unfortunate. But everything else...she's so *close*. The similarities between this woman leaving The Visage, today, and the Victorian "unfortunate" who left The White Swan on the arm of Walter Sickert (dressed as a Grenadier; Saucy Jack did so dearly love his costume) in the August chill more than a century ago, are astounding. Delightfully perfect. As if she has been offered up by the Universe to be your victim, your sacrifice. You can feel the cosmic strings, knotted in your balls, flying up through your body, your arms, out into the Ether to this woman, and from her...to Beyond.

Her real name (Pauline Nizza) is not important. Not yet. It won't matter to anyone till you kill her. Death is the price of her immortality; however ironic, it's the best offer she's going to get out of this life.

You put the mask on. Snug on your face; like it's your own; it's better than your own. You draw the knife...

(oh, that cutting whisper of steel)

...*your* knife.

The steel in your hand is the unfeeling steel inside you.

THE WILL TO KILL.

You pace her. Watch the rhythmic turn of her ass in its tight vinyl skirt. Legs perfect pistons of flesh in the lift of her heels. Meat. Meat and holes. She's perfect. Perfect whore.

The heat in your chest, in your pants (worthless), it disgusts…

(do it, do it, rip her, honor Walter Sickert, be Jack, rip, shed the Boss in you)

…and thrills you like nothing else.

Your oxblood gloves tighten, creak, on the knife hilt.

You're almost there: George Yard Buildings.

She senses you. Senses those cosmic strings that connect you to her. Senses the oncoming rush of immortality.

"Martha…" you say.

You grab her. She tries to scream. You cover her mouth. She bites down, perforating flesh even through your glove. You don't feel it because you're all-over heat. A fire. A living, breathing, walking, killing, consuming fire. The struggle. (Horripilation.) Muscles battling muscles. (Ecstasy.) The animal fear. Yours. Hers. Mingling. Sharp. You can smell it. Feel it like an electric current. She claws at the mask. Scratches your throat. You feel the skin peel away. Know it's under her nails. Hyper-aware. Even through everything else. Evidence. You file it. The knife. You stab. Resistance. The muscle, so hard. Hard as you. Then it gives way. The blade slides into the softness of organ. Soft as her softness. (Orgasm.) The hilt of the knife, blade buried in her like some lethal divining rod, telegraphs every movement; within, without. Telegraphs the beat of heart, the rush of blood through vein and artery. Trembling. You're both trembling. You pull it out. You stab. Pull it out. Stab. You choke back a cry of rage, release, relief. Stab. You stab. (Divine.) You stab over and over and over and over and over…

It must have taken unparalleled devotion, you think. For Sickert. How many papers and clippings did he collect? Scrutinize? He must have tried to collect every detail; he must have tried so vainly.

The sense of power, you know now, is undeniable. You know what no one else knows. In this, in these acts, you are God. The only one with perfect knowledge. But this is the Information Age, isn't it? The world is a Global Village. Home to the interminable, digital galleries of the Library of Babel. Knowledge is instant. Power without sacrifice. The Internet makes your work almost…mundane.

It's been nearly a month since you ripped her. Your Martha (poor stuck Pauline Nizza).

The police are apathetic. Disinterested. Murder is murder. In Whitechapel a knifed-up whore is just as much news as it was in Sickert's day. Which is to say, it isn't news at all. Just another brutal killing. Ho. Hum. Ha. Ha.

You maximize *The Independent* article on your laptop.

Victim identified in George Yard Stabbing
By Kevin Stevens
Thursday 21 August 2013

The young woman found brutally stabbed to death at George Yard Buildings in East London on Wednesday, August 6th, has now been identified by police as Pauline Nizza, 40, a resident of Pimlico Heights.

Dinesh Ongezni, 25, discovered Pauline's body on the 1st floor landing of George Yard Building at approximately 4:30 A.M. after returning from a stay with family in South London.

A student at The University College London, Dinesh told the Independent, "There was a lot of blood. You wouldn't think the body could hold so much blood, you know? My cousin (Dinesh's flat mate) rang the ambulance. I don't know why. She was already dead. Whoever did it, they carved something in her forehead…"

Martha, you think. I carved the name "Martha" in the whore's pretty skin.

"…but I couldn't make it out."

Metropolitan Police sent officers to the scene at 4:50 A.M. that Wednesday. A murder inquiry was opened and forensic tents were erected in the building. No arrests were made and police continue to appeal for witnesses. No other information has been released to the public.

You laugh at the computer. Turn to the easel at your back. You're still painting the acrylic base the oils will be laid over. Your Martha, in repose on a couch with a man you assume is her estranged husband, a little girl on her lap that you know is her daughter. The work is little more than an Impressionistic blur of colors, the shape of things to come still rude in composition. The photo you took from her flat before you "met" her on High Street is taped to the upper right corner of the canvas. You have admired it these past weeks, but you admire the faceless blurs of paint you have created more.

Whores don't deserve husbands.

Whores don't deserve children.

Whores don't deserve faces.

You pick up the remote to your stereo.

PLAY.

Morrissey blares, mid-tune, filling the flat with bleak, lover's tones.

You paint.

The detail of the oils over the acrylic is exquisite.

The oval of untouched canvas that is (and will remain) Pauline Nizza's face is like the clean hole you have left in the world.

This is your Mary Ann Nichols. Canonical victim #1. Dear, sweet Polly, as she was known on the streets Sickert prowled.

HUFFINGTON POST UNITED KINGDOM
Community "not surprised" over new stabbing death
By Roxanne Zulkowski
1 September 2013

The body of Patty Williams, 37, was discovered on Durward Street in Whitechapel at approximately 4:00 A.M. this morning by sanitation workers.

We mustn't forget to put out the trash, you think. Ha. Ha.

According to Muham Choudbury, one of the men who discovered the body, "POLLY" was scrawled on a wall behind her in chalk. "Her throat was cut up. Somebody had taken her pants off and her shirt was lifted up. Her...her guts were hanging out of her. What is wrong with people? It's these kids. These gangs. You hear about that attack in the Heights? No. Not the woman that was killed. The one where those boys knifed that girl when she got off the bus. Stuck her like she was nothing better 'an a pig. Right sick, innit?"

Detective Chief Inspector Edgar Lyons described the victim as a known and convicted drug user, and related that she had been detained recently in the investigation of a prostitution ring. "Frankly, I'm not at all surprised to have found her killed," Lyons said.

The Metropolitan Police are appealing to the public to come forward with any information that might be relevant to the investigations.

This is your Annie Chapman. Dark Annie. Canonical victim #2; what do *they* know?

HUFFINGTON POST UNITED KINGDOM
Third woman found stabbed to death in Whitechapel
Press Association
8 September 2013

Metropolitan Police and London Ambulance Service were called to Hanbury Car Park at 5:50 AM, where the body of an unidentified woman was subsequently pronounced dead.

A postmortem will take place later today at Greenwich mortuary.

Detective Chief Inspector Edgar Lyons, leading the investigation, said: "Another senseless killing. We're working now to identify her. There was nothing found on her person but an odd assortment of items. I urge anyone with information about this incident to come forward. If they prefer to remain anonymous, I ask that they contact Crimestoppers.

I know people locally are going to speculate about the fact that this murder took place in the same location Shawn Chambers was killed in September, but I would like to make it clear that we do not believe there is a link between the two incidents aside from the location."

They give no name? No mention of the clues you left? Are they beginning to understand?

THE GUARDIAN
Victim named in Hanbury Car Park stabbing
Press Association
11 September 2013

A woman found stabbed to death and mutilated in Whitechapel has been named by police.

Nancy Brace, aged 51, was found on the morning of September 8 by a security officer in the Hanbury Car Park. At the time of her death, police were unable to identify Brace.
She is survived by her husband and two sons.

The security officer who found Brace said: "Her throat had been cut and she was.... I'm sorry. Give me a moment. She was disemboweled. Her intestines had been arranged over each of her shoulders. Whoever did it, they scratched 'Dark Annie' in the hood of the car I found her by. There was all this junk around her, too. All laid out just so. Some pills. A comb. Half an envelope. There's a serial killer on the loose. That's what I think. This wasn't about gangs, or drugs. This was like some kind of sacrifice."

Yes. Dark Annie. They do understand. Their eyes are open.

Listen, Boss. Two words: Double Event.

THE TELEGRAPH
Two women stabbed to death in Whitechapel:
Metro Police fear serial killer
By Hattie Anne-James
3 October 2013

The double murder of "Long Liz" and the victim Metropolitan Police have dubbed "Catherine" has sparked speculation of a serial killer stalking the streets of Whitechapel.

Scarlett Thomas with Scotland Yard was quoted as saying: "There appears to be evidence—what I believe to be undeniable evidence—many of the recent murders in East London are related to the quasquicentennial anniversary of the Jack the

Ripper slayings. Items recovered from the scene at Hanbury Car Park where Nancy Brace was found stabbed to death on 8 September have been identified as symbolic with the 8 September 1888 slaying of Annie Chapman."

On 30 September, an unidentified victim was recovered from Henriques Street in Whitechapel at approximately 1:00 AM. The victim was pronounced dead at the scene by Metro police. Less than an hour later a second body was discovered by City police at the corner of Mitre Square. A distance of less than a quarter mile from the crime scene on Henriques Street.

Both victims were found with ritualistically displayed items with possible symbolic links to the Ripper killings of Elizabeth Stride and Catherine Eddowes, killed exactly 125 years ago.

Scarlett Thomas, a Chief Investigator for Scotland Yard, has taken over investigation of the five, possibly six, interrelated killings that began in Whitechapel as early as August this year.

You have transcended accepted "morality"; transcended the social human animal; transcended humanity itself. Woven a chrysalis of action, of determination, of retribution. You have chosen THE WILL TO POWER. Emerged from your cocoon Saved. Saved from the Bosses of the world.

There is but one more act of consecration.

You are not so foolish as to believe you will find immortality in Jack's footsteps, not in this modern world, but you have allowed yourself the hope of bolstering Sickert's. This is just the way of things, you know. The closest you might come to immortality is a TV miniseries.

But for that you must complete Sickert's (Jack's) most sacrosanct act. And you must get away with it.

It is time to make Black Mary.

She is special, your Mary. Oh so special! You bought her in Myanmar. In the Hill Country on the border to Thailand. She was not expensive.

You go down the stairs to the first-floor hall—Flat 6—reach through the broken window and unbolt the door.

The room is tiny. It was always tiny. Twelve-by-twelve whole. Now, with the false wall, the room you enter is a pie-slice four feet wide at its largest dimension. The false wall greets you. Plywood. Painted dark gray. Solid oak door at its center. Padlocked. Chained. In over a year, no one's noticed. No one has reached through the broken window, peeled away the curtain and seen this strange configuration. And if they have… not a one has reported it. Why would they? This is Whitechapel. The intersection of a hellish far right and the scum of the earth. No one cares, here. But they will remember this. For a little while.

Just inside the door is a halogen lantern. You pick it up, turn it on; its clear, blue-white light is like starlight in the darkness.

You key and unbolt the padlock. The chains crinkle, steel on steel on steel, to the floor. The door creaks. Shouldn't it? The hinges haven't moved in months.

She's there. Of course she's there. Bound to herself. Bound in starlight and shadow.

She sees you but doesn't respond. Doesn't shy, or shrink. Doesn't blink. You watch the pupils in her eyes diminish in the lamplight.

"Mary," you say.

Her head lifts on its slight, perfect frame. Like a dog's head will lift when you call its name.

"Hello, Mary."

Cow-round eyes, blank as tinted windows stare up at you.

You hold the lamp up and smile at her. Your most rakish smile. Women have always loved that smile; it is both sensual and disarming. You know. You have spent years studying it, practicing it, in mirrors.

You turn away from Mary. Turn a circle on your heel. An almost perfect pirouette. You have reconstructed the original crime scene as closely, as accurately, as necessary. The floor is the same oak it was a hundred or so years ago. Cut-in with shoddy patches, some of them pressboard. The walls are covered in soundproofing. But there are tables. Three of them. Small, wooden tables. A chair that's never been sat in. The bed in the far back corner. And the fireplace.

"Are you cold, Mary?" you ask cheerily.

"Ye... ye... yesss."

"Let's have a fire then, shall we?"

The fire is for light. Mary will be a cold, bloodless assortment of meat in a few hours. You wouldn't waste warmth on her even if that wasn't so.

In the fireplace there are two cured logs and an old copper kettle. You take a yellow bottle of Ronsonol lighter fluid out of your coat pocket. A box of matches. Shrug out of your coat. Throw it on top of the logs and the kettle. Soak it with the bottle of Ronsonol. Throw the empty bottle in. Strike the match on the brick hearth.

Flick.

The room ignites.

Mary screams.

For one brief moment, you and Mary are standing on the sun. Consumed. The smell of the coat, the lighter fluid, the burning plastic... it's sharp, nauseating.

You laugh.

Mary screams. And screams and screams.

You have her on the bed, one hand crimped over her face so hard you can feel her teeth through the skin of her lips. The other hand is on your knife.

The blade.

The blade has become all.

The focal point. Not just of your life, her life, but all life.

You draw the edge of the blade across her throat. It's not a slow movement. Not quick. There's pressure. Even. Precision. The smile of death must be perfect.

The struggle has become sex. Penetration, penetration. The last shudder of life, orgasm.

The blood comes. Hot. In spurts. In floods that fill all the fleshy hollows. Thick liquid emptying in every possible way. Life. Leaving. Emptying. Emptying. Emptying.

You lean down on her. Put your face to hers. Shadows and firelight cavort, caper, dance to the irregular music of her suffering. You want to see it. The blankness of abuse in her eyes becomes the dullness, the stillness, the nothingness of a passage that is transpiring. It's hard to see by the light of the fire, but it doesn't deter you. You must watch. The emptying, emptying, emptying.

Right now, two miles away in Pimlico Heights, a gang of teens are chasing a fourteen-year-old Bangladeshi boy down with wide kitchen knives. Legs pumping. Lungs burning. Hate fueling. Fear swelling: a thunderhead of dying hope. The boy trips. The gang falls on him. Blades go in. One. Two. Six. Stab. Stab. Feet kick. A small voice says, "Stop." Begs, "Don't do it!" Steel slips between bone. Into organs. It's all hot breath and animal sounds. An orgy of destruction for the sake of destruction. And then it's over and the boy is left to bleed, to die, alone on a dirty pavement that smells of oil and rubber. The gang members tuck bloody knives into socks, then into sleeves. They walk away, breath easing, hearts slowing. What's it about? What was the boy's life payment for? Does it even matter? Do we really care?

You cut into the fat of her left breast. Remove it. Place it under Mary's head—loose on its neck like a broken toy.

Trapped air escapes her lips. You press the blade to them—the silencing finger of her god—drawing cuts as you whisper, "Shhh-hhhhhhh! Quiet, now, Mary. Sh-sh-shhh!"

Three miles away, in the Docklands, through a membrane of time only a few hours thin, a fifteen-year-old girl leads her seventeen-year-old boyfriend to a flat he doesn't recognize. Six young men, aged 16-20, take bats and fists and tennied-feet to him. He's nothing to them. They're less than human. Less, even, than beasts. Even in the most fierce competitions for territory and mating rights, animals seldom kill others of their own kind. Knives come out. Laughter peals the silence (you peal skin from muscle, muscle from bone). Ugly noise. Hate without identifiable source. Hate as human condition. Knives go in. No emotion. No reason. Youth destroyed by youth, without remorse. What has changed? What have we done? What have we become? And have we earned it?

You remove her other breast, knife working in a ragged circle, into the muscle, cutting it away. Once removed, you arrange it by her right foot. Ceremony. Pomp and Circumstance.

You open her abdomen in the prescribed three cuts. Remove the flaps of skin, placing them on one of the wooden tables. You remove your sweat-soaked, blood-soaked shirt and throw it onto the fire. It smells like meat saturated in embalming fluid.

The smoke is hellish. Your eyes sting. Burn. Run tears. The light is too little. Time, running down.

This is your life's labor.

Everything must be perfect.

You pose her. Arrange her organs.

It's almost done.

You stare into her emptied eyes one more time. Her face. Her face is beautiful, even with the thin, silencing cuts of the knife running through the plump of her cocksucker.

You reverse grip on the knife.

Whores do not deserve faces.

You stab, arm working like a piece of machinery. The arm of a well pump. Up and down. Up and down. Up and down. Stab. Cut. Destroy. Erase.

You strip out of your gloves, the rest of your clothes. Add them to the fire. From the deep, commercial sink in the far corner of the room, you wash.

On the door in the main hall you write in chalk:

BLACK MARY
MURDER INSIDE

Naked, blade hard in your hand, you walk casually back up the stairs. To your flat on the second floor. No one sees you. No one wants to. You are truly one of thousands. Not even one of the worst. Your work, at least, is at an end.

An ambulance rushes down High Street, red lights and sirens and then it's gone. Not for your Mary.

You wonder how many murders you will have to wade through on Google News to find her when *they* find her? Will she even make headline (you worry)? Perhaps the front page of the *Guardian*... in print?

Does anyone read print anymore?

Ripping

Walter Greatshell

"You were brilliant up there. I'm a big fan of Louise Brooks."

"I hate to break it to you, but she's dead."

"So I've heard. Yet her hairstyle lives on. Drink?"

"Vodka tonic."

"Make it two. Listen… I may have a proposition for you."

"A proposition? And here I thought you were buying me drinks out of the goodness of your heart."

"Not that kind of proposition. I'm casting a movie, and I think you might be right for a part in it."

"Wow—how original. Did you bring your couch?"

"I'm serious."

"Aren't we all. The problem is, some of us are also full of shite."

"At least hear me out."

"I'm all ears, Mr. DeMille."

"Have you ever wanted to be in a movie?"

"At the price of a bumming?"

"Not quite."

"You offering to make me a movie star, then?"

"No. I think stars are obsolete. Expensive, temperamental…who needs them? Not me. The new face of cinema is not flesh and blood, it's CGI. Motion-capture—do you know what that is?"

"It's like how they make Gollum… or Jar Jar Binks."

"*Exactly.* Everybody knows who Gollum is, but not necessarily the guy who played him."

"Andy Serkis."

"Whatever. He was just a stand-in for the digital character they superimposed over him. You don't need stars for that; all you need is people who embody certain attributes of the character you want to create."

"Let me guess: You think I would be *perfect* as Gollum."

"No, but I would like to screen-test you, yes."

"Meaning you'd like me to remove my knickers."

"Certainly not."

"Then why me? Surely there are starving actresses in abundance."

"You have a specific quality I'm looking for, like you don't give a damn."

"You're describing every dancer in this place."

"But you're the only one with an Irish accent. You also project a certain... bruised innocence—an angel with a broken wing."

"Excuse me while I go have a wee vomit."

"It's a special quality that very much suits the character of Mary Jane Kelly."

"Who?"

"Mary Jane Kelly, age twenty-five—a pretty girl who came to the big city with stars in her eyes and ended up working the streets. True story."

"*That's* the role you want me to play? A hooker with a heart of gold? You've got some bloody cheek. Just tell me this: Are we talking about porn?"

"Absolutely not."

"Then what makes this silly tart's story so special?"

"She was the fifth and last victim of Jack the Ripper."

"Jack the Ripper—is that what your movie's about, then?"

"That's part of it. Our concept is to make a dead ringer for a Hitchcock film. Not just an homage, but the greatest film Hitchcock never made, using the tools of CGI technology to re-create all the familiar Hitchcockian trappings—in spectacular 3D no less."

"Sounds a bit dodgy to me. That CGI business always looks fake."

"Not if it's done well; did you think *Avatar* looked fake?"

"*Avatar* cost a billion dollars."

"But that same technology is now available off the shelf for much less, and we're getting it even cheaper because we're farming the digital effects out to a lot of little startup companies that are begging to compete with the big guys. The soundtrack will be contracted to a wonderful symphony orchestra in Belarus. Think of it: music in the style of Bernard Herrmann, titles evoking the mod designs of Saul Bass, CGI resurrections of such movie icons as Laurence Olivier, Cary Grant, Ingrid Bergman, Janet Leigh; a veritable Who's Who of the dead and famous, so real they'll practically climb off the screen and sit in your lap. There will even be the traditional cameo of jolly old Alfred himself—or a digital facsimile thereof."

"You're not overambitious at all, are you?"

"Have you looked at what amateurs are doing on YouTube these days? Kickstarter? Believe it or not, it's not really that difficult—the major studios are way behind the curve. We are on the cutting-edge of a New Cinema, a true People's Cinema, one without the soul-sucking demands of the Hollywood machine."

"Such as talent?"

"Talent is cheap; nothing is more common than unsung talent... as I'm sure you know. Come on, who wouldn't be excited to see a new film by Alfred Hitchcock? Or if not that, at least a film crassly purporting to be that?"

"So it's to be a Hitchcock film about Jack the Ripper?"

"It's actually a film-within-a-film: the making of a Hitchcock movie about the Ripper case, and how the production is beset by a new rash of Ripper-like murders on the set. All very meta."

"And when do you start filming this masterpiece?"

"We've already started. We're well into it. That's the beauty of CGI: the shooting is the easiest part. As soon as we hire an actor, we immediately get them on the set and shoot their scenes on high-def digital cameras. If more than one actor is in a shot, we can film them individually and composite them together later—in fact it's easier that way. We rent most of our equipment on demand, so we can't afford scheduling conflicts."

"I'm more interested in whether you can afford to pay."

"This is a bit of a guerilla shoot, everything's under the table, but after each day's work you get a hundred quid—cash. Your scenes will likely only take a couple of weeks to shoot, but when the movie wraps you get an extra bonus of a thousand quid."

"In other words, I shouldn't quit my day job."

"That depends on how well the picture does. It could be a big hit, in which case the sky's the limit. Look what happened with *Blair Witch*."

"*Blair Witch* was rubbish. So assuming I'm interested, what happens next?"

"We schedule a time for you to come to the set and do a screen test, preferably as soon as possible."

"How soon could that be?"

"First thing tomorrow morning?"

"Mornings are bad for me, I'm a late sleeper. How about right now?"

"But you've only just come off work. It's nearly midnight."

"Midnight is my favorite time of day. I'm all pumped up and nowhere to go."

"I suppose it *might* be possible... if you really think you're ready to go before the camera and read a few lines. I'd imagine the studio should be free at this hour. Look, I just don't want you to feel needlessly rushed. It's a fairly painless procedure as auditions go, but I do find some people require a certain amount of psychological preparation."

"Mister, I was born prepared. If this all turns out to be a load of bollocks, I'd rather find out sooner than later. Let's go."

"After you."

"By the way, what's the title of this motion-picture extravaganza of yours?"

"One word: *Heinous.*"

"*Heinous.* Well, let's hope it don't live up to its name."

"Welcome to our little film studio."

"This is it?"

"This is it."

"Not much to look at, is it?"

"It's all we need: lights, camera, action."

"Not much in the way of action. Where is everyone?"

"Off for the day, I reckon. It's just you and me, baby. Still ready for your close-up?"

"I can't believe this is what filmmaking has come to: a moldy basement hung with green draperies."

"Don't knock our green screen—that's where the magic happens."

"If you say so."

"Hey, filmmaking has always been the art of illusion. This is just the ultimate perfection of that art, creating almost everything necessary for a Hollywood epic right inside the computer."

"But doesn't that rather take the glamour out of it?"

"Glamour is a luxury we can't afford, love. Fancy sets and exotic locations cost money. Pixels work cheaper than union film crews."

"It's a bloody icebox in here, I can see my breath."

"Sorry, the heat's off. Why don't you go over these lines while I make us a spot of tea?"

"Thanks. And I wouldn't mind a tot of brandy in it."

"I may have just the thing."

"Fuckin' hell, what's this picture?"

"Oh, that's just the coroner's photograph of Mary Jane Kelly."

"I can see that! Why have you got me looking at it?"

"Just a little visual aid to help you get into character."

"I don't want to see that—what are you, mad?"

"Making a movie like this requires everyone involved to use their powers of imagination. This soundstage does not exist! Instead you must envision a gorgeous period-piece that interweaves both the terrifying monochrome of *Psycho* with the lurid Technicolor of *Frenzy*, because those are the contrasting visual motifs that audiences will see in the finished film. The idea is to combine the look of my earliest black-and-white pictures with the psychosexual opuses I make now."

"Come off it, it's not a contender for the bloody Palme d'Or, it's just a cheap horror movie. And to be honest, I'm not sure I care to be cut to pieces."

"Since you're playing a victim of Jack the Ripper, it is somewhat mandatory."

"I don't think so. In fact, you can shove it up your pretentious arse, Alfred—I'm outta here. Whoa… shit."

"Are you all right?"

"Must've had too much to drink… head's a bit swimmy. What's in this tea?"

"Just a little something to help you relax."

"Tastes funny… s'not brandy."

"No. Something slightly stronger."

"Think I better go…"

"Oops—don't try to stand up. I don't want you to hurt yourself."

"Not gonna… hurt myself."

"Just sit back, make yourself comfortable. *That's better.* If you don't mind, I'll turn on the camera now. Ready for your big scene?"

"Don't… feel good…"

"Tell you what: I'll just do my part, and you respond as you see fit."

"*Nuh…*"

"May I see your engagement ring? Thank you. This is quite incongruous; I am aggrieved to think of the man who would *debase* himself with such a charade. One cannot make a decent woman out of a pig by marrying it; a pig is only good for one use. If a man desires the heart of such a creature, there are far more sensible ways of obtaining it. The ring would be far better placed in its snout."

"No... p-please..."

"Four down, one to go. Like all true showmen, I've saved the best for last—we have a long night ahead of us, and I don't want to spoil it by going off half-cocked. The others were simple, just a matter of cutting their throats and copping a few souvenirs. Did you know the uterus feels exactly like a boiled egg?"

"...please God *no*..."

"Bit late to be thinking of God, my dear. But I'm sure you'll soon be joining your sisters in sin: Mary Ann Nichols, Annie Chapman, Elizabeth Stride and Catherine Eddowes—the last two killed on the same morning! That was a busy day. But the pure of heart needn't fear the knacker-man; he only calls on brute beasts. Animals are bred to be slaughtered, the Righteous to bleed them and dabble in their tripes. Do you know which you are? For rest assured *he* does."

"Help me... someone..."

"Shut up, slut. Would you believe there are those who call *my* behavior unnatural? In fact nature is my guide: 'red in tooth and claw.' Did you know the male bedbug has a very similar method? Instead of bothering with the bovine peculiarities of the female anatomy, he violently pierces her belly with a specialized tool... rather like the one I have here... in order to propagate his seed in an orifice of his own making. 'Catastrophic penetration,' some call it. *I* call it... all in good fun."

"And then I just scream and flail around a lot as you're hacking me to bits."

"More or less. I must say that was quite good for a cold read—nice job."

"Thanks—you had all the lines. Not exactly a barrel o' laughs, is it? Is that the end?"

"Just the end of your part. The movie goes on a bit longer after that with a big chase leading up to a climax on the roof of Westminster Abbey—typical Hitchcock finale."

"Starring Hitchcock himself, I assume. Do they catch old Alfred?"

"Of course! But we end the picture with a sense of lingering unease: What if Hitchcock's snuff film inspires other evil men to kill?"

"Or women."

"Hm? Yes, I suppose so. Excuse me, I'm suddenly feeling a bit sick… don't know what that's about. Whew. Never mind. Anyway, once our little epic is finished, we'll be entering it at all the major film festivals. Cannes, Venice, uh, Sundance… Toronto…"

"Maybe you should sit down a moment. You look a bit green."

"Yes… thank you. Strange…"

"Not all that strange, actually. I slipped something in your tea a moment ago."

"You… what?"

"Little habit of mine. You see, I've learned that men are nasty, repulsive brutes who get a sick thrill from seeing women tortured and murdered. It happened to my own mother. As you may well imagine, such a thing can play havoc with a child's mind. One day a man tried doing the same to me, and before I knew it I was covered in blood—his. I found that I liked it. It's really the only thing you bastards understand, innit?"

"Bitch… what've you… what've you done to me? *Ungh!*"

"That'll be the muscle spasms—very painful, so they say. Sorry about that. Good news is you won't suffer long. Bit of a coincidence, really, us meeting like this. Truth is stranger than fiction and all that. Maybe it was inevitable, considering. Quite funny, if you think about it: Jack and Jill."

"You… you… *mmph!*"

"I think that's enough talk for one night, don't you? Time to get down to business."

Something About Dr. Tumblety
Patrick Tumblety

An intruder in my room called my name and lifted me out of sleep. I fumbled for the light on my nightstand and ended up knocking it onto the floor. The moonlight that punctured through the window helped me to see that the intruder was not on that side of the room, so I hopped up and put my back against the wall. The television still played, but its glow was not strong enough to penetrate the darkness at the other side of the room. Had I left that on? I usually leave it on. Keeping my eyes fixed on the angular shadows of the interior space I leaned over and opened the top drawer of the nightstand, taking out and turning on my flashlight. I threw it on the bed and the light illuminated the dark corner. The room was empty. I must have been lucidly dreaming.

That's when the television called my name.

"Tumblety."

A man's deep voice narrated over old photographs of London's streets with the History Channel's "H" at the bottom corner of the screen. The pictures dissolved into a reenactment of a red-haired woman shielding herself from the shine of a lifted scalpel. A female interviewee replaced the reenactment, and though I wasn't completely coherent, I could make out key words such as "murder" and "Whitechapel." It was just another documentary about Jack the Ripper. The calling of my name, surely, was a mere byproduct from the remaining remnants of the dream.

"Tumblety," said the woman on the screen, and I held my breath while a chill of fright crawled up my spine. A yellowed photograph replaced her, showing a man with a bulbous head and a comically enormous Snidely Whiplash-like mustache. His identifier popped up on the lower third of the screen: Dr. Francis Tumblety.

Seeing my last name scrawled on the screen was so odd that I had to physically shake away the confusion.

The deep male voice continued, "Dr. Tumblety had already fled the United States to avoid persecution from both his private and business life, and continued what some have called a 'deviant life-style' while living in London. On the next episode of 'Ripper: Unleashed,' we will explore the facts behind this man's dealings in Whitechapel and why some expert investigators call him the best candidate in the search for Jack the Ripper's true identity."

I was never told a thing about my past. My grandfather killed himself when my father was a teenager, so there was never any knowledge passed down. If my mother knew anything about my lineage, she never told me. If she wasn't working, she was drinking, telling me that I was just like my father, telling me that I had to pay for his mistakes. She died when I was nineteen. If I ever see my father again, I'll tell him what I just learned, that it's not his fault he's an evil, abusive bastard. Evil just happens to run in the family.

Bad luck runs in the family as well. It's almost comical. I had dropped my Prozac down the bathroom sink and had to pick up a refill from the pharmacist. Fishing out a new pill on my way to work, I slipped on ice and the refill rolled into a runoff drain in the street. I arrived at the hospital twenty minutes late with a scraped knee and a coffee stain running down the left leg of my scrubs. During one of my father's angrier rants he had told me, "Son, every man in this family is fucking cursed." Considering the parents I had, as well as the extreme anxiety and the insomnia, nothing in my life had yet disproved that statement.

"You pissed yourself," Dr. Elizabeth Carmine muffled from behind her surgical mask as I walked through the door, looking up from a cadaver's chest cavity. Her judgmental eyes were the only visible part of her body, like Bela Lugosi's eyes in the Dracula films when he's transfixing his victims. Her dagger-like eyes and cold demeanor were the reasons why those who had the pleasure to work alongside her called her Dr. Death. A handful of students laughed behind their notebooks. They would need her recommendation for an internship one day, so it was better to suck up while they had the opportunity. I lifted up my half-filled cup of coffee with a fake "that's life" smile. I needed her to write me a recommendation too.

I worked in the room adjacent from the teaching lab. It was a closet space with two desks and a cot in case one of the instructors was pulling double duty as a medical professional and teacher. I used it a lot. After graduating with a doctorate in Cellular and Molecular Medicine I stuck around the hospital to help pay off my student loans. I spent hours translating Death's bad handwriting into a spreadsheet. The notes were from her personal research into using microscopic proteins to stimulate infected cells on gangrenous limbs in order to slow the rotting process. I did this until Melissa finally arrived, storming into the room at noon and announcing that it was lunchtime.

"Why do all doctors' handwriting look like chicken scratch?" I asked her, holding up the stationary paper. She dropped her surgical jacket and shoulder bag on her desk and leaned over me to look at the notebook. She picked up a pen from my desk and a pile of Post-it notes and slammed them down in front of me.

"Write your name in cursive," she demanded, and then unsheathed her laptop from her bag and placed it on the desk. Playfully, I did as she said and peeled the note away from the stack, lifting it into the air. She snatched it from my fingers and then stuck it to the back of my neck, "Congratulations, it's terrible, you're a real doctor." Though I'd only known her for a short while,

I was closer to Melissa than any other woman I've ever known. She had a unique effect on me that no other woman, including my mother, was ever able to create; she made me feel comfortable.

"I'll believe that when I get my own stationery," and then I saved the document.

The hospital's cafeteria was crowded, but we found a booth near the front. I bought vegetable soup to warm against the cold air that came from the windows. I knew Mel wouldn't take my seat or my jacket even if I offered. She was very strict on not showing that she needed anything. Even as a cancer survivor, she wore a pink ribbon on the inside of her jacket, not because she didn't want anyone to think she had once been sick, but to remind herself of her inner strength. I think I'm the only one who ever knew she was going through treatment. I never saw her family when visiting her in chemo, and mine were always the only flowers next to her bed.

I felt her look up from her parfait every few minutes, most likely wondering why I wasn't making small talk. I couldn't get my mind off of Francis Tumblety. My potential relationship to this man trailed my psyche like a shadow. It was a morbid curiosity, but maybe finding if it was true could fill the hole that was my family's unknown history.

As my mind wandered, fixating on the image of my possible relative, I spooned out the little bits of vegetables from the tomato broth. Apparently, three green beans, two baby carrots, and a handful of those little corncobs from Asian restaurants were enough for the café to call a "vegetable" soup. Mel used to be perplexed with the way I broke apart my food, like the way a soldier field-dresses a machine gun. She had gotten used to it in the eight months we had been working together.

My throat was dry so I reached for my water. Still half asleep, I miscalculated, and my knuckles hit the plastic cup, tipping it over the edge of the table. It fell onto a black leather dress shoe and splashed across a suit cuff. I looked up to see a very large man looking down on me and wearing a bemused grin. I grabbed the cup off of the floor and uttered an apology.

"And this," came Dr. Death's voice as she appeared at his side, "is the man I was telling you about."

Death was holding a tray of food that held two plates. I knew the woman well enough to know that she would only carry someone else's lunch if she could gain something from the action. The man must be important.

"Ah, you must be Dr. Patrick Tumblety," the man said jovially, sticking out a large hand. I shook it and kept my eyes fixed on his, wondering what he knew about me.

"Hello, sir…"

"Doctor," he corrected, "Henry Clemenson."

The Tumblety luck struck again. Henry Clemenson was the Dean of Medicine at Johns Hopkins Hospital, and I spilled water on him after Dr. Death talked shit about me.

"It's an honor to meet you, sir, uh, Doctor Clemenson." I was good at sabotaging myself.

The doctor shifted his gaze over to Melissa and extended his hand again. "And you must be Dr. Melissa Mendoza. Maddy here told me a lot about the two of you."

"I hope it's all good," Melissa said with a flirtatious undertone. She would often ask me why, even in the new millennium, she had to change herself in front of men to get professional attention. All I could ever think to say was, "The more things change the more they stay the same."

"Well, let's hope," Dr. Clemenson said with a huff that sounded like a laugh. "I hear you both applied for residency next quarter."

Mel and I just nod, unwilling to say anything that could disprove our worth to the man. The competition for the handful of open positions was fierce.

"I'm sorry I got your cuff wet, Doctor," I told him, and winced once I said it.

The doctor huffed out a laugh once more. "Nothin' to it, son. Y'all have a good afternoon, and good luck to ya on the applications."

He walked away and Death followed, but before moving out of sight she shot me a look that was full of disapproval.

"Do you believe in karma?" I asked Mel.

"Keep your head up," she snapped jokingly, keeping me from boiling over with anger. "Even if you did something in your past that was so bad that you are doomed for it, I haven't. I've put up with enough shit to get us both into Heaven."

I put the vegetables back into the broth and looked up at Melissa. Though she smiled, her eyes showed the truth, that I could have just ruined both of our chances.

My mother was right; I was paying for the sins of my father.

That evening was spent in bed researching with my laptop. I used various searches on my last name, as well as websites offering extensive research on family trees, one of which I had to pay to unlock information. None of these turned up much about whether or not I was directly related to the man, but I did find that it was highly likely. There are various versions of the name Tumblety, mostly spelled with an "ee" ending. The "ty" ending wasn't common, and the line tracing the name backwards ends with my great-great-grandfather, who travelled from Ireland. The name-line stopped there, only to pick up again with Francis Tumblety. However, it seemed to begin there as well, as his parents' headstone was chiseled with a different spelling: "Tumuelty."

This change in name wasn't too out of the ordinary, as Francis often used aliases as he traveled across America and Europe. Until his death in 1903, Francis had been known as a misogynistic homosexual who spent most of his life on the run from authorities on two separate continents. Though dying a free man, suspicion of several criminal acts are still attached to his name, the most infamous being that he is the likely candidate for the man known as Jack the Ripper.

Francis had been in Whitechapel at the time all the murders were committed, with rarely a credible alibi. He had rudimentary knowledge of human anatomy and an incredible distaste for women so intense that acquaintances had witnessed the man break out into sermons on the evil that women bring to mankind. The murders were of prostitutes, brutally cut and disemboweled, their womanhood torn from their bodies.

Upon investigation, Francis fled to France, and the suspicion surrounding him went global. Even the *New York Times* reported on the search for the doctor. The article was titled "Something about Dr. Tumblety," and that *something* was that he "…is at present under arrest on suspicion of being implicated in the Whitechapel murders."

Every psychological profile on Jack the Ripper fits a man like Francis Tumblety more than any other suspect, and every piece of information about the man I can find points to me as his last descendant.

Out of curiosity, I googled "Patrick Tumblety" in full, and every search result that was listed led to articles about Francis "The Ripper" Tumblety. If Dr. Death hadn't already sabotaged my career at the hospital, any other potential job would be turned away once they searched my name and came across Grandpa Serial Killer. My name doesn't appear until the survived-by article for my mother's obituary on page four, and who looks that far back anyway?

Seeing my name buried under all of that dark information made me think about karma again. What if the tragedy plaguing my family's history was residual payment for the unholy debt accrued by my one ancestor?

That question had plagued me for days. An almost supernatural feeling assured me that by knowing more about this man, I would know more about myself. I had been emailing Death that I was sick for almost a week. When I wasn't in my apartment I would haunt the library, the diner, the bagel shop, anywhere with a strong Wi-Fi connection. One barista commented on my twelve-hour stay by calling me the Phantom of the Starbucks as she finished her shift.

I couldn't argue, especially if she had seen the information on my computer screen.

There were many theories about the Ripper's motivations, from plain insanity to a conspiracy with several men to rid London of the lower class. If I were to conclude that Francis Tumblety was the sole murderer, then I could make some inferences that could have led to his actions. The hard facts about him included that he was a misogynist, an adequate physician, and a person who had no qualms about breaking the law. Could his hatred of women run deep enough to kill them? The women's bodies were mutilated, confirming his rage, but they were also dissected, the way you cut up a frog in a classroom. That piece of information stuck out at me, as though it were the key to a locked door. Could it be that he just didn't understand them? Did he take the women apart piece by piece, not out of hate, but because he wanted to understand how they worked?

Francis Tumblety could have just been a misunderstood and misguided doctor who used his skills to solve a problem. The Ripper could have been a man just trying to understand the world.

Regardless of his motives, the question remained: Since my ancestor was never caught, was vengeance being exacted on me? I never knew why I wanted to be a doctor, but considered that I probably just wanted to be a healer. I also never had a close relationship with a woman, but I figured that was because of my mother. I always felt detached from the world, an outsider. There needed to be a reason, and as strange as it seemed, my father must have been right when he said that the Tumblety name is cursed.

The lack of sleep was making me feel inebriated. I stopped by the hospital and asked Tom, one of the nurses, to grab me some Xanax. He just told me that I looked like shit and to get some rest. I had a six-day-old beard by that point and my eyes were bloodshot from staring at a computer screen for that long.

I resolved to sleep in the office. On my way there I found myself stopping at the morgue and contemplating cutting up a female cadaver. If Francis was family, the only way I could know anything about him was to do what he had done. I'd dissect a body and pull out the internal organs one by one. Some of the bodies had already been used as practice autopsies, so it was not like I would get caught, and if I did, no one would think I was doing anything other than practicing. Could I imagine this woman as my victim, putting myself inside my ancestor's head? I would dress her. Yes, that would bring more realism to the illusion. Melissa kept an extra pair of jeans and a few nice shirts for when she was going out directly after work. I could pretend I stalked the body, seduced her, and then cut her while she was still alive. What better way to understand the man inside me than to bring him to the surface?

I opened the door to the office and froze as the light in the hallway caught the edges of Death's face as she slept on the cot. My initial thought was that this had been a sign to back up and get out of the morgue and leave my curiosity in the past. However, still lacking sleep, medication, and sensibility, my unhinged mind rationalized the situation in a different direction; I had to work twice as hard to get anywhere, from living in assisted care when my mother died, to putting myself through medical school with multiple jobs. The curse pushed me to take the risk. Death was the temptation.

I was able to swipe a vial of sedative and a few syringes. I covered her eyes as I jabbed the needle into her neck. The doctor was in scrubs so I thought about changing her into Melissa's clothes, but Dr. Death was a flesh and blood specimen that I found. I no longer needed the illusion. I wrapped her in Melissa's lab coat and carried her limp body to the lab, straining against the dead weight as I plopped her onto the autopsy table. I didn't know what I was going to do, but the feeling of power over her was intoxicating.

Seeing the doctor on the slab created quite a manic feeling. I had left behind mere curiosity and there was no turning back, so I decided to enjoy myself. I went into the bathroom and shaved off what I had of my week-old beard until all that was left was the outline of a thin, pointed mustache. Had I more foresight, I would have gone all the way: grabbed a nice fitted jacket and a top hat to complete the iconic Ripper look. I also considered that, if I was able to get away with this much, could I commit murder for real? You can't burn in Hell twice.

I threw away my reservations and allowed my forefather to the forefront of my mind. Whatever he wanted to happen would happen.

I undressed the doctor and found myself quite embarrassed with how attracted I was to her. She had a more youthful figure then the hard lines of her face let on. Looking down at her nude, limp body brought up thoughts of my mother. On several occasions I had to strip my mother down and wash off the puke that accumulated during one of her drunken binges. She would be covered in the filth of her own transgressions. After washing her and draining the tub I wondered how someone who looked so pure on the outside could have so much internal chaos.

I put the scalpel to Death's chest and contemplated making a long cut down her abdomen. I wouldn't kill her, but I would cut her. The woman would wake up and never know how she got that scar, but she had seen that kind of incision so many times that she would know how it was made. She would always wonder who had cut her...

I could feel my forefather's disappointment in me, so I tried to push back my hesitation and just kill her like he wanted. This woman might have sabotaged my career anyway, so what kind of future did I have to look forward to? Besides, it was poetic. Francis Tumblety was wanted for murder and fraud in two different countries, but existed without persecution until he died. Francis' work lived on in infamy, and through a history that resided inside of me. I was responsible for carrying on his legacy...

A bright discoloration on the floor caught my attention. Melissa's pink ribbon from the inside of her jacket had detached and fell from the table. It triggered the memory of the day that she asked me to confirm what she had found inside of her body. My hands explored

Melissa's skin, my fingers pushing into her until I found a gross lump underneath her breast. An ugly thing resided and grew inside of her. Her cancer was the same as my curse. It grew and infected until it overcame the host.

Melissa beat her disease. Could the curse, like the cancer, be eradicated as well? If my father, and for all I knew all the men in my family, were burdened with the fallout generated by one man's choice to murder, had any of them ever tried to make up for that evil? Had they been keeping the darkness alive all this time by passing the burden down without trying to push against its influence?

It had plagued me, for sure, but until that moment it had yet to corrupt me like it did to all of the Tumblety men. In fact, every time I fought against it, something good happened. I had to work twice as hard, but I did work, and I was still alive and successful. The men in my family were weak, and so continued to feed the curse. I wanted to fight, to become a healer.

I was responsibility for putting an end to his legacy.

I took the scalpel off of the doctor's chest and took a step back from the slab. My anger toward this woman was fierce, justified, and natural, but my actions were not. Even in the changed state of mind I did not want to hurt this person, proving that I'm not a product of my past. Even though my past influenced my life I wasn't about to let my forefather take me down like he did to all the men that came before me. Even if life was harder because of where I came from I would gladly work twice as hard to be better than Death.

I placed Dr. Carmine back on the cot and left the hospital. I gave myself a shower and a shave and a few days to recover. When I awoke well rested, I had considered how close I came to hurting another human being. I thought of suicide, but that would just be a way out of the curse, a coward's way out. I wanted to heal the horror brought upon my family by the evil of Francis Tumblety, Jack the Ripper.

A few years have passed, and if the curse still haunts me I seem to be doing well with my fight against it. Melissa and I are engaged.

She asked me. Her one condition was that I had to stop dissecting my food. A month after the incident we each received an email from Dr. Henry Clemenson, welcoming us into the hospital's family of healers.

"Maddy always said," he concluded in his letter, "that there's 'something about Dr. Tumblety,' and I trust her instincts. If she thinks you are a worthy investment, then you must be."

Nowadays, when I google my name, the links on the first few pages attach to my accomplishments in the medical field. The name of Jack the Ripper, Francis Tumblety, doesn't show up until page four, and who looks that far back anyway?

The Truffle Pig

T.E. Grau

I am a ghost, a curl of smoke, a whisper told to children to shut stubborn eyes until sleep comes to take them from their sheets. A shadow of a thing that casts none.

I am the wave that washes away the sand castle when the father turns his head. I am a saboteur, a tracker. I am a killer of women, and of men. But so many women.

I am reviled by all who don't know me and hated by the very few that do. And I am the only thing that stands between how our world remains, and how it could be. No one wants to know how it could be, because it will mean the end of everything.

I have been given many names from many quarters, yet none that matter. Bloodhound. Monster. I know myself as the 42nd of my kind, and the success of my art is the last barrier that keeps us from falling into the soundless crush of the eternal abyss.

Presently, I am on the deck of a ship tossed by the North Atlantic, following those whom I and my forbearers have always followed, keeping six measured steps behind, which is close enough to see but not be seen. They never know who I am, or when I am going to strike, although I see them clearly. That is my edge, and the only reason why we are all still alive.

I would kill every last one of them if I could, but I am one, and those behind me very few. We must keep our numbers low, as secrets abhor a crowd. Yet there are so many of them, with their numbers multiplying around us, while ours dwindle in private, as all rare things do. Total eradication was attempted in the 7th century, and our order was nearly wiped out when we emerged from the shadows, drunk on hubris and the lotus of righteousness. We were cut down like chaff and chopped to pieces. Souvenirs made of our bones. So now I follow them like a bloodline curse, do not engage, and destroy their work in whatever way I can.

They make their rounds, and so do I, tailing them on their circuit of ancient outposts, established before time had meaning. After a stint in the red hill country of Southern France, they recently arrived in London, blending in with the bustle of the shrouded city, close enough to their communication base at Solsbury Hill and those things that still live deep in the Pictish Highlands above the Antonine Wall. The calculating Romans never built a wall without reason, let alone two. They knew what was lurking in those caves, what howled from the bottom of deep crags. But those bulwarks had crumbled with forgetfulness, while what they were built to repel waited for the stars to sing to them in melodies none of us could hear.

My work in London attracted more attention than we anticipated, as none of us could foresee the butchery of a few random spares igniting a national scandal that soon spread across the globe. Information moved so quickly these days, and we were guilty of underestimating the modern lust for depravity. During times past, such events would be muttered across a tilled row, accompanied by a sign of the cross or prayer to an ancestor. Murder was still hot in primal limbs back then, and untimely death was an unfortunate neighbor to every house. It was endured, a wintered dip in daily lives. But in these days of lace and buttermilk, death was marched into sitting rooms and made to dance, as a brush with oblivion became exclusive to the point of aristocratic fetish.

Accordingly, in a matter of hours, London exploded with interest in the first girl I took apart. This made my remaining task more difficult, demanding a hastily prepared misinformation campaign to distract the insatiable thirst of pen and populace from my bloody casework on the cobblestone of Whitechapel. Make it appear isolated, spiced with a bit of royal intrigue, so no broadminded Scotland Yardies would put the pieces together. Princes, Freemasons, palace doctors. Occulted journalists and Polish Jews. A smear of horseshit over the lens, ensuring that the puzzle would remain scattered upon the floor while the full picture bled invisible into the planks underneath.

They who continually force my practiced hand year after year are followers of the Dark Man, who was last documented by public record—since destroyed—striding out of a screaming Egypt after blanketing the land with pestilence three and a half millennia ago, before fading into the sand at a Delphic place still marked by the wandering Kharga of the great Western Desert. He had punished his former hosts for turning their backs on him in the name of river superstition buoyed by slave theology, while his legacy of plague was co-opted by various holy books in the years that followed. The Dark Man cared not for the truth or the lies, waiting for his next re-emergence on a timetable only he knew, dictated by the stars and those things that lay in wait far beyond them. In his absence, a growing coterie of acolytes disappeared underground with him, anticipating his next mission of celestial cataclysm, and often taking initiative, sowing anarchy to pave a path of advent. Multitudes went with him. Houses were cleared. Villages. Families within families that kept alive the Elder Ways, and those willing to sacrifice everything they knew to learn. The allure of the glinting black is irresistible to anonymous eyes choking on the monotony of the neverending gray.

That is when we were born, like seeds fertilized by rotting flesh, rising delicate into the morning air, yet still tasting death in our veins. We grew in secretive greenhouses, shaped by the blade, and then were released one at a time to follow across the planet the spoor of the Dark Man and those followers who glorified in his peculiar taste for destruction. But chaos begs for order, and order can only live to stabilize chaos, as water looks for the glass. And so I and others before me were tapped and trained, called by forces that no one fully understood yet dared not question, as the reality presumed by the rational mind is just an onion skin surrounding the deeper mysteries spiraling at the core. We were trained in the secret fighting arts and built a mental foundation grounded in the philosophies of dead moons, before graduating to anatomy and vivisection, memorizing the human form inside and out, as this was the battlefield on which our modern wars would be waged. The flesh. It always came back to the flesh. To hone our skills, we leaned on esoteric surgical techniques far in advance than those of contemporary physicians employed in the enterprise of saving lives, as our craft was always practiced in the pursuit of death. Removal of corruption on such a minute level could end in no other result, for the sake of the infected and the greater world. Much like the Romans and their concealed knowledge of what lay north of their Britannia walls, we had to keep in place a shade over our work and real reasons why we willingly play this game of fox and goose, hoop and stick. Marbles. Bloody fucking marbles.

And so we studied as we fought and learned as we died, finding that the servants of the Dark Man are dedicated, and not merely human. Things that slither, scuttle across the dust, and swim in lightless waters heed the call of this ancient numen, who happened across our reality incalculable eons past, before human and mammal, before the birds and thunder lizards and bright things of the sea. He has been with us since before the beginning, and much like us, named a thousand labels. One for each tribe. Trickster, Loki, Lucifer. He isn't any of these things, yet is all of these things. He is older than the gods of the Israelites and the Babylonians and the Sumerians and more powerful still, yet somehow bound by strictures outside our comprehension, inscrutable to even his followers, who bow low to the riddles. And blessed be these barriers, as without them, none would need my services, because no one would be around. Marbles.

Years we have battled, as the corpses stacked high. I followed their migration, driving them out of Cathar country, before they turned their sights on London. Old black pudding London, gem of the western world.

In between assignments, I enjoyed my stay in The Square Mile. I took tea and the sights, moving through halls of royalty and libertine gutters. Dipping my toes into the Thames, wondering how many skulls were staring back at me. All the while waiting out the stars. Like both sides had always done. The cosmic chess game played on a terrestrial board. I sniffed the air, avoided the food and sampled the humanity around me, which is a relatively painless process. Relatively. By way of my rather unconventional initiation, I was intimately familiar with the flavor of tainted meat, fouled by whatever their side brought through from far-off places and unleashed on our unprepared feedlot.

I had been stationed in London for several uneventful months, when I finally found the scent, which led me into the East End and the warren of brothels that serviced the bent desires of prim English gentlemen of Queen Victoria's empire. Following instructions taught to them in dreams, the Dark Man's followers utilized discarded street girls to spread their fungal stain into London's population. Death from trash, wrapped in a silken doily, this time using humans as the mules instead of fleas like centuries before. Prostitutes were hired and used, servicing clandestine orgies to keep the master plot hidden. Never one at a time, never kidnapped, as that would draw too much attention amongst the working women, and one can never kill the spread of gossip without sacking a city. They took their hosts from off the streets, and deposited spores into vaginas, mouths, eyes, organs, in a closely scrutinized mating ritual guised as fantasy play. Practicing their miscegenation in plain sight, lit by black candle and smoking brazier. After the wounds were washed and bustles retied and before the drugs wore off, the women were set free to spread what they now carried to the thousands of locals and global travelers that took full advantage of the daylight whore trade of fabled London. Catch and release, to grow the herd.

So I cut those mules apart, finding the bad bits and disposing of the disease as only my people know how. Spores were not just left in the womb, but could be anywhere, depending on the vagaries of the copulation, and the physical capabilities of the sire. Behind the cheekbone, spinning in the intestines, buried in the heart. The hosts didn't need to be quality, just female, and alive long enough for the spores to mature into polyps, and then into something more. Those unfortunate Brick Lane dollymops were just incubators, spider sacks to be sucked dry by the grand scheme of tiny parasites who dreamed of rising tall like their fathers. Prodigies from beyond the stars.

That just wouldn't do, so I sniffed them out, tracked them down, and did my business before disappearing into the fog.

Upon seeing my handiwork, draped proud and messy, the local authorities assumed rape, as they always do, but those poor drabs had been raped a thousand times before I ever found them. I was sending a message. To Them. Fucking cunts. This wasn't about murder, this wasn't about a scandalizing of the local whores. That was just collateral damage. My work was about protection, the careful removal of the next generation of those things that lived in the hills and other forgotten spots now shunned by humanity. The intelligent bacteria from far off Yuggoth, that did terrible and unpredictable things when acquainted with human ingredients.

My conspicuous message did the trick, and the fellowship of the Dark Man uprooted again in the middle of the night, booking passage to America by way of Arkham, with private train portage to Chicago in the middle west of the country. They thought that I was unaware of their plans, and especially their end destination, but just as they have tentacles, I have tendrils, and the concentrated wealth of the very few and very old can buy a mountain of classified information. Money can substitute for numbers on many occasions. Not on the field of battle, per se, but in the close quarters of global commerce, which is all that the world cares about these days anyway. That and their appetite for murder, just so long as it will shuffle out the door in time for brandy and cigars. These church pew sadists probably didn't deserve my work, but orders are orders, and our papers say keep them safe while giving them a circus. The clowns always draw the eye away from the cracking whips and creaking chains behind the tent flap.

I'll give them their circus, and do, because it suits my needs, and thwarts those of the Dark Man. It did the trick in London, and has moved the game west, across the frozen sea, following the path taken by so many English three hundred years before. Of course, the circumstances seemed different then, but the roots cause is not dissimilar. The exodus of faith.

A shout goes out, startling me, which is an unfamiliar sensation. I am on edge, and try to blame my seasick stomach. Yet I know something isn't right about the speed of their departure from London, but my pride hides the truth from me. A force bigger than my art and my kind is at work. I will tell myself that it was what I did on those East End streets that tore them from the city, but I know that I am wrong. Gods help me if I'm startled again. Gods help all of us.

Land is sighted and a crowd moves to the rail. New England off the starboard bow. The ship creaks southward past the lightless blot that makes up queer Innsmouth, bearing west again into the harbor, flanked by Kingsport and Martin's Beach to each side. We head up the sluggish Miskatonic to Arkham, where a waiting train will take them to the middle of the country and the expo that will bring in a million pilgrims a few years from now. What the docks did for London, this World's Fair will do for Chicago. Attracting flies of every species from every country on the planet. I will follow my six measured steps behind, and they will not know I am there, until they set up shop again, and I am there. Once again, in the shadows, sniffing the air.

Snow begins to fall, slicking the deck. It's Christmas time in the dying weeks of 1888, but no one seems to remember. No carolers stroll the streets of Arkham. No bells ring in the church houses.

The ship docks, and I disembark down the gangplank, slipping with my seventh step. A sailor catches me by the arm. "Watch yourself, miss," he says with a grin, revealing a sporting history in several missing teeth. "Don't want to drown yourself a foot from shore."

I just nod, feigning a coquettish blush that hides the burn of anger at my unsteady stride. For stumbling, even slightly, while the black seawater waits and watches below me.

"You arrived from London, then?" the sailor asks while escorting me to the pier, stepping lightly on the plank so as not to disturb my balance.

"Yes," I say, scanning the wharf.

"Terrible business happening there, with that Jack the Ripper running the streets."

The name snaps me back to attention. "Indeed, sir. A woman is lucky to make it out alive."

"Old Bloody Jack wouldn't like your type, I don't reckon."

I shoot him a look.

"Begging your pardon, ma'am," he sputters. "Just meanin' that you bein' such a fine lady and all, not like those brothel slags who got carved up proper."

I say nothing, as there is nothing to say.

"A bird's gotta keep her eyes open back home. Never know if Jack's headin' your way."

I can't help myself. "What if he's headed *your* way?"

The sailor is about to respond, but swallows his words. He tips his cap and hurries back to his ship. The fear has spread, as the game continues.

I called myself Jack in Londontown, but that's not who I am. That was just the latest mask, the newest nickname, and just as insipid as the others. And there will be others.

My name is the Truffle Pig, hard trained to root out the fungus. I am your protector, the 42nd of my kind. I was yours truly, and I will be again soon.

So next, Chicago.

Ripperology
Orrin Grey

"It is a blessed condition, believe me.
To be whispered about at street corners.
To live in other people's dreams, but not to have to be."
                    —*Candyman,* screenplay by Bernard Rose

It was my grandfather who taught me the difference between a man and a monster. I remember him saying, "When a man dies, that's the end of his power. A monster is different. When a monster dies, its power is just beginning." We were watching Bela Lugosi as Dracula at the time, on the big old black-and-white, wood-panel TV that sat in my grandfather's living room until the day he died.

He died in his sleep. Nothing terribly dramatic. They said that his heart just stopped. Though he had always seemed old to me, he never seemed weak or sick. In his last years, he often sat very still, staring off at nothing, or at something only he could see. He seemed like a golem, like a figure carved roughly from stone, hard and unyielding.

My grandfather was Jewish, by birth but not by practice. He had survived the Holocaust, had a number tattooed on his wrist and everything, just like in a movie. My mother said that he had been religious when he was a boy, but that the Holocaust had knocked his faith right out of him. I asked him once if he still believed, and he told me, "I believe in the God of Abraham, and that God is a motherfucker."

My mother and I lived in his house when I was growing up, until he died. When I broke one of his rules, he would whip me with his belt. I can remember the sound that belt made when he took it off; a clear, purposeful sound. I was afraid of him, but I was also enthralled by him. When he told me something, I listened as I never listened to anyone else, before or since.

When he died, my fear and my fascination died with him. I guess he was just a man, after all.

Why do we have a name for the study of Jack the Ripper? Why are men fascinated by him after all these years? Why the books, the movies, all of it? Jack the Ripper killed five people. Just five. And that's assuming that all were killed by the same hand. Others have killed more, in much more spectacular fashion, before and since. Sawney Bean and his clan, eating people in the Scottish hills of the 15th Century. Just five years after the Ripper murders, H. H. Holmes killed as many as two hundred people in ways a thousand times more fanciful and grotesque than anything the Ripper was ever accused of, but hardly anyone knows his name today. What's the difference?

It's really quite simple. With Holmes we have a name, a face, a photograph. We feel that we know him. We can say, "He did these black deeds, but he was still only a man." The power of the Ripper comes from the fact that he isn't a man. The hand that held the blade may have belonged to a man, or a woman, or to several people. That isn't important. It doesn't matter if the name was Sir William Gull, Lewis Carroll, or Mary Pearcey. That is why the legend of the Ripper is immune to every explanation, every suspect. No theory will ever satisfy, because the Ripper was much more than the hand that held the knife. Something that probably didn't yet exist at all when the first throat was cut. Something that may not have existed yet even when the last woman was dead. Its first faint stirrings could be felt when the killer was given a name. The heartbeat quickened as letters began to pour into police stations and newspapers, claiming to be from the Ripper. Suddenly, the Ripper was no longer just a killer, but had become something that was alive in every heart, sending letters out not by human agency, but from Hell itself.

No theory, no proof, will ever quench men's thirst for the Ripper legend, because the Ripper can never be contained by any one suspect, or conspiracy, or narrative. In Madame Tussauds' Chamber of Horrors he is represented only by a shadow, the last and final word on the Ripper's legacy.

—from *Every Man Jack*, by Derek Midwinter

Derek's table was next to mine at the Ghosts and Gangsters Convention in Chicago. During one of the many lulls between people walking by and listlessly fingering our books before moving off without buying a copy or asking for an autograph, he leaned over and introduced himself. "I need a beverage if I'm going to make it through this," he said. "You watch my table, and I'll bring you back something?"

He wore a three-piece suit, even though most of the other people aimlessly making the rounds were dressed in black t-shirts and jeans. His hair was long and white, with a beard to match, though he seemed to only be in his energetic fifties. When I shook his hand, I noticed that it felt strangely dry and smooth, like worn leather, like he was wearing an expensive glove. When I notice things like that, I try to imagine myself writing them down in a notebook in my head, so that I'll remember them later, when I'm back in front of my computer. I picture the words appearing in the notebook, written down by a phantom pen, *like an expensive glove*. It's my process; it works for me.

When Derek came back from the bar with a glass of beer in each hand, we got to talking, and that's when we learned that we both lived in Kansas City. If you spend any time at all in any kind of niche hobby, you quickly figure out that it's a small world. Anyone who does anything in it gets to know almost everyone else, and that goes double if you live in the Midwest, rather than New York or LA or someplace. It may not have been a lot, but it was enough to get us talking that night at the convention, and that was enough to get things started.

Derek stood out. He was what you'd call gregarious, though it also didn't take him long to put people off. He spoke like a lecturer, and I wasn't surprised to learn that he'd been an attorney before going on disability due to an undisclosed condition. He walked with a slight limp, but rumor had it that it was a psychological malady that kept him from practicing, rather than a physical one. Whichever it was, Derek never shared the nature of it with me.

He'd written two books on Jack the Ripper, one on Ed Gein, one on H. H. Holmes. All of them nonfiction, none of them really about the murders themselves. Instead he concerned himself with the cultural repercussions of the crimes, the narratives that had been built up around them. The ties between Ed Gein and *Psycho*, *The Texas Chainsaw Massacre*, and our modern idea of the serial killer, that kind of thing. "People like to compare actors and superheroes to the gods and demigods of Greek myth," he said in a lecture at that same convention, "but really it's the murderers who form the backbone of our cultural mythology. What does that say about us?"

He was at the convention peddling his second Ripper book, and from talking to him I quickly learned that, while he had come to Ripperology rather late in his career as a ghoul (his word), it had rapidly become the focus of his mania. He'd gotten his start in the field as a collector of murder memorabilia. The old-fashioned wire glasses that hid his dark eyes were actually part of his collection, worn by a clerk who worked the Holmes case in 1893, painstakingly restored and fitted with Derek's prescription. "No reason to assume that they saw anything to do with it, of course," he told me once, leaning conspiratorially over his beer, "but then again, no reason to assume they *didn't*, either."

The first time I went to Derek's big house on Holmes Street—not an accident, he told me—it was to see his collection. I was writing my third and longest book for Cold Blood Press, purveyors of local-interest true crime fiction, about the Bloody Benders. When Derek learned that, he told me that he had, in his collection, several pieces from the old Bender Museum in Cherryvale, from when it got shut down and turned into a fire station.

Derek was a bachelor, with a grown daughter from a marriage that had ended fifteen years before I met him. His house was nice, clean and meticulous, filled with books and real wood furniture. He had a wine cabinet, though I only ever saw him drink wine on two occasions.

He kept his collection in the basement. It wasn't at all dim or disordered, like it would have been in a police procedural or a scary movie. Derek was a collector, not a hoarder, and his collection was as meticulously organized as a museum vault. Carefully preserved, coded and catalogued, grouped together by murder and ordered by year. Nothing very new, aside from a few Ed Gein pieces left over from when he was researching his first book. Mostly, he was fascinated with murders from around the turn of the century. But there weren't any Jack the Ripper pieces in his collection.

When I asked him about it, he just shrugged, but then he brought it up again, out of the blue, later that night. "I don't really know why," he said, suddenly, in the midst of a lull in conversation. "My mania for collecting just seems to have petered out about the same time my mania for the Ripper really came on. Not that Ripper memorabilia is exactly easy to come by, anyway."

He may not have known why, but privately I think that it was just the evolution of his obsession. While he may have started out as a collector, it was always the way that we mythologize killers that really interested him. His collection was just an entry point to understand that process, beginning with fetishizing the accoutrements of the crimes, and moving from there to the metaphysics of the crimes themselves. Though Ripperology was never my thing, I'd read a few books on it before, and I read both of Derek's, and Derek was the only Ripperologist I ever knew of who didn't have a theory as to Jack's identity. In fact, Derek seemed to think that there was more to the Ripper mythos than any one identity could ever contain. That was essentially the thesis of his second Ripper book, *Every Man Jack*.

After Derek's death, the police asked me if I was his friend, and I wasn't sure how to answer. I guess that I was probably the best friend he had. We were both bachelors, both writers, both in the same field. We lived twenty minutes away from one another, in good traffic. I went to his house a few times, he came to mine more seldom. We used to meet for drinks at a bar on the Plaza called Sullivan's. I knew him for six years, but I never met his daughter, he never even told me the name of the firm where he used to work. When we got together it was our interests we talked about, not our lives. For the first two years, I assumed that Midwinter wasn't even his real last name, just something he put on because it looked better on the cover than Jones or Meyers, until I happened to see a utility bill on his kitchen table addressed to it.

Unlike my grandfather, Derek didn't die quietly in his sleep. And unlike my grandfather, I wasn't the one who found his body. He had a lady who came in twice a week to dust and vacuum and do the laundry, and she found him sitting in a chair in his basement, surrounded by his collection, a cutthroat razor in his lap and both of his hands nearly hacked off. The wrists not just slit, but sawed through, cut all the way around to the bone, as though he was trying to remove his hands like gloves. The coroner said that the tendons were severed in both hands. They had no idea how he'd managed to hold the razor at the end. The working theory was that he gripped it in his teeth.

He left behind no note, no indication of why he had done it. The police conducted an investigation, but there was no sign of forced entry or burglary, and they had no leads. Derek kept a careful catalog of his collection, and every item in it was account-ed for. All signs pointed to a bizarre and inexplicable suicide, case closed. It's what everyone assumed, his daughter included, and in their assumptions you could hear, unvoiced, the old refrains about his undisclosed mental condition, about the morbidity of his hobbies. I was asked only cursory questions during the inves-tigation, and I didn't have anything to add that would shed any light.

I went to Derek's house for the last time when the estate sale was happening. His daughter lived in Seattle, and while she flew down for the funeral, she had everything sold through an agency. Derek's collection went up on an online auction site and brought quite a bit of money. I didn't buy anything from it, though I bought a chair from his house at the regular auction, one that I used to sit in next to the bay window when we would drink and talk about crimes committed before we were born.

They moved most of the furniture out onto the lawn to sell it. Somehow, doing that divorced it from him, made it into just stuff, all disarrayed and random. Like a dissection or an anatomi-cal chart, just shapes now with numbers tacked on, nothing left that resembled a person, resembled a life. People were wandering through it in the fall weather, kicking dead leaves off the lawn and pulling the drawers out of dressers. I was standing on the front walk, looking up at the house, and my glance fell on the cupola window above the front porch, where Derek used to sit and watch the traffic go by when he couldn't sleep. A figure was standing there, just a shadow against the glare of the window, but one that I knew instantly, though I had never seen it before. It was a figure that anyone alive would recognize. Tall and indistinct, in a top hat and cape, his white-gloved hands crossed at his waist.

Maybe I should have gone in then and investigated. Maybe I would have found that it was just some eccentric collector, another enthusiast come to gather memorabilia from Derek's old life. But seeing that figure there, feeling his unseen gaze on me, I felt sick, like the sidewalk was buckling under my feet, and I turned and walked away, sat sweating in my car on the side of the road until I felt well enough to drive home.

The day after the estate sale, I got a package in the mail from Derek, postmarked the day that he'd killed himself. I called the post office, and they said he'd left instructions to delay postage. They'd assumed that it was a birthday present or something.

Inside there was no note, no explanation. Nothing to clarify the nightmare jumble of his death. Just one object, carefully wrapped and sealed, something that hadn't been listed on his exhaustive collection manifest. A single white opera glove, with a brownish-red stain around the cuff.

That night, I had a dream. In it, I watched myself sleeping from a vantage point somewhere up near the corner of my ceiling. From there I couldn't see the glove extract itself from its nest of packaging on my kitchen table, but I heard the rustling and I saw it appear like a plump, pale spider in my bedroom doorway. Bodiless as a dreamer, powerless to intervene, I watched it creep across the floor and up my sleeping body. When it fastened itself around my throat I felt its grip, dry and smooth.

That was the last night that I slept. I spend a lot of time now sitting and looking out my own window at the street below, waiting for a familiar shadow to cross my path. In life I was fascinated by Derek Midwinter. In death, he terrifies me. I guess maybe now he's become the monster after all.

Hell Broke Loose

Ed Kurtz

HELL BROKE LOOSE,

Could Not More Appall the Good
People of the Capital
City

Than the Dark and Damnable Deeds
Done in the Blackness of Night
By Fiends.

—Headline from the *Fort Worth Gazette*,
December 26, 1885

I.

BLOOD! BLOOD! BLOOD!

So screamed the headline Christmas morning, bellowed by news agents on every street corner, howled mournfully by a thousand terrified neighbors. So screamed his brain the night before, Christmas Eve, as he staggered between houses and through dark alleys, avoiding the streetlamps lest they betray the slick, dripping red that coated his form, stains that could never be washed clean. His hot breath shot gusts of steam from his gasping mouth, each

wheezing huff expelling her name into the erstwhile silent night:
Luly!

Out came the dogs, the policemen's hounds sent free and wild,
snarling into the shadows in pursuit of the annihilator, the killer
of girls, now a chimera none of them could fathom. Heretofore
the fiend slaughtered colored servants only, a heinous crime but
nothing to overly concern the society ladies when they lay in their
dark bedchambers at night. But now…

The muscles in his back and legs burned with exertion, tighten-
ing and tiring as he pressed on, dodging the lamps and lanterns
and frightened gasps as the news rapidly spread—the annihilator
had murdered again. Sweat boiled out of his skin, mixing with the
blood spattered on his face and sluicing down to sting his eyes. His
voice whined through hitching breaths, the hobnails in his shoes
scratched at the hard dirt of the unpaved lanes he desperately traversed. *Did you hear? Did you hear?* cried voices he doubted were
real, phantoms risen from his fear- and guilt-addled mind. The
too-bright moon sent spears of silver light to the earth, illumining
the pink-white stones piled around the nascent capitol building
at the head of Congress Avenue, firing at him like Jupiter's thun-
derbolts. He scrambled south, ever sliding through the pitch as
insects that fear the light, tumbling into the city's terror until at
last he reached the comforting embrace of the First Ward.

II.

Blake Prentiss threw back his head to finish off a glass of beer; he
had his hand up at the serving girl before he swallowed the last
gulp. The girl, a pale complexioned beauty named Delilah, gave a
sharp nod and bustled to the bar to pour another glass. All around
Blake in the dim, smoky tavern rowdy men sang and cursed and
groped the half-dressed girls squirming in their laps. Farmers and
lawyers alike, they rose one by one to palm a dollar to the bearded
attendant guarding the darkened back rooms, the sporting girl of

their choice in tow. Such was the pattern and purpose of the First Ward—*Guy Town*—though this was not what drew Blake to this noisy, lascivious sector of Austin. He wanted nothing more than to drink until he blacked out, and though he could do that practically anywhere he wanted, Blake deigned to do it in an assignation house's first floor saloon for the anonymity it afforded him.

Delilah came sweeping through the dense, odorous throng with Blake's beer glass in hand, floating carefully so as to not spill a single drop. She deposited the glass on the table and immediately eased herself onto his lap, her face the picture of gloom, whereupon she locked eyes with him and awaited his reaction.

"No, not today, my dear," Blake said apologetically.

Delilah pouted and knitted her paper-white brow.

"You don't go to a cattle auction just to smell the cow shit too, do you?"

Blake grinned, took her hand and dropped two dollars into it.

"Christmas is the day after tomorrow, you know," he said to her. "I pray you have a happy one, Delilah."

"With some smelly cowboy sweating and grunting over me, and while you'll be singing carols and eating rumcake? Don't be stupid, Blake."

He shrugged, unsure of what to say so he said nothing at all. She stood up from his lap and dropped the two coins in her apron pocket.

"Whoever she is, I reckon she can't be worth it."

"Why would you say that?"

"Because no one's worth it. Not in the end."

She offered a bittersweet smile and turned on the balls of her feet before melting back into the hollering mob. A moment later she shrieked as her head and shoulders flew up above the seat of pomaded and hat-covered heads. Some rough fellow had swept her up like so much chattel and was barreling through the crowd toward the back rooms with her slumped over his shoulder. Her face was grave but she wasn't resisting her fate. This was, after all,

Delilah's lot in life. This was Guy Town.

He drank a quarter of the beer and left. Just outside the batwing doors a tall woman leaned against the saloon's façade, her red curls cascading down and over her shoulders like liquid flames.

"Evening, Blake," she purred.

"Mona."

"Do me a favor?"

"I'm not looking for company tonight."

"Neither am I—that's the favor. Could you just walk me back to May's? Nobody'll bother me if you're along."

Blake sighed and failed to suppress a small smile. He offered his arm and Mona accepted it, and if she had not been one of the better known whores in Austin they would have looked just like a pair of amorous lovers out for a late stroll. They spoke little during the long jaunt to the southerly end of Congress Avenue where an unassuming three-story hotel stood. No outsider would ever have given the plain structure a second glance, but May Tobin's knocking shop was infamous to locals. Like a half dozen other girls Mona lived there, more or less, so long as she kept a steady stream of paying guests visiting her in her room. Why she was eschewing her professional obligation tonight Blake did not know, but as a longtime friend and client of the capital city's working girl contingent he knew better than to ask prying questions.

They stopped before the front door where Mona delivered a kiss to his cheek. He replied by way of a soft squeeze on her shoulder.

"You're a prince, Blake Prentiss," she said with a wink before opening the door and vanishing into the hotel.

"Ain't I just," he whispered to himself as he turned back the way he came. The rhythmic clop of mules' hooves sounded behind him, the arrival of a carriage at the Tobin House. Blake shook his head and laughed quietly, remembering the rustic little town Austin had been a mere fifteen years back. The thought of a May Tobin—never mind her thriving success or the city fathers' un- voiced acquiescence to it—would have sent any number of the town's mere five thousand citizens into apoplectic fits then. Now lewd women were a given, an assumed aspect of life in a rapidly growing city. *How quickly things change*, Blake thought.

He paused under the light of a streetlamp—another recent introduction—and watched as the mule driver stayed his beasts and the carriage slowed to a halt. Presently the driver stepped down to the unpaved street and opened the carriage door, from which came a woman in a billowy dress the color of a robin's egg. Blake fairly stared, his mouth agape. It was her. It was Eula Phillips. And she was not alone.

Next emerged a tall and reedy figure dressed in black, a wide-brimmed hat perched on his head. The tall man paused to confer with the driver, leaning in close to speak in private. Then the driver climbed back up to his seat and the tall man opened the hotel door, which he held for Eula. She glided in like a ghost and the man stalked after her, shutting the door behind him. In the next instant the driver jerked the reins and the mules went clopping north on Congress, trotting right past Blake and off into the night.

Blake froze, his mind reeling. What on earth was Eula, a married woman, doing at a house of assignation with a strange man? That he loved her and chose drink over adultery only exacerbated his bewilderment. Out of respect for her Blake did everything in his power to avoid her company lest his baser instincts get the better of him, yet here was undeniable proof that she cared nothing for her matrimonial bond with Jimmy, for the man who escorted her into that house of ill-repute was most assuredly not her husband.

Thunderstruck, Blake stepped away from the halo of light that bathed him from above and slinked through the inky night to the nearest window on the hotel's first floor. The lace curtains were only slightly parted, though enough that he had a direct line of sight into the parlor. A pair of half-dressed girls sang and served drinks to a trio of inebriated men in black suits while May herself played an out of tune melody on the piano. Abruptly one of the fellows, a fat man with a handlebar moustache, grabbed a yellow-haired girl and tore the whalebone brassiere from her torso with a single deft stroke. The girl screamed and covered her bared breasts with her arms as she sped from the room. The man laughed uproariously, and every other person present soon joined his mirth. May switched tunes—"Sweet Betsey from Pike"—and the party continued as though nothing had transpired. Blake frowned and snuck to the next window down.

Here Blake found a hallway lined with closed doors and a staircase in the middle. One of the doors on the left cracked open and a young girl's head poked out. The party in the parlor fell into song and the girl grinned.

"Oh, do you remember Sweet Betsey from Pike
Who crossed the wide prairie with her lover Ike?
With two yoke of oxen, a big yellow dog,
A tall Shanghai rooster, and one spotted hog."

She smiled more broadly still and stepped out into the hall, fully naked from crown to toe, and added her warbling voice to the proceedings:

"Hoodle dang, fol-dee-dye-do," she hollered at the parlor. *"Hoodle dang fol-dee-day!"*

"That's the spirit, Amelia!" May Tobin hollered back.

A spattering of low, throaty laughs followed. Blake moved on.

At the fourth window down from the street, he peered into a chamber weakly lit by a sconce on the wall. He sucked in a sharp breath upon seeing Eula seated stiffly on the edge of the bed in the center of the room and her escort facing the opposite wall, his hands together behind his back. The man still wore the wide-brimmed hat and stood so still he seemed unreal, a statue or manikin. Eula's shoulders bounced as she softly wept.

"Luly," Blake whispered. "What have you gotten yourself into?"

He lowered himself to a squat and sat on the ground beneath the window where he listened to the love of his life sob beside an uncaring stranger.

III.

She was only seventeen, a fair-skinned beauty with dark brown curls she usually wore swept back from her soft and pensive face. Already married and the mother of a young boy when Blake first laid eyes on her, he knew immediately that he would always be relegated to admiring her from a distance, loving another man's wife in the cold isolation of his aching heart. For a time he tried to choke it off at the roots, to suffocate the unwanted emotions without pity, but he learned in due time it could not be done. Blake Prentiss loved a woman he could never have and there was nothing he could ever do about it. From the moment this realization dawned on him, Blake sought refuge at the bottom of a bottle—a thousand bottles. Branded a layabout as things stood, he should become a roustabout, a "rowdy" like so many of the rough types who populated Guy Town in the First Ward. A cur, a scoundrel, a useless wretch. Though lately a bucolic cowtown, Austin was fast approaching cityhood and that made room for worthless rascals and dipsomaniacs who whiled their days away with drink and whores. The only trouble Blake ever foresaw was his inability to lie with any woman who did not happen to be Eula Phillips.

If he was fortunate, Blake oft-times reasoned, the drink would kill him before he had to take a more direct approach. Otherwise, there was no shortage of trains that shuttled through the center of town in front of which he might just lay down and close his eyes and…

The scent of rosewater and sweat filled his nose, cloyed in his throat. His head swam and he was back at his father's apothecary—not eight blocks north on Congress—that same heady aroma sweeping into the room and nearly knocking him over. The other woman came in first, blocking his view of the downcast girl trailing behind but not the scent, not the scent. Chamomile flowers, cottonwood extract and ergot was what she wanted, her eyes ever drifting back to the pitiful looking girl at her side, and Blake was no blockhead, he knew what manner of potion this alchemist aimed to throw together. The young girl was to induce an abortion, perhaps by this stern woman's urging, though perhaps not. What was certain was the girl's desperate despondency, an aspect of her mysterious aura that only heightened Blake's utter fascination with her. He fulfilled the order and put the charge in the ledger, debited to one James Phillips. As they left, the escort barked, "Come, Luly…"

Luly.

Five days after Christmas it was, an easily memorized date not only for the importance it held in the chambers of his wounded heart, but in the terror and mystification of anyone who heard tell of the Negro servant girl's murder. The poor girl, name of Mollie Smith according to the newsmen, was discovered back of her wealthy employer's estate, stripped to her underthings and left behind the outhouse with a yawning red hole in her skull. December the thirtieth, the day Blake's soul shriveled up inside of him and an unfortunate young woman fell afoul of the business end of a fiend's ax blade. And though he witnessed the grisly aftermath, the neighbors who came scuttling at the screams and the policemen who looked on stupidly with lanterns held aloft, his thoughts remained focused on the frail girl in the apothecary, desperate to prevent the birth of the child in her womb. His eyes stung and tears spilled down his cold face while he watched the police turn Mollie's violated corpse this way and that, offering baseless suppositions to one another and poking probing fingers at the grinning red mouth the ax made.

"Did you know the Negress?" a corpulent officer of the law demanded of him. "Did you observe the killing? Who did it? What do you know?"

But of course Blake knew nothing apart from his envy of the late Ms. Smith, her suffering in this atrocious game put to an end. Perhaps, he considered, they would apprehend her killer, whereupon Blake was certain he would be tried, convicted and hanged with all the efficiency and aplomb the Great State of Texas could muster. What would never be so much as whispered by anyone was the great favor the assassin had bestowed upon poor Mollie Smith. All life was pain and disappointment, white and colored alike, and this black angel came to relieve her of that anguish.

"No," he muttered to the officer. "I saw nothing."

He saw plenty while he fitfully slept that night, however: visions of murdered girls, their skulls split in twain, nude but for the concealing dresses of red-black blood that swung majestically about them like the finest fabrics. Luly Phillips was chief among them, the queen of the dead, unrecognizable due to the total removal of her face though Blake could never mistake the tiny steps she took, the way she directed her gory head to her bloodstained feet with shame and self-loathing. Her bare-boned jaw flapped on its hinges and incoherent sounds roiled out of her throat, crying out for release, for an end to the myriad miseries life inflicted upon her. He reached out for her, stretched aching limbs to just touch her fragile, pallid skin, but at his touch her flesh turned liquid and sloughed off like mud in a rainstorm.

He awoke at noon, his eyes swollen from sobbing in his sleep.

IV.

Spring arrived before he was tortured with a second visitation from Luly Phillips.

The five-month interval had done nothing to calm Blake's frayed nerves, but for the most part Austin no longer gossiped about the gruesome demise of the servant girl Mollie Smith. Her common law husband, it was revealed, was also attacked and survived. Mollie herself was determined to have been outraged by her attacker, a nasty detail that led detectives to the doorstep of her former lover, a man named Lem Brooks. The bewildered man was promptly arrested, beaten within an inch of his life, and tried. To the astonishment of a breathless city, he was freed when the court failed to nail down sufficient evidence to convict him of Mollie's murder. In weeks, the outrageous crime dissipated like smoke, all but forgotten.

Then, in May, Blake Prentiss espied the annihilator of his peace and well-being ambling down Cypress Street, a parasol in her hand and a dour-faced gentleman at her side. He swooned like a woman in a melodrama, fell to his knees in the street. A threesome of cowboys rushed to assist him. Luly did not notice.

As a train shuttled noisily over the nearby railway track, a white-haired man in an equally white suit waddled from the expansive porch of a house set back from the street. A colored woman stood in the doorway, wringing her hands as she watched the man hurry to Blake's side. The cowboys had him sitting up, though his face was besmirched with dirt and his eyelids fluttered, struggling to stay open.

"All right, boys," the older man said with deep-voiced authority. "Best we get him up to the house, then."

The man led the way as the cowboys dragged Blake from the street and up the walk to the porch. The woman leapt out of the path of the charging man, who barked at her, "Eliza—hot soup for our guest."

"Yessuh," the girl answered softly, and she scurried off to the kitchen.

The cowboys trampled through the parlor leaving a trail of mud in dust in their wake. They clumsily dropped Blake on a divan and as quickly as they came in, they went back out. The man stood over Blake like a conquering warrior, his hands on his broad hips and a slight smile on his lips. Blake tried to sit up, but the room spun and he fell back into the soft cushioning of the divan.

"No, don't try to move, son. You've had a spell. My girl's bringing you something to get your strength back up."

The man shoved a meaty pink hand at Blake and announced, "L. B. Johnson—I'm a doctor, so don't you worry. You're in good hands."

"Mr.—Dr. Johnson, I'm embarrassed terribly," Blake muttered, turning his head away from the older man's staring face. Johnson merely laughed as Eliza returned from the kitchen with a serving tray balanced atop her hands.

"Our Eliza's a fine cook, son, a fine cook. Pea soup, is it?"

The woman nodded as she set the tray down on the adjacent table where Blake could see a ceramic bowl filled to the top with a steaming green goop. His stomach flipped. He sat up at once, his face hot and vision blurred. Somewhere in the blur Eliza lingered nervously, eyeing him with something like suspicion but not quite fear. Blake stood up, shakily.

"I mustn't impose, Doctor," he said. "I'm wanted elsewhere, you understand."

"But, young fellow…"

"Thank you, Dr. Johnson. And thank you, Ms. Eliza. I'm sure your soup is lovely."

Johnson sputtered and Eliza took several long strides toward the kitchen as Blake staggered for the door. The woman's perfume intercepted him halfway, striking his senses like hammer on nails. Did servants permit themselves such niceties? Perhaps, he reasoned, it was a gift from her employer. Perhaps the venerable physician insisted upon Eliza smelling pretty in his presence. Blake reached for the door handle and fell gasping out of the house as he lurched down the steps from the porch and hurried back to Cypress Street. Behind him Dr. Johnson appeared in the open doorway.

"Be careful, son! Be careful!"

As his head cleared and his stomach settled, Blake rushed around the corner to Jacinto Street. He glanced back at the doctor's big house and saw Eliza exiting from the back through the servant's door, holding up her skirts as she traversed the tall grass to a shack on the far end of the property. She was a pretty woman, if in a deeply glum sort of way, and Blake could not help but notice how gracefully she moved. He shook it off, disinterested, and kept on until the house and the shack and the sad servant girl were far behind him.

There was only one woman who could fill his thoughts beyond his desire for her to do so, and she had ruined him. He had no room for another.

Still, when Blake found himself wandering the streets in a drunken stupor in the wee hours of the night that followed, he was surprised to discover that he had returned to the corner of Jacinto and Cypress streets, the address of Dr. L. B. Johnson. He paused on the very spot upon which Luly stood when he saw her early in the day, stayed there for several minutes as if he could absorb the air she breathed and exhaled into his skin. He wondered if she ever laughed, and if so what it might sound like. It occurred to him that he had never heard her voice at all. She was a spirit, a creature of smoke and mist. Was it her utter unavailability that twisted his guts so? She was a dagger in his ribs, poison on his lips. He felt his knees buckle and his heart started to pound a savage tattoo against the inside of his chest. Blake dropped to the ground, buried his face in his hands and cried.

He invoked her name and the name of Christ in the same desperate moan when a high-pitched shriek split the air and his skin grew cold. A policeman's whistle pierced the night and a woman's voice screamed, "Murder! Murder here!"

The policeman tramped by Blake and over Johnson's property, blowing his terrible whistle all the while as lights flared up in nearly every window in the house. People poured out of the back, each in possession of a lantern or lamp, and a confused chorus of shouting voices rose up.

"Dead!" the woman screeched. "My god, she's dead!"

"Look out!" a deep voice boomed. "Get the women inside."

Before he realized what he was doing, Blake was bounding for the shack. The door stood open and the policeman was already inside, frozen with horror at the bloody tableau before him:

A pile of pillows on the dusty floor, soaked with blood, atop of which the corpse lay.

Her head cleaved in half, clear down to the chin, exposing brain and skull and a pool of syrupy blood.

Eliza Shelley wore only her nightdress, badly torn to expose both her breasts and her nether regions. Like Mollie Smith before her, Eliza had been outraged.

In a dark corner a child whimpered and wept. The policeman raised his lantern to illuminate a trembling colored boy, grasping a blanket tightly and staring with wet, wild eyes at the mutilated corpse. At once Blake deduced the boy to be Eliza's son. He put a hand to his mouth, horrified that this child must have seen the entire horrible spectacle.

"You, get out of here!" the policeman roared at him. "Go on, get out!"

Blake obliged, having seen more than enough of the abused remains of the woman who served him soup mere hours earlier. In the yard Dr. Johnson paced nervously like a new father, a pipe in his hand and a fretful scowl on his face. More policemen arrived, including an imperious man with a walrus mustache and a high brown bowler. Blake recognized him from the Mollie Smith event the previous winter. The man shot a squinting glance at Blake on his way to the shack. Blake stole away to the street, his cheeks flushed hot and his heart racing. Behind him, the mustachioed man shouted, "Who is that man?"

But Blake kept on. Soon he found himself at the batwing doors of a saloon where a tinkering piano clinked away at a clumsy tune. He leaned against a lonely corner of the bar and drained a bottle of rye whiskey into his gullet as quickly as possible, ignoring the sloshing spittoon by his feet. When he saw through the bottom of the bottle he demanded another one. The barman brought it over as a pockmarked roughneck sidled up to the bar and declared, "Another nigra got kilt!"

Blake promptly vomited into the spittoon and collapsed onto the sawdust covered floor.

V.

The implication was clear. He failed to wrap his addled mind around it, to comprehend how it was possible or why it should be, but Blake could see plainly now that his love for Eula Phillips was *dangerous*.

Love, he now knew, had its consequences, though he knew not how it could be. His sorrow—all-consuming as it was—not only haunted him like an ever-present black cloud, but that cloud seemed to deal out bloody strikes wherever his nightly wanderings took him. Absurd, yes, but inescapable. Even if Blake was no murderer, murder appeared to precede him. His heart was filled with the horror of solitude, and in the largely inebriated weeks that followed the gruesome death of Eliza Shelley, he could sense the horror spreading, ever outward.

On the twenty-first of May, Blake once again espied Luly in the company of her rakish husband, sucking oysters by the street-side window at Bulion's restaurant, and his misery ran rampant. He stomped directly to Guy Town from there, sucked down a gallon of strong beer in the tavern before climbing atop a table and pronouncing his intent to take the first whore who caught his eye. Unaware that tears spilled from eyes while he shouted thus, Blake dropped to a stoop and scanned the rowdy assemblage until his eyes fell upon none other than the pretty, ashen-faced harlot Delilah. A cruel grin cut across his face, whereupon he announced, "And it came to pass that he loved a woman whose name was *Delilah*!"

The whore blanched, her mouth agape, and scuttled back behind the bar while cowboys guffawed and the tinkerer at the piano resumed his tuneless key pounding. Blake laughed too, but in a moment his eyes blurred and his head reeled like a child's top—his shoes slipped out from under him and he dropped freely backward, meeting the hard-packed dirt floor with a shower of twinkling sparks that heralded the end of his consciousness.

He awoke, piecemeal, to cool water trickling down his brow. Blake had never been in a sporting girl's boudoir before and was surprised to see, through narrowed eyes, how clean and conservative everything looked, never mind the lingering tang of male sweat and seed. There was lace atop every surface, from dresser to end-tables, and a vaguely Oriental-looking basin sat sloshing in the lap of the bedside girl, who dipped a kerchief into the clear water and let it drip, drip, drip onto his flushed face. His head was half-sunken into a mound of feather-stuffed pillows and his body covered with a pink and yellow quilt. He turned his eyes toward the girl beside him, and for the briefest moment bethought her to be Luly—a dream vision that dissipated like mist in the sun when the girl leaned close and smiled with what few teeth she had left.

"Took you a nasty spill there," she drawled. Her breath smelled like caramel and gin.

Blake lifted his head and felt it slosh, his brains liquefied, just like the water in the basin. He was still drunk as Cooter Brown.

"Nobody cares about them, you know," he rasped, the reverberations of his own voice like hammers crashing against the inside of his skull.

"Who, darlin'? Who don't they care 'bout?" She kept on with the kerchief and water ran in rivulets, spilled over the ridge of his brow and into his eye. He did not so much as blink.

"Negresses," he explained. "By Christ, you whores will be next. Why, were it my Luly, old John Ireland himself would hunt the bastard down."

"What's all this 'bout Negresses and Gov'nor Ireland, sugar? You're plum drunk and you ought to see a sawbones on account o' that fall you took."

"By Jesus, you whores'll be next," Blake said.

VI.

The end of summer brought subtle relief from the stifling heat, and also a fresh spate of killings. An eleven-year-old colored girl was discovered in a backyard wash house, ravaged by her attacker and ended with an iron rod that entered one ear and exited the other. When Blake heard the news, he laughed even while tears rolled down his drink-reddened cheeks. He had not been to the apothecary in weeks by then, selecting instead a series of gambling dens and cathouses for the working hours. Proper Austin life was all but behind him now; Blake had transformed into a resident citizen of Guy Town.

The child, name of Mary Ramey, engendered as much outrage as the city could muster, considering. Yet when the next servant girl met her end, no one whispered Mary's name—it was already forgotten in light of the phantom murderer's freshest victory. Of poor Gracie Vance's state upon discovery in the stable back of the boss's house, the *Austin Daily Statesman* roused most of the capital's horror with lurid descriptions of the woman's jellied brains, spilled out of her split skull. Said the sporting girl whose bed Blake shared the night of the Vance killing: "At least her husband hasn't got to mourn her—he took an ax to the back of the head."

Still no one seemed to inquire as to *who* was behind the savagery, nor what could be done to put a stop to it. Not seriously, at any rate.

"Dime novel fascination," he muttered furiously, slipping away from the boudoir in search of a bottle. The girl remained where she lay in a blur of dust motes suspended in the dim lamplight, the *Statesman* spread out before her as though it was a map to secret treasure. "Damn your eyes."

Outside the clammy air of the whorehouse, the warm September night embraced Blake like a mother. He paused beneath a streetlamp and glanced back at the building, the same "hotel" to which he had trailed Luly nearly a year hence, the night the first of what were now six bloody murders took place. Blake rolled on his heels, grasped the lamppost for support, and squeezed his eyes shut while he tried to remember all of their names. *Molly and Eliza and Irene and wee little Mary and Gracie (and poor Orange Washington too).* He did not really have to try at all.

Christ Jesus, but what was she doing here? he wondered, peering at the window through which he watched her—her and that strange, reedy man. Her, an heiress to founding Texas families for the love of God, secreted away to a stinking knocking shop...

The whores will be next, he reminded himself.

Blake reached up to scratch around his collar and was surprised to find he wasn't wearing one. In fact, he stood on the street, some time past midnight, in his shirt sleeves like a vagrant. He shook his head, still feeling the spectral irritation from a collar that was not there, and somewhere distant a crackling report sounded. Rowdy cowboys, Blake knew, raising hell. Elsewhere, Austin's gentry—perhaps Jimmy Phillips and his bride Eula among them—toasted their gilded glasses to this new Gilded Age for Texas.

And still elsewhere: a devil crept the night, punishing Blake Prentiss and his overburdened conscious for the crime of adoring an unattainable heart. Fraught with horror at this knowledge, he dropped to his knees and wept into his hands, hands that might as well have dripped with the blood of six butchered corpses.

His mind reeled with hazy images of the frail, alabaster brunette whose utter perfection brought apocalyptic judgment to those who deserved it least. For love, for grief, for terror, Blake sobbed at the night.

"Luly...Luly...Luly..."

VII.

If it had been boiling up, beneath the surface, those last twelve months, Hell broke loose on Christmas Eve.

Whilst the Good Reverent Snoot sermonized his flock at First Presbyterian on the birth of Christ and the gifted voices of unseeing children were heard to raise carols to the heavens at the Institute for the Blind, the lower sort remained in Guy Town and those lower still huddled for warmth on the periphery of the railyard. Blake Prentiss, former apprentice pharmacist, huddled amongst them, waving his red raw hands at the guttering camp fire near the tracks. The yard bulls bothered these transients little on the night before Christmas, left them to their quiet misery for once, though sharp eyes were kept upon them lest any man of their number try to jump a moving box car outward bound.

When the rye ran out someone produced a bottle of Laudanum, from which Blake took a deep belt before the next man wrestled it away from him.

"This chippie's half-Indian," the man barked to a round of phlegmy chuckles.

Blake grunted and pulled his coat closed around his sunken chest. The filthy, bearded men with whom he had kept company these last several nights were brutes at best, vagrants and criminals who boasted of taproom killings and bank robberies and rapes. One of them, a small and wizened man with a shock of white-blond hair, even confessed to killing President Garfield and pinning it on Guiteau. No one listened, no one apart from Blake who drank in every word the unfortunate tramps about him spoke lest the devil's instrument be uncovered before his eyes.

But though many murderers surrounded him during his days at the railyard, none was the murderer he sought. The devil, it seemed, was slyer than that.

Round ten o'clock the wizened man started to bellow "A Babe Was Born in Bethlehem," inciting a tremendous bear of a man called Joshua to suppurate and announce his every sin before God.

"By Jesus it kilt my mama, the things I said and done," Joshua burbled, tugging at his great, tear-sodden beard. The singer interrupted himself to assure Joshua that there was no God left to tally his misdeeds, and when fisticuffs ensued Blake removed himself from the assemblage to begin his stumbling trek back into town.

He made it as far as Fifth and Guadalupe, his left foot throbbing from the silver-dollar-sized hole in the sole of his shoe, when Delilah came swaying through the batwing doors of the tavern with an arched eyebrow and a canted smirk.

"May's looking for you, you know."

"I guess I owe her some money."

"I guess she don't want to forgive it, even though it's Christmas and all."

Blake nodded and Delilah said, "I'd ask you to come inside out of the cold, but I don't work on no credit."

"A girl's got to eat," he said, averting his attention to a pair of mongrel dogs feasting on a bloated dead pig. Everything in the First Ward was looking for something to scavenge, something to violate, but that, Blake reckoned, was just how things were here. The status quo. It was the landed gentry who had cause to worry, even if only for their servants' well-being. The devil was not punishing the whores and gamblers and adulterers and dope addicts; he selected outrages that would be noticed but quickly forgotten. The devil played his fiddle well with Blake for a bow. And Blake was growing weary of that catgut sting.

He teetered for a moment, the opiate squeezing his brain like a gigantic hand, and he tucked his chin further down into his coat for the march up to Congress Avenue. His breath came out in uneven bursts of grey mist, the sweat on his brow felt like ice against the skin. He checked the contents of his pockets along the way, ensuring that he was flush enough to see his errand through—ten dollars to May Tobin to settle his debt, another dollar and a half for a roll with one of May's girls, and however much it took for a man to drink until he plain gave out.

The final count came to twelve dollars and a nickel. He sighed and halted, sat down on the ground beside the road and counted again. The count was the same—enough for the first two tasks, but with nothing left for the end. Blake sighed heavily and stared down the length of the street. A pair of policemen was pounding on a woman on the corner of Lavaca; plenty of people were watching, but no one moved to help her. Blake made a thin line of his mouth and hoisted himself back up again. His head seemed to keep going up, even after he reached his full height. *Christmas,*

Christmas, he thought.

"And where's my pudding?"

He chortled and missed a step, stumbling over the paving stones until he regained his balance, and then continued on to May Tobin's bordello. The front room was in full swing when he arrived, let in by a half-dressed mulatto girl no older than fourteen.

"My debt," Blake mumbled, stabbing a fist stuffed with paper notes at the madam of the house.

May accepted the payment with a thin smile and an ironic curtsy.

"And a merry Christmas to you, Mr. Prentiss."

The girl from Blake's last appearance at the house of assignation appeared at his elbow, winding herself around his middle like a snake, and May scrutinized what little money was left in his hand. Blake shrugged, and May said, "Oh, what the hell—it's a special night, isn't it?"

"And a bottle of—anything," he added to the bill on his way to the back rooms, veritably dragged by the girl.

Together they sat and drank, he ten times as much as she, from the jug of cheap rotgut May had sent back to them. The girl made several attempts at idle conversation, each rebuked by Blake in turn, as were her clumsy overtures that they get to the business at hand. At times he feared that he would begin to weep again, but he was successful in maintaining composure apart from a violent shiver that rocked his bones. The girl politely pretended not to notice.

When the liquor was gone and the clock struck ten, Blake left the room without a word, leaving the bored and frustrated prostitute to breathe a sigh of relief. His heart slammed unevenly against his ribs, his hairline spilled sweat in rivulets that slicked his unshaven face. He found himself facing the hallway window through which he had peeped a year before, and right beside the door to the room in which he spied Luly Phillips and her startling escort.

Was she in there now? With the same cadaverous man, or another, or whom?

For a moment, Blake considered the dubious wisdom of kicking the door down to see for himself. Instead, he lurched toward the window, hefted it open, and climbed out into the cold black night. A pervading sense of déjà vu overwhelmed him, a mirror to the past wherein he crept alongside the dark hotel as would a thief and rose only high enough to peek through the window into the lamplit boudoir. And his heart stopped.

For on the narrow bed beside the fluttering flame of the sconce, a sallow-skinned man Blake had never seen before was grunting like a rooting hog while he rutted with Blake's beloved Luly. The man—his eyes small and black, his nose upturned to an almost comical degree—wore a battered slouch hat and black stockings on his feet that were riddled with holes. As for Luly, she was stark naked, her chocolate hair undone and spread out over the pillows like tentacles. Her small breasts, so white that the skin was webbed with translucent blue veins, shook violently as the man rammed into her, baring his teeth and gripping the bedposts tight.

Blake whimpered like a beaten pup. He dropped back down to the cold, damp ground and pulled his knees up to his chin. The night seemed to shatter all around him like obsidian glass and fall away, with nothing left but him and sweet, frail Luly who was neither sweet nor frail but filthy—degenerate and dripping with sin.

And Blake hissed aloud, "You whores will be next."

VIII.

A scant few carolers were to be seen on the streets of Austin this Christmas Eve; most of the capital's women remained at home behind locked doors while their husbands eyeballed strangers passing by or joined up with armed militias to prowl the shadows in hope of putting down the "servant girl annihilator."

To a one they all felt certain that the killer lurked somewhere among them. They traveled only in pairs and groups, firing suspicious glances at one another and whispering *sotto voce* whenever Blake passed near. He paid no mind.

He floated up Congress, a man possessed, his eyes streaming tears and lips gibbering madly after the loss of love and life, the betrayal of Luly and his own heart and everything that made the slightest bit of sense to him. Pure and chaste she was, belonging by right and fate to that violin player, that *rake*. All lies: the devil did not walk in Texas. Just a murderer, whose madness and motivations were his own and had nothing at all to do with the hell through which Blake had walked, burned, loved, hated, wanted desperately to die. He had given up his livelihood, his standing and his sanity, and for what? A dream? That his love for the girl who needed his father's potions to flush the life from her womb was so wretched the whole world needed to be punished for it?

But what to do? What to do?

For worship of a false idol, Blake had nearly died…

He collapsed onto the crisp, yellow grass of somebody's sideyard and vomited up a belly full of liquor. "Luly…"

He blacked out, and the night reassembled itself, shard by jagged shard. Only it was not the same night as before, before it cracked apart and took Blake's soul with it to Hell. This night was much blacker, and though it did not return with his soul, it came back with purpose. Seconds later, or perhaps hours, he found himself being shaken roughly and a tenor voice shouting at him to rouse himself, to go back to whatever reprobate hole in the earth from which he crawled. Blake opened his eyes to thin slits and beheld the grey-haired man looming above him. The man's face was pinched with annoyance. He wore a dressing robe and cursed enough to bring the law down on himself for coarse language in public. Blake had seen a dozen people hauled off to jail for saying considerably less.

In time, he sat up. His skull pounded, felt much too small, and his stomach roiled again. He pressed his fingers hard against his temples and focused narrowly on the scars the night bore from its reconstruction.

He said, "I am sorry, sir."

"Just fuck off, trash," the man grumped and he stomped back into the house. Blake watched him go, and when the door shut and the lamp went out, the moonlight illumined the woodpile beside the house, and the broad chopping stump before it, and the well-used ax protruding from one of the stump's many clefts.

His head stopped hurting him. So he rose up and went directly to the ax.

"Moses?" came a tinkling voice from back of the house. "Mose? What is it?"

"There is no devil," Blake whispered, yanking the ax free. "Only me."

He went boldly around to the backyard, where he discovered the voice's owner: a birdlike woman clutching a heavy red cape to her throat.

"Moses?"

"Only me," he repeated for her benefit, hefting the ax. He grinned through his tears and took three long strides to close the distance between them. "And I am from Hell."

Though dulled from overuse, the blade cleaved through the top of the woman's skull with relative ease. Its trajectory halted half-way down, at her nose, and she emitted a hissing noise like steam from a teapot before falling limp. Blake planted his right foot at her groin and gave the corpse a shove; the ax came free and Moses' wife crashed to their winter-dead lawn.

Blake wiped the tears from his eyes with his free hand and squatted beside the dead woman. Her head was an impossible tangle of hair and blood, bone and brain. The selfsame moonglow that showed the ax to him now brought a sparkle to a hairpin, having come loose from the now bifurcated head. He pinched it between forefinger and thumb, examined it closely as though it were some artifact from an undiscovered civilization. Blake had never before given much thought to the accoutrements of feminine beauty, something he always took at face value, so to speak, but he thought now of Luly's heavenly locks and how high she usually wore them on her head. The work of hairpins, he did not doubt.

A small, sad smile formed at his cold-chapped lips. He then jammed the hairpin deep into the corpse's brains, pushing it all the way in with his thumb until it vanished completely.

"Merry Christmas," he said.

IX.

Hell came to the Phillips' house round about midnight.

Blake stood at the foot of the couple's bed, breathing slowly through his nose and watching them sleep, man and wife. There was frost on the bedroom window and the faint odor of cinnamon in the air. The smell was stronger on the first floor, near the modest Christmas tree in the main room, yet somehow the reek of heart-rot overwhelmed this erstwhile pleasant sensation. Eula's rot permeated everything.

It even poisoned her marital bed—mere hours after fucking some John of May Tobin's custom, here she lie beside her lawfully wedded husband (worm though he was) in defiance of everything noble about the world before the night smashed to pieces. Sleeping like a milk-sated babe, her small hands pressed palm to palm beneath her snowy cheek as if in supplication to God.

"I am down on whores," Blake said aloud, causing Jimmy to rustle the blankets. "I will *rip* you, my lady."

"Whuh," muttered Jimmy Phillips, turning his head on the pillow and sucking in a sharp breath. "Who—who's there?"

Blake moved round the bed and brought the flat end of the ax down upon the back of Jimmy's head. The blow thudded dully and Jimmy moaned, quick and low. Thereafter, he questioned Blake no more, so Blake lifted his weapon high above his head to finish the job but he froze dead away when Eula shrieked, "NO!"

Eula—*Luly, his erstwhile love*—sat up straight-backed and wide-eyed, her face radiantly silver in the moonlight sifting through the window. She trembled all over and moved her thin lips as to speak, though she made no sound. Slowly Blake lowered the ax until it rested softly on the bed. He met her terrorized gaze head on, a challenge. He did not blink. And when Eula began to quietly cry, he felt his own eyes spill warmly over his face.

She rasped, "It was you. You murdered those girls."

"They did not deserve it."

"And Jimmy. My Jimmy."

"Will you mourn him?"

A small sob shook her and she whispered, "No."

"I loved you," Blake said, as matter-of-factly as one speculating on the weather.

"I don't know you."

"Still."

"I want only to get away," she said, her voice nearly too hushed to hear, each word tremulous. "Stow enough to make it out west, California maybe."

"You earned every penny."

"God," she moaned, and Blake said, "He is not here to help you. And the devil never came. When Hell opened up, it belched me out. And you have earned this too, darling Luly."

He roared then, an animal sound, and in a deft movement swung the ax in a wide arc at her. Eula sprang from the bed at the roar, and the blade merely nicked her shoulder, though the cut bled liberally. The ax blade drove into the headboard, sending a shower of splinters into the air, and while Blake jerked it free his quarry bolted screeching from the room.

Blake groaned with frustration, spun about to look upon the spotty trail leading from the bedroom to the stairs. *Proper red stuff,* he thought with some queer satisfaction at the sight, and he gave chase.

The blood spattered the steps and the cold floor of the foyer, then angled sharply to a hall that led to the kitchen. Blake sped over the gore, clutching the ax and huffing, and he burst into the kitchen in time to see Eula pass through a back door. Blake followed, light on his feet, and could only barely make out her shadow in the dark back alley beyond. She kept ahead of him, just out of reach. So Blake reared back and flung the ax at her; it spun head over handle into the pitch until a resounding crack filled the silence and Eula screamed. The scream struck his heart like a hot needle. He paused, winced, and went gradually to where she fell in the alley.

Her back was wet to the touch, tacky with blood. He seized her by the shoulders, turned her over and brushed her cool face with his sticky fingers. She shuddered from cold and fear, and sobbed, "Why?"

"Because no one else will," he explained. "And so it falls to me."

Clinically, he commenced stripping her of her nightclothes, down to the birth-state in which she enjoyed her work at May Tobin's whorehouse. He now had his own work to do, and in the doing he saw how this job undid the sin inherit in every other killing he had made. This time, now, in the inky dark of an unlit alley, Blake Prentiss was saving his own life by snuffing hers out.

Eula struggled then, thrashed beneath him. He grimaced and, spying a pile of timber at the end of the alley, got up and dragged two lengths back with which he pinned her to the ground. She screamed again and Blake screamed with her. Somewhere in the night a hound howled plaintively. Eula shook her head from side to side, burbled like an infant. Her skin so white and eyes so large and brown, filled with faux innocence and a helpless desire to go on living...

The sallow man pumping away, his beady black eyes and piggish nose and rotten slouch hat, a clown thrusting into her, and she with her tendrils of shiny brunette and hands so small, so delicate, clutching the edges of the bed...

Blake smashed the side of the ax against her brow, crushing the bone. Her eyes sank in and he hit her again, this time caving in her face. Tears and blood and pretty, pretty hair...

Luly, sweet Luly, demoness Luly, was finished. Flushed with

madness and fury and grief, Blake set the ax down beside her and lay atop her for a long while, brushing the blood-soaked hair away from her demolished face and telling her, softly, that Austin would be safe now.

X.

John Prentiss wept openly in front of his son for the first time Christmas morning upon discovering his lost boy asleep on the divan. The elder Prentiss fell upon Blake and kissed his face, waking the younger with a start.

"My boy, my darling boy," the old man sobbed. "You've come home."

"I'm finished with all that, Father," said Blake, his voice gummy with sleep. "I'm sorry to have worried you so."

No explanations were demanded and none given. Duck was served for Christmas dinner and there was pudding and rum punch, and even Jake and Helen Slaughter, old friends of Blake's dearly departed mother, dropped in for a toast and a bit of yuletide cheer. Blake washed up and shaved and presented himself as fine a young gentleman as ever, wiping away his time gone and that was all in the past anyway, so far as Father John was concerned. He spent as much of the day grasping his son's hands or squeezing his shoulders as Blake would allow him, and resisted letting the lad get on to bed for hours into the night.

And on the morning, as news of the nightmare slaughter of two *white* women spread like a blaze across Austin—BLOOD! BLOOD! BLOOD!—neither John nor Blake cared a whit for it. The world, as both of them knew, was restored.

Epilogue.

August in England was a marked improvement over the tyrannical heat of late summer in Texas. Most evenings were cool enough by then to be deemed brisk. For Blake, it felt like a sort of reward for surviving his first English winter, and he celebrated by throwing open the windows in his small rented room to feel the night air on his face and neck. The stink of Thrawl Street below was ripe in his nostrils, but no worse than the myriad odors of Guy Town, back home. Blake was a slummer, it was in his blood, and he was more than accustomed to the vile odors and noises and faces and threats that came along with that. Indeed, once he had overcome the initial shock of the strange, often incomprehensible accents and bustling, well-paved streets—and by Christ, those *bridges*!— Blake decided that the East-End of London was not very different from Austin's First Ward at all. The streets were stacked with animal shit, drunken men beat each other bloody, and wanton women lifted their skirts at anyone who dared to glance their way.

Home sweet home.

Shifting his gaze from the rabble on the street to the tintype of his father on the desk, still vibrant and healthy, before the cancer ravaged his body and left him wasted and dead the summer previous, Blake sighed. He missed him deeply, more than he had ever missed his mother, and felt terribly lonely in this room in a foreign city five thousand miles from home. He came because he was done with Austin, and with Texas, and with the whole of America. He wanted to start anew, be born again, and the first ship he found in Galveston was bound for Europe and that was all he wanted to know. Now an ocean separated him from the graves of everyone he ever loved. The distance eased the loneliness to some small degree. But not the nightmares, nor the heat he felt in his blood.

At half past one in the morning, an argument broke out directly beneath Blake's window. One of the two voices he recognized instantly: it belonged to his landlady, Mrs. Neely, who barked, "Fourpence, you wanta kip 'ere to-night. Elsewise leave me be."

The other voice, also a woman, drawled drunkenly, as voices in Whitechapel very often did. "I'll 'ave your fourpence, you wretched bitch, and more besides. Me new bonnet'll 'ave the lads lookin', and me cunt'll do the rest, won't it?"

Mrs. Neely growled, "*Bloody 'ores,*" and Blake wrinkled his nose. Shouts and clopping hooves filled the night all around, and the foul-mouthed whore laughed raucously as the landlady slammed the door shut.

Blake leaned over his desk and peered down at Thrawl Street. Below him, a grey-haired woman in a cheap, tattered blue dress staggered away from the rooming house. His temples throbbed; the hair of his neck stood out straight. A squat man in a tall black hat shouted out to the woman, and she babbled something back at him before turning on her heel to face him. The man squeezed his crotch and leered. The woman reached into her bodice and scooped out her left breast so that it flopped over the top like a dog's ear.

"Wot, then?" she challenged him. The man chortled as he made his way across the street to her.

"Ah, Mary Ann, Mary Ann," the man cooed, taking her in his arms and kissing her roughly, "'ow I love ya, ya saucy bitch."

She was thick about the waste and not a day younger than forty, this Mary Ann, yet when Blake narrowed his eyes he nearly swore he was looking down at the spirit of Eula Phillips. For this reason, though not this reason alone, he reached into the top drawer of the desk and withdrew the long, razor-sharp knife he kept there. He had never used the knife, not since he procured it from a street vendor in February, a peculiar whim he could never quite fathom until now. For now, standing up and secreting the blade away beneath his black topcoat, Blake Prentiss recalled the last words dandy Jimmy Phillips heard before the ax head knocked him down—

"I am down on whores."

Which he was. Even after he slit Mary Ann Nichols' throat and sliced up the body's abdomen he was. And the notice that went up on every wall and door in Whitechapel in the coming weeks only strengthened Blake's resolve, his need, his hellbound duty.

GHASTLY MURDER
IN THE EAST-END.
DREADFUL MUTILATION OF A WOMAN.

Because when Hell broke loose, there was nothing anybody could do to send it back again.

Where Have You Been All My Life?

Edward Morris

The sailor awoke before dawn. Something was wrong. Like he'd wound up on the wrong side of the city, on a map no cabbie could read.

His work had been interrupted. Here lay the Winter of Nepenthe.

Across the room, a single gas lamp burned low, sticking out of the wall above the battered chestnut vanity like a beckoning finger. Simple things. Almost familiar. Gray walls, wood floor. A men's rooming-house, Spartan, nearly bare, with a piece of dirty white muslin draped across the dresser. Atop the muslin was a washbasin full of dirty, soapy water; beside it, a shaving-mug and brush, and a little pearl-handled French razor and strop.

This is how it begins. Anew, now, but always the same. He rubbed the long, twisting scar etched across his stubbly scalp, unsure where the thought was coming from. *In the dark. In a one-night cheap hotel and restless, or under a bridge, or even a cozy doorway in the middle of that great, roaring dark, full of coal smoke and the clopping of hooves on cobblestones and the fog. The fog. The fog—*

But this darkness was different. The fog outside his open window smelt different, tasted different. The air was so much cleaner. He could smell shite, and coal-gas, but the breeze beneath that had a smell which made no sense to him whatsoever. Above the window, most of the smoke was gone from the puffy blue-white cumulus clouds.

Even the sky made no sense. It was too blue, blue as cobalt glass, bright as a hateful operating-theatre where there were always slop-buckets of guts to cart to the incinerator, nurses with mobcaps and round arses and skin as pale as cream…

Green girls, all, within, who nonetheless scowled at him as though they knew. And the damned sniping doctors he could have been, once, whose looks were far more imperious, their every order barked at their little resurrection-man with a mop, their whipped Quasimodo who nightly quaffed the same Nepenthe that got him there in the first place.

"It were the drink that did for you," Mollie and Mum always said, but Mum was long in her grave from the bad heart she had, and Mollie was—

Oh, but his head was coming undone, or perhaps fusing back together in this refiner's fire that crawled along the scar from within. This healing, healing itch where there'd but been a rift.

A rip. In his sour-milk-sweat-stained undershirt and the drawers to a set of long-handles, all stinking of whisky, he trembled out of bed and put his head out the window.

"Better," he rasped, breathing that clean, clean breeze that tasted of little he knew. He was in a long block, by the look, with many other windows like his above and below. Most were shut. Occasionally, one was propped open with a pine board or a piece of lath.

There was snow in the air. He could smell opium sweet as perfume, and *tsa tsui* cooking someplace.

"I'm in Piccadilly, most like," he mumbled as the headache took his eyes and he rubbed them, backing away. "Cor. How long's it… How long's it been? Needs must, I s'pose, but… What kind of piss I been out on, t'come to'n such a state?"

But he knew everything he was mumbling was wrong. It was the fog that told him, the air, the sky… and the cold, cold room. More than that, it was the other occupant of the bed. A woman.

A *woman*. He shuddered. No woman had fouled his bed, not since Memory permitted. But Memory was slowly permitting now. *Not since Mollie went off her head and tried to do for me, all that time ago, the dirty bitch.* His lower lip trembled. *All that time ago, when I was still me. Before me own blushing bride took me own razor to my... to my... When I was sleeping, she...*

His hand dropped to the other scar, and the damage there. The incomplete damage that still half-worked. *She were mad, Mollie were. I were never no whoremonger. Never done what she said, what she shrieked, before I bent her wrist back and took back me razor and I—*

"Nnnn," said the skinny whore in his bed, turning over and wrapping herself in the whole lot of the bedclothes, now that he was out of bed. Blonde locks rustled on her bare, tattooed shoulderblades. He saw a face tattooed on the right one, that looked of heathen Indian design, like a totem-pole, and something that could have been a mermaid, an angel or a demon in the dim light, crawling down the slattern's arm.

He could smell rut in the room, and it made him sick. *Not opium, not absinthe, not morphine. Nowt could'ha' caused this thing to be. She's a woman, for one thing, no rent-boy I take and use and send away. Could never make it wi'no woman, even if I wanted to. Can't even make it wi'the rent-boys, half the time, like, but...*

The thought was gone. That window'd had frost on the outer sill, he remembered, and trembled back to shut it. *I never knew she was expecting, when I did for her. Mad and maybe a month along, and what expecting mother ain't a little bit mad? What's done is done, but if I'm damned then by God I'll have my Day of Judgement, I—*

CRASH. His eyes went white, and the headache took him hard, right through the scar. Right through the itch. His knees buckled and he almost fell, but made it close to the direction of the pillow on the right.

At that, the whore in his bed (*Ay, she's got to be... No ring on the left hand that... Ah, down a bit, yes, lay me flat, there's a dear*) stroked his scar tenderly, kissing his cheek but planting him as firmly prone on his back as though she were a nurse, and he a patient, and…

He made a noise. "Shoosh, shoosh, sailor," she whispered, in a marvelous raspy voice like the rattle of half-crowns in a purse. "Your wound must be excitin' you again. You Limeys just keep going until you drop. Must be the English way."

"Sailor." He sat bolt-upright. "I'm… Wot? No sailors, here. I've never been to sea. I… I work in a bleedin' 'ospital. I—"

And then a strange thing began to happen. He blinked, taking her in,(*Cor, that's a lot of tattoos she's got, but,*) her bright green eyes focused visibly, and her serpentine mouth pursed. She spoke with her hands a lot, like his Mum.

"You're just like that other sailor," she said, almost to herself. "I had a john last year who couldn't remember his own name." Her laugh was nervous, and sounded a little sick, but held the fatalism of the streets, the cold fog and the warm doorway and the big night, the long dark… "He'd been Shanghaied."

When he said nothing, she seemed to understand his blank look. "Great big knot on his head. He worked on a freighter. Said some crimp in London did for him with a cosh to the back of the head when he took to drinkin', and put him on a ship. There was just an X on his papers where the name was, he told me, so he just called himself Ishmael, like in the Bible."

He felt the cold sweat begin to bead on his face as she spoke. Every sprout of beard-stubble itched. His heart was pounding. "Don't fink they can fix me, just yet," he sighed. She didn't ask what he meant. He knew she thought she understood. Hell, he almost understood himself.

Outside the window, the bloody fingers of Dawn pointed at him from the East. But East was the wrong way. The whore was still talking.

"I remember—" She frowned. "In *Collier's Weekly* or one of those magazines from out East, something… Something about this railroader, years back. His name was Gage something. Took a tamping-rod right through the head, and lived, but it took him years to come all the way back to himself. *Years.*"

Again, the fatalistic chuckle, the wide white smile. He saw a silver incisor, and smelled his own sweat on her sweet breath. She took his hand in both of hers.

"My name's Mina," she told him. "Do you remember yours?"

He pushed her hand away, but gently. "I... I'm not sure." He was, but she didn't need to know it. She was insistent, and took it again. "Do you remember where you live?"

He sighed. This was getting intolerable. She didn't need to know that, either. Or why. *No reason to lie...* "I fink I know me own address, dear," he muttered. "It's... in Prince William Street. Whitechapel. 'Ow... 'Ow close are we t'... "

She relaxed a little. "Oh, we're in Whitechapel. That's a very good start, mister, sure enough. But there's no Prince William Street anywhere here. You're on B Street, sir. B Street and Fourth Avenue. The old Phillip Hotel... I'm not even supposed to be here."

It was a good start for him, too. A little. He tried to smile. "Wot, no respectable place for a lady?"

Now wasn't the time to betray the true thoughts that screamed through his head, begging him to be up and gone. There was important work to do, and so much lost time. He could feel how much lost time. But the time wasn't now.

"Ha," Mina smirked. " This is Skid Road. There's no lady anywhere in Portland, *Oregon,* comes this far west of Wash'nton street, English! You're too kind. No, that day man on the Front Desk doesn't like me. Hisses and spits like a cat, and then gives me the bum's rush. I think he's a fairy."

Portland. Oregon. America. Dear God. Dear God... "Oh, aye? As you say. Doin' for a woman like that. Never a policeman near when you need one..."

Now he understood why his heart was pounding so hard, the cold sour sweat springing anew. The strange breeze. The sky that wasn't gray soot, the streets so empty. "Can you tell's one more thing, love?"

Mina twinkled. "Anything, English. Speak."

He was insistent. "The year."

This put her off a little, but only momentarily. "Sakes alive, you really must be like that Gage fellow." But her smile came back, and grew a little warmer. "Eighteen hundred and ninety-two."

Red lightning ate his eyes again. The itch in his head was all there was. *Three years. Maybe almost five. So much lost time. So much work left to do...*

The window full of Dawn before him was red, too, and the light fell on a new field bright for reaping, reflected back double from the vanity mirror and the mother-of-pearl inlays on his straight-razor.

So much lost time. So much work left to do.

"Clever, you are," he managed to whisper. "I fink I'm... 'ow'd you put it... comin' back to meself already." His heart was in his throat. "I'll set this town alight..."

He loved his work. He wanted to start again. He could only wait a little longer.

No time now. No time to squeal. The whore was lying flat now, with the bedclothes off. Waiting. Blushing to the tips of her shell-pink ears. Mina smiled again as he got up to lock the door.

FOR HARLAN ELLISON

Juliette's New Toy
Joseph S. Pulver, Sr.

for Robert Bloch and Harlan Ellison

Expunge
Erase
Delete
Rub out

wipe out

obliterate

child's play…

Juliette smiled. Her mouth cradled the color of desire. Settled into her pillow. Closed her eyes and peered into a dream…

…Lustrous knife. Sexy blouse. A whisper of cleavage.

She could climb to heaven on flesh. Be born in the flight of color. Blood in the moonlight. Her eyelids flutter. Her lips, larks above the bones.

Red.

Glimmering.

She hears a violin in the vineyard. Sees a drunkard's wrist, throat, beholds the spectrum of fruit. Hears the lyrical beauty of a scream.

Temptation.

Action.

The soul of a man. Guiding her. Prey healed of the world's chain of suffering and pain. The frequencies of her philosophies slow ...s...l...o...w... Or you'd spoil the game. Deprive fun its bursts and frolics.

16 going on 722. Ready to bloom... Again...

A street attired in poor shabby roofs. Unhurried clouds begetting shadows.

Juliette's red lips sip forever from a vial. She has returned.

He came. A monster carved by the full moon. Entered her Perfect. Carved Hell in her war paint, shamed her belly with his rooting snout. Closed the theater dance in her eyes.

Jack

White skin.

Nest of black hair.

Slippery Jack.

He touched. Thickened. Exhausted her years with between. Howled in her deepest ruts, in the lanes and alleys she kept under lock and key. Took the stars from her seams. Gave her slave language. Surprised her lightning with taboo. The ages and branches of her fields traveled from ash to dust to void. His "Ah" peeled her rind. Brutal, swelled by absolutely, bars her from azure and the moon. His hectic teeth—reading, inquiring, spit lust, as they wandered, flowering her tender with void. His open mouth won't be sidetracked by her wings and eternities. Open. A waterfall of Jolly. When he clipped off her ear.

Left her in the desert street for rats.

Then he took the path of Future... Again...

Dead, but she did not die... in the litter of the dead she crawled... found a shaft... tasted the supplies of life... ate the storms of nothingness… opened what was forgotten with breath…

She waved down the taxi. "Flower & Dean."

"Out for a pint, Miss?"

Of blood. "Yes."

A knowing grunt. A cluttered smile.

"Calms the cursed swords of a godforsaken day it does… Breaks the blacks of the horizon's unforeseen events."

The cabbie nods in agreement. "Up and on it is, Miss."

Chariot of yellow and chrome deposits her at the door of The Little Blue Book. Lightyears swing low and flee the club's windows.

The demon and the hulk employed as bouncers smile and let her pass.

IN.

Bump and grind on FUNK. The star children and thumpasorus people ridin' lowdown are out. Gamin'. Watching for getten'-to-know-you and surprise. Comin' for ta carry you to love, or sure-shot fever.

Glasses of Ride On and escape ecstasy shine in the senses;gladly flashing laser light. Wide RED hooks under the summer night religion of BLUE. Strobes translate hands and faces harvesting the flavor of silk soft altitudes. GREEN loose at the hip and Emphasis-ORANGE fly to free your mind.

Thrust.

Nuthin' but a party bangin'.

Shake.

Shake.

In 3-D.

Feet perfumed in getaway burn with fire-method, hoping to persuade careful princesses to points where trembling sears skin in overnight.

"Soul food." Juliette smiles at the fruit of life.

Let them sing. Let them dance. Let them drink. A playground should thrill.

She needs to stretch, needs a little taste

before

Jack.

Before she climbs the streets and the stars in search of the death-rattle of his heart…
Jack.
The flower.
The hanged man.
Baked.
Burned by the hunger of her ink.
Jack.
Deep in PAIN.
Jack.
Never existed.
Never had color.
Jack.
Just raw material.
To feed to the black stars.
Soul food.
A bird at her shoulder. A pale courtier. Smooth-shaven. Lion's jaw. Climax eyes. I celebrate what pleases you in the tango of his words.
She'll have him barefoot and sailing the unavoidable.
This one will do.
And they do.
Curtains down. Stories of violence open. Getting down. No textbooks.
Chest…
Belly.
Massacre without explanation. Juliette's silhouette gestures as she operates.

Her ringmaster-need bites as her sculpture clings to the scream.
Time is dragged off to another shore.
It's mouth and hands and wounds smell like

"Jack."

She puts on her stockings and her bra.
"Here are my hands."
Runs her fingers through her hair.
"I am motion growing... An ancient lamp to unlock the truth
of your chapters."
Bends to take in the perfume of a bundle of peach-hued flowers
united in a vase.
"I will show you the petals of silence."

(Parliament Mothership Connection)

Villains, by Necessity

Pete Rawlik

It took five days for Thomas Newcomen, formerly Inspector Thomas Newcomen of Scotland Yard, to come out from under the influence of the pipe. He hadn't always used opium, but he like so many others had developed a taste for it while in Afghanistan. His occasional use continued after he came home to London and found employment with the Yard, but never while on duty, and only in moderation. It killed the pain, dulled the memories of the things he had done in the war, and made being a civilian more tolerable.

All that changed after he botched a case; when he couldn't see what was, in retrospect, quite plain. Who would have thought that the events of what became known as The Strange Case of Dr. Jekyll and Mr. Hyde would have destroyed his career. How he had missed the obvious; after years of soldiering, of hunting and tracking, was inexplicable. Afterwards, there were reprimands and a review board. His use of opium and prostitutes came out. That he was fond of young men who could stand the lash seemed particularly troublesome. So was his war record; the incident in Dewangiri, for which he had received a commendation, was being scrutinized. Had he killed all those boys out of necessity or simply wanton bloodlust? How could civilians judge what had occurred in the heat of battle?

Rather than defend himself, he took early retirement, with a significantly reduced pension. Whether it was the boredom or the depression, he eventually began using regularly, and lost weekends or weeks, depending on how much dope he could afford, became common. He had been thusly incapacitated when the thugs came for him, so strung out that he couldn't even put up a fight. They locked him in a room with a jug of water and a bucket and let him sweat it out. At times he screamed until his throat was raw, but in the end his gray skin gained some color, his eyes returned to normal, and his thoughts became his own. They fed him porridge with some bits of dried fruit, and he gained some strength. Gin and tonic water helped settle his nerves. Even so, when they came for him again he didn't resist.

Despite the hood he knew from the smell that he was near the Thames. The bag they had used to cover his head reeked of dead fish, but even that wasn't enough to cover up the Stink. That he was near the river was clear, but when his abductors moved him roughly through a door and then down several flights of stairs their clumsy footsteps echoed back at him. From these observations he concluded that he was in the basement of some kind of large open building, most likely a warehouse or some similar structure. The men who had taken him had smelled of green tea and rice water, but they barked at each other in a language that he did not recognize. They could have been speaking Japanese, or perhaps even a dialect of Malay.

Without warning he was shoved into a chair, wooden and ornate by the feel of it. He flinched as a knife cut the hood apart and grazed his ear in the process. Even in the dim light he could make out the shadowed forms of guards armed with guns and large daggers. These he knew were only hands, tools to be manipulated, those in control sat on the dais before him. The man on the right was Chinese, taller than others of his kind, with evil green eyes. His imperious attitude would have been evident even if he had been dressed in rags rather than in the fine silken robes embroidered with golden dragons that currently draped his form. The other man was Irish, dressed as a gentleman, but not as a dandy. His frame was bent, and the unobservant might consider him older than he actually was. His face was gaunt, such that his thinning hair made his visage appear almost skull-like. When he spoke it reminded Newcomen of the headmaster at his son's school.

"Inspector Newcomen, do you know who we are?"

The old policeman nodded and spoke respectfully. "I do, Professor. Though I've never seen either one of you in person before, I know you by reputation, and from blurry photographs at the Yard, though the analysis suggests that the two of you in the same room is something that would be considered very unlikely."

The Professor grinned maliciously. "Circumstances make for strange alliances, temporary though they may be. I and the Doctor," he gestured at the Chinaman, "find ourselves with a common problem, one that we think you would be interested in resolving for us." The Professor turned to look at his partner, and the Chinese Doctor gave an almost imperceptible nod of approval, but before either of them could say anything Newcomen protested.

"What makes you think I would do anything for either of you?" He tried to maintain a tone of respect even as he attempted to rebuke them both. "If you want favors you have an odd way of asking for them. Why me, surely there are plenty of other constables and inspectors in your employ?"

"You come highly recommended. Your former commanding officer says you are quite skilled with a gun. He would be here himself, but he is indisposed at the moment. He reports that excluding himself, you are the quickest shot he has ever seen. He also says that you lack certain moral compulsions that might prevent weaker men from accomplishing the task." At the implication that the Colonel had recommended him for the job Newcomen relaxed slightly and motioned for the Professor to continue.

"These murders in Whitechapel; the Ripper, the Torso Killer, the Strangler, it is all very bad for business, not just in Whitechapel, but throughout London. People are scared. They are staying home at night. Pub patronage has dropped ten percent. Prostitutes have become uneasy, and some twenty-two have left the city for safer venues. Their clients are afraid as well: Of being wrongfully accused, of being attacked by nervous girls, of being targeted by George Lusk and his Vigilance Committee. Revenue from gambling has decreased by twelve percent. The use of opium has declined significantly." The Doctor sighed heavily. "As long as these murders continue to be in the public eye our operations will suffer, our employees will suffer, and tensions between our two organizations will build. We sit on a powder keg, Inspector Newcomen, and with each murder a new match is lit. We have ordered our men to remain calm, but like two empires who are openly at peace, the actions of our client states may precipitate a war we would rather avoid. We need these murders to cease."

Newcomen was perplexed. "I am sure that the police are doing all they can. Abberline is a fine man, as is Bond. I am sure they will catch the perpetrator of these horrid crimes, and the murderer will be brought to justice."

"You misunderstand us, Inspector; we do not care about justice. We want these killings to end, and we want you to be the instrument we employ to end them. Perhaps, in doing this you will no longer be haunted by your failure to deal with Mr. Hyde." The look on Newcomen's face made the Professor elaborate: "Additionally, we will use our influence with certain agencies to create for you a new position. Not law enforcement mind you, but a place for you in one of our many legitimate private security companies. We have ties to the Continental Agency. A man of your talents has a place with us, if you want it."

Newcomen smiled. "That's a fair deal, and I would be more than willing to take it, but for certain obvious problems. I have no suspects. I don't have access to the files, the evidence or the resources I would need. Even if I did, I'm not sure I am smart enough to figure out something my betters can't. You need to approach someone else, perhaps Mr. Hol—"

"THAT IS NOT AN OPTION!" the Professor roared. "That man cannot be involved in this, though his interference is expected. He will be dealt with, managed, and misled. False leads and patsies are being created to distract him. This is one game he will not be joining." He took a deep breath and coughed with a wheeze. "As for the files, that has all been taken care of. The Gentleman Thief has supplied us with copies of all the evidence and files available to Inspector Swanson and his underlings. We supplemented this information with our own investigations and observations. We have resources, capabilities; a lack of restrictions that allow us to do things the Police cannot, or will not. In this manner our logicians Mr. Fogg and Mr. Loveless have not only identified those who have committed these crimes, but their motives and hiding place. Even now our agent, a man we recently recruited from Paris, an expert in the art of remaining unobserved, and of subterranean labyrinths, has them under observation. When the time comes, he will act as your guide."

"So you've confirmed that there is more than one man committing these crimes? That has always been the suspicion, but surely they cannot be working in together? With such varied methods, that would be almost inconceivable."

Suddenly the Chinese Doctor was clapping, but his eyes were not on Newcomen, but rather on his fellow crime lord. Finally, the Devil Doctor himself spoke: "Congratulations, my dear Professor, your point is made. Your theory concerning the minds of those in law enforcement, as opposed to those involved in criminal exploits, is all but proven." He turned to look at Newcomen. "It seems that we must lay things out for you, dear sir. The murders in Whitechapel have indeed been committed by more than one person, but it is not a pair of men that have done these deeds. There are twelve of them. A dozen maniacs stalk the streets of London seeking revenge on those they believed have harmed them, twelve individuals and most assuredly not men."

"Not men? The Whitechapel murders were committed by a gang of women? Surely not?"

The Professor was suddenly sniggering. "Please, Inspector Newcomen, London has not been beset by the Dowager Calipash and her daughters. The culprits are all male, the sons of your nemesis, Mr. Hyde." Newcomen's face went pale as the man continued. "Surely you realized that Mr. Hyde was, how did Beccon put it, 'Sowing wild oats'? What did you think he was doing with all those London whores, playing cribbage? He impregnated them, and they like so many others in their profession gave the children away. Now they have come home, and they seek revenge on those who have harmed them, their own mothers.

The aged inspector's mind reeled as something dawned on him. "But Hyde was only with those women five years ago. His children couldn't be more than four years old."

The Devil Doctor sat back down. The Professor wrung his hands before grudgingly speaking once more: "Is that a problem? The Colonel did say you were the man for the job."

Inspector Thomas Newcomen reflected back on his life and what was being offered him. The massacre at Dewangiri had been twenty-five years in the past, but he could still see the faces of the child soldiers that the enemy had sent in a futile attempt to drive back the British Forces. The Colonel had ordered a retreat, but Newcomen had refused, and instead held the position. He had killed dozens before the opposing forces had fallen back. Even then he kept firing at the fleeing boys who had been armed only with daggers and wearing little more than rags. The company surgeon had wanted him discharged, but the Colonel had ignored such nonsense. Newcomen would never forget those faces, the screams, and the sight of blood and gore exploding from bodies. He should have been discharged, for what he had done still haunted him. It was because of these memories that he had turned to opium in the first place. Not to drown the images from his mind, but to quench the desire he felt to relive the experience. He hated those memories, not because of what he had done, but because he couldn't do it again. And now, he was being offered another opportunity to kill children, monstrous children, but still just children.

A smile crept across his face as they handed him a rifle. The weapon felt good in his hand, like it belonged there. "A problem? No, not at all." For the first time in years, he felt complete.

When the Means Just Defy the End
Stanley C. Sargent

London, East End, late night November 8, 1888

A bone-chilling cold pervaded the late night air, and those few individuals out and about on the streets were not immune to the chill. They were brave souls indeed, ignoring not only the cold but the persistent warnings that the savage killer who had of late been so generously providing the newspapers with shrill headlines was likely still stalking the streets. The fog, actually more pollution than anything else, blurred visibility as it lingered above the slippery cobblestones. This eerie, almost impenetrable atmosphere conspired with those who lurked with ill intent, hiding them from sight till they should emerge to pounce on the foolish and the unsuspecting. Somehow the predators, at home in the clammy miasma, could see through it, counting on their prey being equally unable to see any more than a few paces ahead.

It was generally considered that those who haunted the particularly restive, poverty-stricken streets late at night were little more than human refuse, although many of them truly were penniless, homeless and desperately attempting to survive. It was not uncommon to encounter entire families huddled beneath makeshift shelters in an attempt to remain warm and safe while sleeping.

The rest of the nightly population was fleshed out by scatterings of pathetic drunks, gaudy "daughters of joy," men of every rank seeking sexual satisfaction for a few paltry shillings, simple-minded miscreants, filthy street urchins, and other ne'er-do-wells. Nor was it rare to stumble upon a corpse lying in a gutter or secreted away in some dark doorway, the victim of the cold, starvation or foul play. Most residents had long ago learned the importance of keeping a bloodshot eye cocked skyward in order to avoid unannounced splashes of urine and fecal matter tossed from the windows of doss houses that reached as high as two or three stories. Along with the stench of offal that crept from gutters and many shops hereabout, the Whitechapel and Spitalfields districts had earned from London's *Daily Mirror* the unflattering honorific of "Satan's Cesspool."

On this particular night, one lone figure, different and apart from the others, remained in the deepest shadows, quickening his pace only when forced into view by the dull luminescence of distantly separated gaslights. For over an hour, he continuously stalked a small area around Church Street, slipping from doorway to alley, intent on remaining unseen without losing sight of the main entry to the Ten Bells Public House. His was a very different mission, a mission indeed unique. Arthur Belmont would not have thought to call himself a hero, but if someday someone should call him one, he could not disagree. But in fact no one would ever call him that.

He had taken his name years earlier, not so much to conceal his identity as to sever all connections with his past. Unlike most, he did not despise everything and everyone in this urban hellhole; he knew the vast majority of people who populated these streets yearned for better lives and living conditions but were able to do little or nothing to bring about such improvements. This knowledge had been personally ingrained in him during the first eight years of his life, which were spent in Whitechapel before a stroke of luck brought him to better station elsewhere. He still retained deep and jagged scars within his soul from those early years, scars that relentlessly reminded him not only of what he himself had suffered in this place but of the countless other youngsters whose lives were still being destroyed on a daily basis. And yet he himself had performed terrible, unspeakable things in these very streets.

Every fifteen minutes, he stopped, momentarily standing motionless despite the chill and dampness of the night air that seeped into his flesh. Thus he had contrived, these many nights, to escape detection whenever the light of a bullseye lantern signaled the familiar patter of a stalwart police constable's boots passing uncomfortably near.

It was equally vital that he remain alert to sweet little Mary's anticipated exit from the Ten Bells. She would not be in good condition after an evening of heavy drinking and, if he were lucky, she would be alone. She had already taken leave of the place once, nearly two hours earlier, taking just enough time to service a staggering client in a nearby alley before hastily returning to the pub. Arthur had observed her actions but decided to do nothing until he could get her alone.

Fleeting glances of her since that tryst revealed her carousing in the pub, surrounded by friends, while clasping a pint of bitter.

Arthur was reminded of the first time he had seen Mary and how difficult it had been for him to believe anyone could look so much like his late mother. He took it as a sign from, if not on high, then below. After all, Hell for many, including himself, began with "mother." He had followed Mary to her home that very day, only to discover she resided in Miller's Court, in the very same room in which he had spent the first eight years of his life. All of this seemed so far beyond the realm of coincidence that he immediately dismissed any and all lingering doubts about including her in his plan. It was almost as if he was being guided by some unseen hand beckoning him toward a preordained destiny.

The very next day, he had returned to the doss house at Miller's Court in an effort to collect as much information about Mary and her habits as he could without arousing suspicion. He learned she had lived in her rented bedsit with a man for more than a year. According to neighbors, the man had recently moved out, apparently fed up with Mary's constant drinking and whoring. Arthur's father, a merchant seaman by trade, had left Arthur's mother for the same reasons when the boy was only five years of age. He remembered how he had often prayed his father would return for him until the day news arrived that his father's ship had gone down with all hands somewhere in the vast Atlantic. She continued to receive a portion of her seafaring husband's pay for a time but, when it ran out, Arthur's mother was compelled to seek some other means to pay the rent and keep food on the table. Decent-paying jobs for untrained laborers were exceedingly rare, so mother and child struggled endlessly just to make ends meet, and too often the ends were left dangling. In time, like so many before her, Arthur's mother had taken to walking the streets each night. Here was one skill she could turn to her advantage. It was disgusting and degrading work and, as time passed, she felt obliged to consume more and more alcohol to fortify her tolerance for it. That was the only way it ever got easier.

As a mere child, Arthur did what he could to bring in extra money, but he could earn a mere tuppence per week at best. Thus, it was inevitable that, in the end, his desperate mother felt compelled to follow the example of her gaggle of cronies, all low-grade prostitutes living, like her, in Miller's Court, or in nearby Dorset or Thrawl streets. What she did was to force her terrified son to submit to loathsome sexual encounters with some of the strangers she brought back to her room. With this added thrill for clients who were pederasts, she was able to double and, at times, even triple her nightly income. For the next three years, Arthur suffered abuse he considered worse than anything Hell could offer. Plying herself with boozy assurances that it was for her son's own good, since otherwise he should most likely starve, his mother soon became stolidly immune to his suffering. Sometimes she would hold the struggling boy down as a client buggered him. The most unnerving part of the ordeal was the way his mother seemed fascinated by the agony young Arthur endured, staring intently into his eyes as it occurred. She would cover his mouth with her hand to stifle his screams until they died away from weakness. Afterward, both mother and son avoided each other's gaze while she washed the blood from his legs and torn behind. He never forgave her the betrayal, refusing to be in the same room with her when she chose to drink away the extra earnings rather than use them to buy food. The boy made no serious attempt to run away because he knew he would likely fare even worse by himself in the streets. And so he drifted day to day in a waking coma of dull despair.

To his great astonishment, Arthur had eventually been rescued, albeit due to very dismal circumstances. One night after drinking more than usual, his mother brought a novice client home with her, hoping the man would be interested in a more expensive session that included her son's unwilling participation. She assured the fellow he need not fear anyone interrupting them as her husband was deceased. When she suggested the boy join in, the man was shocked and repulsed. As he prepared to depart, his self-loathing was palpable, and he refused even to listen to any alternative offer the woman stammered out. When Arthur's mother realized she was not about to change the man's mind, she launched into a mad rage and lunged upon him with an upraised butcher's knife she kept under the bedclothes. Shocked and terrified, young Arthur witnessed a life-or-death struggle for which he was ill prepared.

Instinctively he grabbed his mother's arm in an attempt to stop her from stabbing the man. Moments later, man and woman were struggling on the bed, entangled in blankets and sheets, all in a semi-darkness relieved only by the dim illumination of an oil lamp. When the lamp toppled from the bedside table, the combatants were deprived of all light. The breathless, sweat-soaked man eventually managed to extricate himself from the covers and rekindle the lamp, only to find himself staring at a fount of dark blood gushing from a horrendous slash across the woman's throat. Her jugular vein had been severed. The knife lay beside her, having fallen from her hand in the darkness. Taking great care to avoid getting blood on his clothing, the man carefully checked to see if she was still breathing while the boy sat calmly to one side of his mother's body. He found neither signs of breathing nor a pulse. Although he had no clear sense of what had occurred once the light was extinguished, he very much feared that he might have accidentally knocked the blade into the woman's throat while attempting to fend off her clumsy assault.

Suddenly recognizing the position in which he found himself, the man panicked, unsure if, despite all the chaos, he might be held responsible for the woman's demise. He was nearly out the door before he glanced back briefly at the pathetic little boy still poised helplessly by his mother's motionless form. Fortunately for Arthur, the good-hearted gentleman found himself incapable of leaving an innocent child alone with a corpse. He knew the boy would inevitably be relegated to some foul orphanage, forced to fend for himself on the streets or, worst of all, be charged with matricide should his recounting of events not be believed. Fighting the natural urge to flee, the man encouraged Arthur to go with him, promising him a good home in the country where he would be treated as if he were the man's own offspring. Perhaps in this way the man sought to atone for his uncharacteristic yielding to the temptation of infidelity.

What choice had Arthur than to trust the man and believe his promises? After pulling from a stinking heap a threadbare coat to protect the already shivering youth from the chill outside, the would-be rescuer hurriedly shoved a few necessities into a pillow case; they then fled the scene together. Hailing a hansom cab, they headed for the train station where both slept until morning. They boarded the first train from London to the man's family residence in Reading.

While on the train, the first he had ever ridden, Arthur learned his benefactor's name was Robert Ornin. He owned a small but thriving demolition and clearance concern based in London. The pair put their wits together, devising a story they hoped Ornin's wife would find believable. The couple had no children of their own, despite their great desire for a family, so it might work if Ornin introduced Arthur as a half-starved street urchin who had won his heart begging on a cold street corner. The boy, they would tell her, had been abandoned by his father after his mother died of consumption, and had survived by totting, rummaging through garbage and refuse for salable items. Unfortunately, Ornin would say, they dare not attempt to legally adopt Arthur for fear of his step-father returning and making trouble. The man and the boy agreed not tell Ornin's wife the truth of how Arthur's mother had died, fearing any slip of the tongue by either of them might lead to Ornin being accused of murder. Both of them knew Ornin had not intentionally harmed the woman but, for Ornin, the details of those crucial moments would forever remain unclear in his mind. He and the boy believed that the less his wife knew, the better it would be for all concerned.

After learning something of the horrors the lad had endured, Ornin found himself yielding to a warm, parental attitude toward him. The more Ornin thought about it, the more he dismissed all possibility that his wife would receive the boy with anything other than a lovingly embrace. Together they would provide Arthur with a fine home and a good education. And, assuming all went well, they would eventually make him their legal heir.

Arthur, realizing he was being offered a far better life than he could ever have hoped for, he readily consented to the plan. Ornin's ready kindness and generosity quickly won the boy's loyalty and affection as well.

It came as no surprise to Ornin when his wife took to little Arthur instantly. At last she had a child to love and nurture, the single missing element in her otherwise happy life. Arthur initially reacted with guarded caution, but he soon found in her the motherly love for which he had always longed. She and her husband were a decade older than his actual parents had been, but that meant nothing to him if he even noticed the fact. They loved him, and that was more than enough. For the first time since his real father had vanished from his life, Arthur was truly happy. This gave him the strength to repress much of the pain and trauma he had experienced, although the memories would continue to haunt him for the rest of his life. He and Ornin avoided referencing the night they had met, apart from those infrequent moments when Mrs. Ornin gently probed for more information. She stopped her prodding after a while, fearing her curiosity, if carried too far, might somehow ruin the happiness of her newly established family.

As the months and years went by, Ornin let it be known that he hoped Arthur would eventually take his place as the owner of his successful business enterprise. He did not force the issue, even after he and his wife made Arthur their legal heir. He knew it would be best for his new son to choose his own path once his interests and abilities should blossom. And that path, it seemed, might as easily lead him into medicine as into business. His "grandfather," Damon Ornin, M.D., had taught anatomy and physiology for many years at a local medical college after retiring from private practice. He grew so fond of his clever "grandson" that he encouraged the youth to follow in his footsteps. In private sessions, Dr. Ornin taught young Arthur much about the human body and the surgical methods required should he choose to pursue medicine. When the boy reached the age of sixteen, old Dr. Ornin invited him to assist him in performing a series of autopsies for the benefit of his students. Much to his disappointment, however, Arthur, though an able apprentice, evinced only a passing interest in medicine. Nonetheless, some years later, the knowledge he gleaned from the anatomical demonstrations would prove quite invaluable once his true path finally became clear.

The dark memories buried deep in his subconscious did not prevent Arthur from enjoying his new life to the fullest. Yet, having no one with whom he could share his inner turmoil, he kept to himself much of the time. He made friends easily, but inwardly he brooded over the past. He never doubted that someone must do something to prevent other innocent children from enduring such abuse as he had suffered, but he failed to contrive a remedy. It was a dark period in England's history, when the poor, both young and old, became mere fuel to fire the engines of the country's booming industries. But amid that smoke-choked darkness some small sparks appeared, as prominent men like the popular writer Charles Dickens used their influence to bring attention to the plight of the destitute. Arthur wished he had some influence to bring to bear, but he had none.

Only after both Ornin and his wife passed away did a daring plan begin to clearly formulate in his mind. Having reached maturity as the thirty-year-old owner of Ornin's company, he finally felt truly free to set the initial elements of this plan into motion. Before long he had brutally murdered four of his mother's old friends without arousing the least suspicion of either Scotland Yard or the detectives of the Metropolitan Police. It wasn't that his crimes went without notice; on the contrary, the outcry was at once very great. The greater the popular panic, the greater the urgency of the authorities to find the culprit. But none ever glanced in Arthur Belmont's direction.

He found it amusing when an upstart author by the name of Arthur Conan Doyle offered Scotland Yard his services and expertise as an amateur detective. The man's credentials amounted to little more than having published a fairly popular mystery novel the previous year. When Doyle announced the identity of the killer, Arthur watched with interest as, after arresting and questioning the accused, Scotland Yard released the suspect after the most cursory interrogation; Doyle had accused an innocent man. Embarrassed, the "great detective" returned to writing. It seemed he was a brilliant sleuth only on paper.

So far, Arthur had outsmarted them all. The officials and even the torch-wielding vigilante groups were seeking a vicious, sex-driven madman, a slavering, inhuman monster, thereby launching their own investigations in the wrong direction. There were many who were convinced the killer was a Jew, because of what some thought might be a message from the killer, scrawled in chalk on a wall near where one of the earlier victims had been found; it contained an obscure reference to Jews, though none to the murders. Arthur knew nothing of the confused graffiti, but the public was in such an uproar that the police felt obliged to obliterate the message lest it become a pretext for violence against London's Jews. No one knew how many suspects had been hauled in and questioned at length, but there had been many. There had even been rumors that the killer might be a woman or a member of the Royal family. The greater the furor his efforts created, the more Arthur was delighted. He most assuredly did not want anyone else to receive either the credit or the blame for his deeds.

It had proven a challenge for Arthur to avoid detection for so many months, to be sure, but he felt confident he could accomplish his purpose before getting caught. After all, his plan demanded he kill only once more, albeit using methods even more dramatic and vile than those he had applied to any of his previous victims. If his luck held, Mary would present him with that opportunity before morning.

During his investigations, he had learned that, like his own mother of ill memory, Mary had permitted, even encouraged, some of her clients to misuse her two children. Oh, there was no doubt she deserved the end Arthur had in mind for her. Her children, unlike so many others, had been fortunate enough to escape further torture when Mary's elder sister heard of the abuse. She had become so enraged that she had taken both children, against Mary's will, to live with her in the country. The sister later convinced Mary to give her custody of both children by pointing out how her life would be easier with two fewer mouths to feed. On her own, Mary's drinking had increased but, by working the streets, she had managed to support herself despite frequently falling behind in her rent. Currently, she was twenty-plus shillings in arrears, with but a single day remaining before she and her ratty belongings would together be thrown into the street. She certainly had not earned enough from the single client with whom Arthur had earlier observed her in the alley, so he felt quite sure he should see her on the prowl again at any moment. How pleased he felt at how very nicely all the pieces of his plan were coming together!

The sound of a woman's voice, singing "Sweet Violets," prevented Arthur from continuing his musings, snapping his attention back to the present. Glancing toward the source of the song, he saw Mary stumble out the front door of the Ten Bells. She had plainly had too much to drink. Immediately behind her, two other drunken Megs emerged from the smoke-filled pub, clutching each other in an effort to remain upright. They bade Mary a good night before turning to toddle away in the opposite direction.

After allowing Mary a few moments to regain some semblance of sobriety, Arthur began walking toward her slowly, pretending he was headed away from the direction of her home in Miller's Court. He dared not want to approach from behind as that would certainly frighten her. He stopped a short distance away from her and softly whispered, "Are you all right, Miss?"

Surprised at the sudden emergence of a stranger out of the darkness, she angrily snapped, "Who wants to know?"

"Oh, I do beg your pardon," he said. "I was just passing by, on my way home, when I noticed you. It struck me that you might be in some sort of distress. My mistake. Please forgive the intrusion." With a benevolent smile and tip of the hat, he wished her a good night and made to depart.

Disarmed by his demeanor, Mary's thoughts returned to the important matter of her unpaid rent. "Cor..." she said, waving her hand to demonstrate that she had overreacted. "You was just bein' a gentleman. I shouldn't be so gruff. It's me that should apologize, sir."

He relaxed. It was going to be simple to convince her to take him back to her room. He would pretend to be a novice at this sort of thing, ignorant enough to agree to an extravagant amount in return for the intimacy her residence would provide them. As this was a method he had not previously used, he had nearly hesitated to try it, unsure if the act would fool this woman. Obviously, his luck still held.

She immediately began flirting with him, subtly and with respect. He played the naive foil well, allowing her to suggest he accompany her home as all the talk of a killer on the loose made a "poor girl" like her nervous. And he had expected this game to be difficult!

He leaned down to retrieve a valise approximately the size of a doctor's bag before offering her his arm. They made small talk along the way until she once again spontaneously burst into song, prompted, no doubt, by her lack of sobriety. She had a rather charming voice, he noted, encouraging her to continue but not so loud as to attract unwanted attention.

It was a short walk to Dorset Street, then Miller's Court, where they encountered a man who knew Mary. He insisted on asking her if all was well, while simultaneously doing his best to get a better look at her unfamiliar companion. Despite his efforts to see Arthur's face, it was too dark and Arthur's hat made it impossible for the man to get a clear look at him. In addition, his large handlebar mustache served to obscure more of Arthur's features. Mary thwarted her friend's curiosity by emphatically bidding him good evening as she guided Arthur away from the street and into the court. Resuming her singing, she did not even find it odd when her companion redirected her stumbling gait away from the stairs leading to the second-floor landing. Had she been sober, she surely would have thought it quite peculiar that he apparently knew the way to her room as well or better than she did.

Upon reaching the door, she giggled mischievously and turned away. She mumbled as she explained that she had recently misplaced the key, although a female friend who had been staying with her for a few days might have possession of it. Walking to a window, she carefully reached inside through a broken pane. Moving a flimsy curtain aside, she easily unlatched the lock from within.

Bitter memories flooded Arthur's mind as he followed her into the small, sparsely furnished room that he remembered only too well. Mary lit a candle, perching it on a large table opposite the bed. It seemed little had changed since he had lived here as a child; the same old headboard stood at the top of a single bed wedged into a corner by the window. He took care to avoid knocking over the piles of old newspapers and of stray clothes carelessly stacked near the fireplace. A bedpan and jug near the unmade bed completed the depressing setting. Difficult as it was for him to revisit his past this way, it was vital that he steel himself for what he was about to do. He placed his bag upon the table and stood, unmoving, in the dim candlelight.

Feigning awkward shyness, a few moments later he mumbled, "Well, my dear, now that you're safely home, I should probably be on my way."

"Oh, no, please don't leave," she begged. "I don't feel like being alone just now." She fumbled with his coat, eagerly trying to convince him he should stay. There had, as yet, been no mention of sex or payment, so she carried on about the kindness she saw in his eyes and how lonely she was, confident he would soon warm to her advances.

In time, he agreed to remain, pretending to find her pandering all but irresistible. Encouraged by indications of progress, she displayed her delight by dancing wistfully around the room. She apologized for having nothing to offer him beyond a bit of leftover whiskey mixed with water from a common spigot just outside her room, but he refused the drink, telling her there was no need to fuss over him.

She snatched the hat from his head, humming the same tune

she had been singing earlier. She then ran her hand affectionately across his cheek. His attitude, though she finally persuaded him to remove his coat, remained stoic. She could see this man was somehow different from the ones she usually met, and thus she decided to bide her time before cautiously broaching the subject of payment. If she acted too hastily, he might decide to leave. She urged him to sit on the edge of the bed, then sat next to him, resting her shoulders against his arm with her back to him. When he raised his arms, she awaited his embrace.

She felt very confident of success until he lowered his arms and slipped his woolen scarf around her neck. She felt the unexpected bite of the scarf tighten about her throat, depriving her lungs of air. She thrashed about desperately but, as she faced away from him, she could barely reach him, let alone overpower him or escape his grasp. The pain of being strangled was instantly preempted by her desperate need for air.

Arthur held the woolen noose taut for a full five minutes, long after her struggle had ceased. The last thing he needed or wanted was for her to wake up during that which was to come. Suffocation was definitely unpleasant, but it was the kindest means to an end as far as he was concerned. When the heart stopped beating, blood stopped circulating through the body, a vital factor to be considered before cutting anyone's throat. This way, the blood did not gush from a dead body. If he were to cut her throat while she lived, it would splatter wildly onto everything in close proximity. He had carefully worked out this portion of his plan in his head long before approaching his first victim on the street. Once his victim was dead, he could easily move to avoid the slow-moving blood draining from the body. He wondered if the police had yet realized this was the reason no one had reported seeing anyone covered with blood fleeing the murder scenes.

Over the course of the next three hours, Arthur Belmont forced himself to remain as aloof and objective as possible. His was a task so gruesome that, without distancing his thoughts from his actions, he would not have the fortitude to complete it. The training he had received from his "grandfather" alone provided him the ability to work while remaining so totally detached from that which his eyes could not avoid.

He placed the once desirable body on the bed before proceeding to clumsily remove her clothing, then much, but not all, of his own. Fetching his bag from the table, he pulled out several large, very sharp knives that he had carefully wrapped in the change of clothing he had stuffed inside the bag earlier. In order to see what he was doing, he required more light, so he quickly gathered together all of the newspapers and loose clothing in the room; he would burn them in the grate as needed. Although this provided the necessary illumination, the resultant heat caused sweat to pour freely from his body, quickly soaking his clothes. He could only ignore this inconvenience and return to his main objective, the creation of a masterpiece of unbelievable horror.

Slowly and with great care, he began to cut and peel the unmoving form. Pulling the table closer to the bed, he placed her viscera neatly on the flat wooden surface. He deftly sliced off her breasts before arranging them neatly on the table next to her intestines, meaning to lay them back onto the body once he was finished. One by one, other organs were removed and carefully deposited next to each other. It was as if he were emptying her torso, piece by piece. He went on to mutilate her arms and peel the skin from much of her face, transforming her beyond all recognition. Her blood saturated the bedclothes before flowing down to form a large pool on the floorboards beneath the bed. It was a very nasty business, but he forced himself to continue. Having attacked the vaginal area, he concluded his task by denuding the front of her right thigh all the way to the bone and carving flaps from the skin of her torso and posterior.

Exhaustion set in as he transformed an attractive woman into a hideous mass of blood and guts. At last he was convinced he had done enough. He placed one of her arms across her chest, resting the hand on the opposite shoulder in imitation of the royal Egyptian mummies his fellow countrymen delighted in unwrapping at parties for the entertainment of their posh friends.

He finally stood up and crossed the room to fetch water from the spigot in the hall. It took several more trips to the spigot and trough before he was satisfied that he had rinsed as much of the blood as possible from his body and tools. He removed what he had been wearing and tossed the garments into the fire, exchanging the wet clothing for fresh, dry garments from the bag. Wiping the perspiration from his brow, he prepared to leave, extinguishing the candle while allowing the slowly dying fire to continue burning. The experience had all been very matter-of-fact for him. He had displayed none of the sexual frenzy, depravity or insanity the police were so sure were the driving forces behind his heinous crimes. Now all he sought was an undetected departure and a good night's rest, free of dreams forcing him to relive what he had done.

No one had yet guessed his clever means of eluding capture, though it was actually quite simple. As the owner and head officer of a demolition company he was required by the City to inspect the sewage tunnels in all of the areas where destruction was planned. He had been officially entrusted with the keys to the great metal entrances that led to the brick labyrinth of tunnels beneath the streets. In addition, those same oh-so-considerate fools had given him a map to ensure he would not become lost within the arcane sewer system.

London, East End, late night November 9, 1888

Having been accepted into the London Metropolitan Police only a year earlier, twenty-year-old Edmund Setlock retained the low rank of a simple Constable. He was just another Bobby on the beat, despite being the nephew of Chief Commissioner Sir Charles Warren. His uncle had insisted the familial ties be kept secret from the rest of the force and warned his sister's eldest son that no special preferences would be accorded him. Setlock had readily agreed to those conditions before going on to prove himself a most excellent recruit. In truth, PC Setlock harbored no real desire for high position; he was satisfied to perform public service while enjoying a very real sense of freedom as he patrolled the streets each night. The only disadvantage was having to witness the deplorable poverty, pitiful desperation, and appalling rate of crime not only in his assigned district of Whitechapel, but in the adjacent district of Spitalfields as well. He did not much mind the feelings of isolation he frequently experienced while walking the night, especially since the number of PCs assigned to the "murder area" had been increased from twenty-seven to eighty-nine in recent weeks, each constable's beat having been carefully formulated to ensure that at least one man patrolled each block once every fifteen minutes.

As he passed by St. Mary's Church on Commercial Street, he noticed a figure standing in the middle of the street ahead of him. He could not explain it, but something about it just felt wrong to him. As he drew nearer, he realized it was a woman standing quite still with her back to him. She was wearing a flimsy nightgown and no shoes, so she must be freezing. Perhaps she was the victim of a crime or was mad. He approached her slowly, not wanting to spook her. If she did not have all her wits about her, something not so uncommon in this neighborhood, she might even attack him.

When he was within three meters of her, she emitted a jarring, "Stop!" without so much as turning around. Damn the Met's hard-soled police shoes, he thought to himself; had they just switched over to footwear of a different material, as had been repeatedly proposed, he could have approached her without being heard.

Constable Setlock did stop, just as she whirled around to face him. A great dark stain marked the front of her clothing; there was not enough light for him to be certain, but intuition told him it was a terrible stain of blood. Had he stumbled over another of the killer's victims, one who had somehow managed to escape before Red Jack could finish the job?

He began to move closer to her, but after he had accomplished only one step, she again insisted he stay where he was. "I've been waitin' for *you*," she said. "I'm pleased to see yer on time."

Still puzzled, he asked if she needed help. When she didn't answer, he proffered further inquiry. "When you say you've been waiting, do you mean you have been waiting for a constable to come along or do you mean you've been waiting for me in particular? I'm not sure if I can help you, but I'll do whatever I can. Shall I blow my whistle to fetch more help? Another constable is surely close by, so it's guaranteed to bring an all but immediate response."

"Put y' whistle away," she ordered him. "It's *you* I been expectin'. There's no other Bobby what can serve me purpose. I aim t' help *you* as well, I might add. You boys've been seeking this mad killer, this 'Red Jack'? Well, I mean t' take yer directly to 'im."

"You don't say!" he exclaimed with genuine surprise, betraying a high degree of skepticism in his voice, "and how might you know his exact whereabouts?"

She laughed at his foolish disbelief, then blurted out, "I need some facks which only 'e's got, and you must help me obtain 'em. Don't worry; I guarantee you and yer uncle, the high and mighty Sir Charles, 'll get to 'ear the bloke's confession in person so's you can clap 'im in old irons an' do yer worst. But I'll do th' questions, got that? Me and my friends, that is. Once he's told us what we need to know, we leaves 'im to you an' Sir Charles. That's fair tit-fer-tat, wouldn't you say?"

Young Setlock now knew the shadowed form must be that of one of the many who sought to lend some color to their dull lives by inserting themselves into the events of the day. Scotland Yard's men regularly bemoaned the amount of wasted time such false leads cost them. Before he could mollify her with a polite declining of her assistance, the woman rushed at him with surprising speed, stopping only when her face was a hand's width from his own. Startled, he jumped back until further escape was impeded by the brick wall now immediately at his back. To his displeasure, she kept pace with his every move. The flurry of events drove from his mind the momentary thought: How could she have known of his personal connection to Sir Charles?

"So, ducky, do we have a deal or do we not?"

Her behavior made her less credible, not more. She was obviously a nutter, yet he found himself stammering, "As to this deal, just exactly what is it you require of me?" He was distracted as his eyes narrowed in an attempt to get a closer look at her features, which were somehow still obscure even up this close.

She seemed happy to have intrigued, even intimidated, the young man, but she could tell he needed further convincing. "I 'ear yer uncle resigned 'is office two days ago, right before last night's awful murder. Can't say as I blames him, not wi' th' way Scotland Yard and the lot have 'ounded him for not catchin' no killer, and at the same time 'oldin' back th' facks they got on their own. Poor old sot's been set against the lot of 'em, though they's few wot knows it, which puts you 'n me ahead o' th' game, if ye takes me meanin'. Now, do ye spose yer can convince Sir Charles to meet yer a few blocks from 'ere, over by that block uv old buildin's they been tearin' down for th' last few weeks?"

"I know the block you mean, and I'm familiar with the house you've indicated. I pass it on my nightly beat. But I'm going to need something more if I'm to convince Uncle Charles to meet us there. I'm sorry, but he'd insist on more than your word to motivate him. And, by the way, how do you know he's…?"

She gave him a churlish smile. Drawing her right arm back, she suddenly rammed it into and through his chest until the palm of her hand was resting flat against the wall.

Setlock gasped. Slowly overcoming his shock, he dared to look down. She had thrust her arm, nearly to the elbow, into his body, yet he felt nothing. Confused and on the verge of total panic, he looked to her for some kind of explanation. He tried to speak, but found he could not utter a single word.

"'ow's that fer a reason t' believe I speaks the truth?"

Still short of breath, he finally managed to stammer, "What... How...?"

Feigning compassion, she pretended to comfort him. "Now, now, don't fret yer pretty little 'ead; you're just fine." Looking down at her arm, she continued, "I should think this'd be enough to convince you that I'm t' be taken serious. Don't yer agree?"

"But I... I don't understand!" he managed to exclaim, his eyes wide, fixed once again on the arm protruding from his sternum.

"Calm down, luv. I said yer just fine an' I meant it. Watch this!" She slowly withdrew her arm from his body, waiting until her hand began to emerge before snatching it away with a nerve-racking squeal of delight.

Setlock nervously permitted himself to exhale, slowly.

Glaring at him now, she said, "That's better. So, that should convince you I know what I'm sayin'. Seems pretty clear one of us is dead, a *ghost*, an' since yer still breathin', it must be me that's the goner!"

Once he showed signs of relaxing, she added, "Now there's a good lad. So like I told yer, go to th' only 'ouse still standing in all th' mess an' wait just outside until I lets yer in. Your Jackie will be inside, along with me and me gals. It oughter be quite th' lovely reunion, eh? You and Sir Charles can jot down all wot 'e says befo' 'e even knows yer there; I'll see to that. After that, as far as I care, you can send the bastard to prison or to Hell. I'll have no use for 'im after 'e spills th' beans we needs to know." She stared at him for a moment. "Yew keepin' up wiv all this, dearie?" She emitted an eerie chortle, a half-humorous, half-maudlin moan such as one hears from drunks reluctantly facing the dawn, or the noon.

Putting his fear aside, Setlock reminded himself that he was an official representative of Her Majesty's police, not some driveling idiot. "Yes," he proffered, "I've got it, all of it. I know where Uncle is right now, and I could try to get him to meet us, but it is quite late. He's in his office packing things up at present as he wants to elude the press once news of his resignation is made public. But since you already seem to know about that, I guess he's wasting his time. Are you absolutely certain you know the exact whereabouts of Red Jack, Jack the Ripper or whatever you choose to call him?"

She nodded affirmatively.

"Then give us an hour to get there. So, if that's agreeable, you have a deal."

"Deal," she firmly acknowledged. "I'll expect you two in an hour. Keep out o' sight somewhere nears th' house 'til I fetch you. I'll make a grand entrance for yer uncle's sake, I will. Now, get your arse moving. Fetch me Sir Charles."

He turned away a moment at the sound of a child's shout from up the street, and when he turned back, the peculiar old crone was gone. He looked up and down the street. He was absolutely alone. He briefly wondered what he might have gotten himself into, but he could not deny he relished the thought of what the rest of the night would bring. In all honesty, he wouldn't miss the opportunity to attend this little get-together for the world. And here was a chance to vindicate Uncle Charles as well as to secure his own reputation.

He paused long enough to gather his thoughts before breaking into a trot. Two blocks later he stopped, anxiously scanning the street around him. He was sure that Henry, an orphan who haunted the dismal area, would be around even at this late hour. He was a good lad despite his lowly circumstances, and he was clever enough never to pass up a chance to make a few coins in return for an errand. It was the only way to keep himself fed.

"Henry!" the PC called out, hoping not to attract unwanted attention. After all, he had abandoned his beat. "Henry boy, it's Setlock. I must talk to you right now. Come out! I know you're here somewhere. Nothing to fear, chum. I need you to deliver a note for me in exchange for enough shillings to make your eyes shine."

He didn't have long to wait for a return call of "Set, that you?"

Receiving an affirmative answer, the ten-year-old manifested, stepping out from the shadows and into the light. "What's all this you say about a packet of shillings?" he eagerly inquired.

Five minutes later, Henry dashed off with the note Setlock had given him with express instructions to deliver it personally to Sir Charles Warren. The police station was not far, and Setlock trusted the lad would find his way to Uncle Charles's office without problem. The boy was resourceful, even sneaky when necessary, and he was always reliable. The contents of the note should do the rest.

Setlock made his way to the meeting place. This was most definitely going to be a night he would long remember. His immediate concern was how he was going to explain all of this to his uncle.

Just a few streets from his destination, he spied some all-too-common nocturnal activity occurring in a reeking alley behind a pub. A man was engaged in riding a heavy-set prostitute who had simply pulled up her skirts as she bent over a barrel. Such public sexual activity always unsettled Setlock, but to interfere would be overstepping his boundaries. He could only ignore the scene and keep walking. Such was the law, at least for certain parts of the City.

Nearly an hour passed before Setlock heard the clatter of horses' hooves on the pavement a block or so away. He stepped out into the open a few meters from the predetermined meeting place. The dog-cart came to a halt directly in front of him. His uncle, Sir Charles, along with a grimy-faced Henry, descended from the buggy. He noted his uncle did not look particularly pleased, although Henry was grinning from ear to ear.

"Here he is, guv, just like as you asked. Now how's about those lovely shillings you promised?"

Setlock politely nodded to his uncle, as he shoved his hand into his pocket. He handed a number of coins to the lad, thanking him profusely and promising to give him more the following night.

"Blimey!" Henry whispered. He had not expected so much, and more coming. He felt as if he had just won the Sweepstakes.

"Sorry you have to wait for the rest," Setlock explained, "but I try not to carry too much coin on my person while on duty. You know I'll do right by you. Now you'd best run along, my lad. There's danger ahead and it wouldn't do for you to be involved."

With a cry of "Right oh! I'll be a lookin' fer you tomorrow night!" Henry retreated once again into the dark.

Sir Charles glared at his nephew impatiently. "Now, Edmund, would you care to explain what is so urgent that you found it necessary to drag me away from my duties in the middle of the night? I might add that this had better be good."

The older man's features, now habituated into somewhat of a perpetual scowl, remained impassive as his nephew related the details of his brief encounter with the street harridan. Even as Setlock spoke he began to feel foolish, sure his uncle would think him foolish for taking an old woman's fanciful promises at all seriously. He found it even more difficult to confess he truly believed the woman was a ghost.

To his considerable relief, it was soon evident that his improbable narrative was being accepted, at least to a certain extent, by the great man without so much as a probing question.

"Are you quite certain, Edmund, that you are not the brunt of some master trickster using cheap chicanery to fool you?"

Setlock paused, seriously considering Sir Charles's legitimate concern. After a few moments, he bucked up, replying, "Yes, sir, I'm sure."

His uncle expressed his acceptance with, "Very well, then." Setlock suddenly felt quite proud of both his uncle and himself.

The pair continued their discussion, Sir Charles requesting further details. This went on for a few minutes before being brought to an abrupt halt when a light suddenly appeared at the door of the one-storied house in question.

Although startled, the two men slowly and quietly approached the house, making their way through the wreckage of wholly and partially destroyed buildings. No one was visible at the door, which remained closed. Sir Charles stopped a few meters from the door and watched. His nephew followed suit. Neither of them knew what to expect, so each braced himself in his own way for almost anything, attention fixed unflinchingly on the door. They did not have long to wait.

The white door seemed to blur about a third of the way from the top, but the ubiquitous fog was so thick and the night so dark, that this did not seem too far out of the ordinary. Young Setlock reminded himself that his uncle standing next to him was scarcely more distinct. A few seconds passed before the hazy image became clearer and more complete as the drifting miasma became momentarily thinner. Intrigued, Sir Charles fixed his eyes on a woman with long, curly blonde hair. He detected a degree of beauty in her pale, hard-set features. As more of her came into view, he realized she was somehow manifesting through the still-closed door. She took one step forward, her entire body now coming into view, before raising one arm in a beckoning motion, as if welcoming guests otherwise too shy to come nearer.

Sir Charles turned to Setlock and nodded, a look of wonder on his face. Together they moved closer to the house, hesitating only long enough to glance at the ground every few steps to avoid stumbling over loose bits of brick and debris. The strange apparition smiled at them before turning to open the door for her guests. She then led them into the dimly lit interior of the house and down a large hall. In total silence, she approached a doorway to the left, gesturing for the men to enter what appeared to be a study. A single candle cast the only light. Shadows danced and loomed about them as they followed her across the room to a second door. The woman raised an index finger to her lips, calling for silence, before opening this second inner door ever so slightly, just enough to allow her companions to peer into a bed chamber. A fire smoldered gently in the grate near a poster bed they could see was currently occupied. Once both had noted the main elements of the room, she closed the door slowly so as not to disturb the sleeper.

With the door to the bed chamber closed, she finally spoke,

inviting the two gentlemen to take seats in the overstuffed chairs facing the desk behind which she sat as if she were the authority before whom they had been brought for questioning. "You gentlemens must 'ave many questions to ask, but I'm afraid we ain't got time for all that. That man you saw in the connecting room? I believe you like to call 'im Jack the Ripper, the mad butcher of whores. His real name ain't important right now. You can get that from 'im later on. But 'e changed his name early on, taken in by a family in Reading when he was eight years old.

"His victims, including Mary Jane Kelly, the poor child he cut to shreds less than a day ago, are here and they 'ave their own questions to ask him."

Sir Charles was confused, quite sure that either he or the garrulous woman had got something out of order. He made to ask for clarification, but she raised an index finger to her lips and silenced him once more.

"All this should prove quite useful to you coppers, so go on and take as many notes as y' like. Me, I can't neither write nor read. There won't be much light, but I'm sure you'll manage. He mustn't know yer listening before we ladies obtains the answers we wants. Y' see, we've a bit of a trip to take, an' we're runnin' outer time. We got to know some fings first. Wot a relief to be free of all this rot! Once we get wot we wants, you kin 'ave 'im to do wiv as yer please. We wants 'im stopped, but 'at's your job, not ours."

"Quite so, dear lady," Sir Charles said, just beginning to feel this bizarre woman might possess real information, that he and his nephew might actually be on the verge of capturing the Ripper. And if she could really elicit a confession from this man, her delusions about his victims were neither here nor there. So he asked her where they were to stand while listening to the questioning.

"At this 'ere door, naturally! Bring chairs over, if you likes. And a candle too, if ye wants to take it all down."

"What if he hears us or notices the door is open a crack?" Setlock asked.

A self-satisfied smirk crossed her face. "You needn't worry about that, I reckon. There's only th' one lamp lit in there, so it'd be hard for him to make you out in the dark."

"Madame, tell us one more thing. Since you knew where to find the Ripper, you must be acquainted with his movements. How has he managed to elude us so completely?"

"This ain't just an 'ouse he hides in, mind yer, Sir Charles. He owns and runs th' company what's doin' all the tearing down around 'ere. He uses this place like an office and a home-away-from-home, as you might say. This place'll remain standing amid th' general ruin only so long as he needs it as a base to see to 'is killin's. Once that's done, it'll come down like the rest. An' 'e's got keys to every sewer tunnel below Whitechapel and Spitalfields. That's how 'e goes wherever he wants as quick as a flash wivout bein' seen." She stopped long enough to chuckle softly, relishing her next revelation.

"They's always odd gases and fumes to contend with down in them tunnels, but 'e's rarely affected as he sprints through 'em wivout stoppin' long enough to breave in much o' th' awful stuff. Trouble is, after 'e spent three hours carvin' Mary to bits this mornin', 'e wuz worn down to the bone, so to speak. He wad'n 'alf way 'ere before 'e passed out from suckin' in some foul gas or other with each breaf. He laid on 'is back in th' muck for hours before 'e managed to pull himself together and crawl back 'ere. It's a wonder 'e didn't die down there; 'e wouldn't be th' first!"

Fascinated, her audience remained silent, unsure how to respond, or whether indeed any response was required. So their hostess continued. "Once 'e made it safely back, he 'opped inter bed an' 'as been sleepin' there ever since. Can ye smell a touch of sewer stench in th' air? Well, once we has yer in place, we'll wake 'im and begin our questions, just like they do at Scotland Yard." She leaned back in her chair with a look of satisfaction on her face. "Well, it's time we gets to work. You blokes still with us?"

Sir Charles would have preferred to discuss the illogical situation in which they found themselves a bit more before agreeing to her terms, but she had made it very clear that it was now or never. Setlock reluctantly nodded his agreement, still however a bit unclear as to the men's role. When she said "we," did she mean to include him and Uncle Charles? Or were they to settle for a more passive role as observers?

"We agree to listen, observe and take notes, just as you suggest, without interfering with your interrogation of this man, assuming you keep your word that, er, none of you physically assaults him in any way and, of course, that he convincingly confesses to being the criminal known to us as Jack the Ripper," Sir Charles summarized.

She seemed pleased as she rose from her seat. "That'll do just fine." She grinned as she extended her right hand toward Sir Charles to seal the matter with a handshake. He made to respond in kind but felt foolish when he somehow missed her hand. It was, he supposed, the gesture that mattered. Serious doubts arose in his mind concerning his nephew's belief that this woman was indeed a ghost, although he was unable to explain her emergence through the front door.

They proceeded to arrange themselves as previously discussed. Once the men were set and in place, she entered the bed chamber, leaving the door slightly open behind her. Something subtle in her backward glance suggested she was opening the door for their benefit, not her own. They looked at one another in puzzlement, unsure of what they had seen, then shrugged.

She approached the bed and called out to the still-sleeping man lying therein. Receiving no immediate response, she repeated herself several times, increasing the volume each time. There was a plaintive note beneath her reproving sharpness.

The bed clothes shifted as the man began to stir. He sat up slowly, still fully dressed, and peered about the half-lit room in response to the summons. Gathering his wits, a still groggy Arthur Belmont stared in disbelief as he recognized the figure poised at the foot of the bed. He squinted his eyes as he struggled to convince himself he was fully awake.

When finally able to speak, he expressed profound confusion. "Good Lord! Mum, is that you? How can this be? You must be a hallucination from that ripe gutter gas!"

"I do reckon it's a bit of a surprise, a happy one, I 'ope, to see me again after all these years. Tell me, me boy, 'ave you missed yer sweet mum?" Her sarcasm was palpable if the rest of her wasn't.

Terrified, a wide-eyed Arthur demanded to know why she had come to him and what she wanted.

"Now, now, don't get yer knickers in a twist, dearie. I just got one thing I need to know before I can move on, and it seems yer the only one what knows it. So 'ow's about it, son, won't you tell your ol' mum who it was that run the knife across her throat, killing her dead? Were it that fella I brought home or did I do it meself during the tussle without even knowing it? You're the only one what knows. So who really did me in?"

He stared at her with a blank expression on his face.

"Come on, out with it!" she demanded. "There's others waitin' to pay you visits, so answer me and be quick about it!"

A wheezing sound gradually escaped Arthur's lips. He grinned and began to chuckle. "By God, without a doubt it *is* you, Mum! After all these years, too. Well, I'll be damned!" His laughter rose nearly to the point of hysteria as he spat out, "And you're damned as well, if there's any justice, either in this world or the next one!" Catching his breath, he challenged her, "So you want to know who cut your sweet little throat, do you? Well, I'm more than happy to fill you in as to the culprit's identity, luv. It was *me*. I did it, and I can honestly say I've never regretted it, not one jot. Now I ask you, are you pleased now that you know?"

She was taken aback by his words, only able to mumble, "But 'ow? And why'd a boy want to harm 'is own mum?"

With a smirk, he told her, "That's easy enough to answer as well. If you recall, I was on the bed when you and your client were fighting over the knife, flailing about right next to me." He surged with a mix of delight and fury as he continued. Recounting it and gloating was like killing her all over again. "You both forgot about me. If you recall, the two of you were conveniently located between me and the window. Just enough moonlight penetrated the curtain for me to not only see you both clearly, but to see the gleam of the knife as well. When I saw he had you by the wrist, I reached up and grabbed his cuff, jerking his arm down, across, and just under your chin. And I'd gladly do it again! But by your own words, you're dead, so there's no need. No need to thank me. With that issue settled, tell me, are you happy now? I hope so, as I'm more than ready to see the back of you."

Obviously enjoying her shocked expression, he proceeded to taunt her. "Oh, I beg your pardon. You asked what reason I might possibly have for killing you. Well, let's ponder that for a moment. Allow me a moment to look down the list. I'll try to narrow it down a bit. Let's call it even with all those men you so graciously encouraged to rape me."

His crestfallen mother screamed, again and again. Catching her breath, she prepared to refute her son's words, but when she attempted to speak, she could only emit guttural rasps and incomprehensible gibberish. Her own terrible guilt, so long suppressed, was getting the better of her now. She should have known it was better to let sleeping dogs, er, sons, lie.

Arthur greeted his mother's demonstration of inarticulate ire with mild amusement and an incomparable sense of complete vindication. He was enjoying himself intensely. Applauding her performance, he caustically reacted with, "Now that we're finished, you have my permission to go to Hell where you obviously belong."

Seething, she shouted, "Oh, yer not done. There's more to come, and a right lot of it, too!" As she began to fade into the dark shadows of the room, she called out, "Come forward, me lovelies, 'ere's your chance to confront th' bastard what butchered you all!"

From the dark recesses they came forth, those whose flesh had so woefully endured the savage surgery of Jack's blade. Each appeared as he had seen her last, pale and cold, slashed and torn, no longer denizens of this living world.

He puffed himself up as if pleased to see the shuffling corpses. He seemed to be thrilled to have the opportunity to greet them by name as they approached the bed.

"Ah, there you are! Good evening to you, sweet Mary Ann! And how delightful to see you, old Annie, standing there with Elizabeth close beside. Oh, and we mustn't forget *you*, Catherine, you old slag! Draw closer to the light, my dear, so I might get a better view of your wretched self."

He tilted his head slightly, searching deeper into the pitch surrounding him. He gently beckoned, "Mary? Mary Kelly? Come now, don't be shy! Hurry along and join the others!"

From the furthest corner of the room came a muffled, sloshing sound. In the adjoining room, Sir Charles and Setlock, still faithfully maintaining their vigil, leaned away from the forbidding noise and accompanying odor. That very morning, they both had viewed the remains of Mary Kelly, all laid out on a slab in the morgue. Little beyond the general body framework and bones testified to the fact that only the night before, this had been a vital human, an attractive woman who loved to drink, sing and dance. The attendant mortician had claimed he had never witnessed a more "brutal job" in his decades-long career. There was no mistaking either the identities or the condition of these once-women. The bizarre dialogue between their informant and her supposed son might be dismissed as shared delusion, but—*this!* Uncle and nephew alike fought to retain consciousness as their minds sought to shut down in a faint, unable to accept the truth of what clearly confronted them.

Arthur openly relished the opportunity to revisit his most diligent handiwork. He smiled warmly as the carcass hobbled closer, balancing on the sole leg Arthur had left semi-intact, her face and torso all but denuded of any actual features and flesh. "*There* you are," he cried, "how kind of you to drop by for a visit!"

When they had all gathered near, Arthur's mother insisted on returning to intrude on the reunion. "Ye've answered me fair enough, but these ladies can't rest till they knows what they done to you to make yer treat 'em so 'orrid. They can't speak their own peace; you saw to that. Now don't be shy. We're all anxious to hear your reasons!"

Arthur rose to the occasion. "I must say, I can't tell you how grateful I am that you've all come here together just to visit me. Much easier than trying to explain my actions to each of you, one at a time. It's all rather simple, actually. I'm sure you overheard the exchange I just had with my mother. If you think back, all of you were well acquainted with her, except for Miss Kelly, of course. The rest of you may not recognize me now, but you knew me when I was just a wee nipper. I had the privilege of knowing some of your darling little brats as well. One day, I overcame my shame and told the others what my loving mother had done to me. One by one, all the others had similar tales to tell. *Your sons and daughters*, damn you all! That's why I chose you specially for my carve-ups. No one who treats children like that deserves to live.

"As for the unfortunate Miss Kelly here, she looked uncannily like you, Mum. So much like you that I couldn't help wanting to know more about her. And it proved quite interesting. Not only was I gob smacked to discover she occupied the very same room I'd once shared with you, but I learned she'd subjected her own little ones to the same treatment I endured.

"I've never fully recovered from all that I suffered, nor have hundreds of others who've been forced to tolerate the same. When I grew to manhood and my own desires began to appear, I could only greet them with horror. Every arousal immediately sickened me. Marriage was quite out of the question. Finally I reached the bitter conclusion that the only way to divorce myself from sexual desire was to castrate myself. I paid a failed medical student desperate for money to assist me. I was well aware I should bleed to death should I undertake the procedure on my own. In this way I survived, freed forever from all revolting temptations.

"Some time after, it came to me that there just might be a way for me to bring about change for the better, not only for the off-spring of cold-hearted whores like yourselves, but also for those poor souls forced to live in filth on the streets, starving. I knew I'd have to do something the country could not ignore, something to shed light on all of these problems. A light so bright the world would be outraged to learn of the horrors not only permitted but regularly encouraged in the very capital city of the British Empire. I soon saw the best way to do it was to commit crimes so appalling that fear and scandal would spread far and wide. I harbored no desire to inflict pain upon innocent people, so I turned to those already deserving punishment. You ladies were the first to come to mind. I'd already killed my mother, so I sought out any of her old cohorts who might still live in Whitechapel or Spitalfields. I sought you out and ended your lives, one by one, thrilled to see the excitement grow with each death. I didn't especially want to make you suffer, so I didn't take the knife to any of you until you were dead and beyond all pain."

In the next room, Setlock and his uncle listened in stunned silence, struggling to keep up with what they were hearing, all thoughts of note-taking forgotten in the moment.

"Newspapers across the world eagerly published sketches of the crime scenes and even of your corpses, enhancing every gruesome detail. I intentionally increased the mutilation with each murder, adding volatile fuel to the flame. But I limited myself to five murders, lest I should come to enjoy it. The newspapers portrayed me as a demented sexual pervert desperately seeking more intense thrills with each additional death, but such was very far from the truth. I swear to you I didn't enjoy what I did in the least."

It was plain to the policemen that Belmont had long rehearsed this diatribe, as if bursting to tell someone his astonishing secrets. And now he was taking full advantage of the opportunity.

"It seemed I was well on the way to achieving my goals as I exposed fair England's darkest shame to the eyes of the world. I needed only one more victim, one final killing that would be far more scandalous and unpalatable than its predecessors. Well, as impossible as it sounds, it's already begun to work, so my work is done. As long as Jack the Ripper is never found, the fear and the shame will force Her Nibs up there in Buckingham Palace to make this a decent place to live, where the laws are enforced and prostitution is illegal. If there were no prostitutes on the street, there would be no need for the police to waste their time trying to protect them.

"So there you have it, my dears. My wind is long indeed, but I want you to know that you didn't die in vain. And, for what it's worth, I will kill no more. I plan to sell all of my business interests and donate the proceeds to charity before leaving the country. Don't know where I'll go; it makes no difference really. I deserve to die for what I've done, I know, no matter my motives, but I haven't the courage to do myself in. So I'll go away. No one will ever know whether I'm still out there lurking in the night, set to kill again. If they know I'm gone, there would be no further improvement as the fear and shame would soon subside."

The women, the ghosts, were fading from sight, their features blurring as if, having heard all, they could move on to wherever their tortured souls were destined to go.

A sudden sound of breaking glass caused the two men nearly to jump out of their seats. They kicked the door wide open, scanning the room.

Arthur, they realized, had knocked the hurricane lamp from the night stand by the bed. It appeared he had done it purposely. The resulting splatter of oil and flame set the bed clothes and rug afire instantly.

The pair burst in to the room, determined to drag the murderer away from the surge of flames already consuming much of the room.

"You!" Arthur screamed. "You, whoever you are, if you've been listening, then you know who I am and what I've done. Get out! Leave me to the fate I deserve! Whatever the truth, the world must believe Jack the Ripper has never been captured or killed. Save yourselves and save my soul by allowing my plan to bear fruit! For the love of God, I beg you! This house is isolated; there is no danger the fire will spread. When they find bones in the charred ruins, they will deem them to be those of a simple businessman, no one of real note. Now go," he ordered, "that the legend may live on!"

Setlock looked to Sir Charles.

"He's right," Sir Charles told him. "By God, he's right. We need to turn around and leave all this behind, putting it out of our minds as completely as possible." They hurried out of the growing inferno, making sure they were not seen by anyone. Nor, for that matter, did they actually see what may have become of Arthur Belmont.

For Joe and Kat Pulver, the Beast and his Beauty

A Pretty for Polly

Mercedes M. Yardley

"Dear Boss," he wrote in his careful, exquisite hand. "I keep on hearing the police have caught me…"

Time. Care. Dipping the pen in the ink pot again and again. Making love to the paper with his words. Handwriting perfect. Everything, perfect.

"I am down on whores and shan't quit ripping them…"

He was a man of precision. A man of great attention. Spectacles always clean, shirt always tucked neatly. It was all about appearances, wasn't it? To show your esteem? To show your respect?

Even a prudent man has demons. Even a quiet man has something sinister inside. He never would have believed this, but then, that was before.

"Daddy?"

"What, Polly?"

"Mama said I should run in and tell you goodnight."

He turned away from his letter, stopping the ink pot. He opened his arms and his little girl ran into them.

"Be good, my darling one. Dream of sweets."

"I will, Daddy."

She was ribbons and lace and sleeping slippers. Smelling clean after her bath. He slipped her a candy from the drawer of his desk, and put his finger over his lips slowly. She smiled back, and flew to the door like a bright bird.

"The next job I do I shall clip the lady's ears off and send to the police officers just for jolly, wouldn't you?"

A promise is a promise is a promise.

He was good at keeping promises.

Three days later. One night, two women.

The first? Ah, what a disappointment. He was almost immediately interrupted by a man in a carriage. As he fled, he regretted the sloppy slash and dash. Regretted the way it left him numb.

He felt tears in his eyes but didn't wipe them away, and they didn't fall.

He made up for it with the second woman. Took the time. Explored her face and body with his knife, more deeply and in depth than any lover. Kept his promise, as he is wont to do, and left her earlobe barely attached.

He hovered in the dark alleys of the East End, his coat neatly buttoned. His eyes full of shine. His knife tucked securely in his belt, the blood going brackish and ugly on it, but he didn't want to clean it, not yet. It was proof. It tied him to her.

Find me, he thought. *Just find me. Here I wait.*

The police ran around in a shiny-booted panic. Ran past him, several times, even. Each time, his mouth parted in breathless hope, his eyebrows arched in expectation.

"I have a daughter," he said calmly to one as he scurried past. "She deserves better."

The policeman cast him a look over his shoulder, but that was it. That was all.

The London fog rolled past. Like a man shunned for an invitation, a husband whose wife didn't look up when he entered the room, he felt small.

Time passed. He cleaned his knife thoroughly with a rag. Tossed the bloody scrap on the ground. The rag catching the moonlight like something ghostly, the remnant of a person once special to somebody. He waited some more.

Nobody came.

He walked slowly home.

They never found him. They never found him even though he
stood there, even though he *waited*. Time to up the ante, to force
them to look in a way that they hadn't been looking before.

A box. Small and precise. Something imprecise inside. Something that had been a treasure, something necessary and function-
ing, but now it was nothing.

His hair fell over his eyes. He pushed it aside.

"Sor," he wrote. His penmanship was long and loopy, scrawled
and uneven. Ink dripped on the paper and he cursed gently, tried
to wipe it away. "I send you half the Kidne I took from one woman and prasarved it for you..." He frowned at the words. Was
this how he spelled that? Why did everything look so odd? He
was a gentleman of education, of taste, but this looked like it was
written by another hand, by another man or monster entirely. He
took a deep breath and calmed himself. Shut his eyes, hard, and
thought of his schooling, of his business, of the successes that he
had earned for himself. He was that man. This was only a letter. It
is easy for a man of learning to write a simple letter.

He dipped his pen in the ink pot and touched it to the paper.

"...tother piece I fried and ate it was very nise."

He steepled his fingers and put them to his lips.

A knock on the door. Soft. Gentle.

"Daddy?"

"Just... just a minute, darling."

The box. He closed it, slid it under his desk. It smelled of blood
and wine, but surely a little girl wouldn't realize that, yes? Surely
she'd be too busy thinking of pretty things. Of kittens and trinkets
and perhaps something that her father could buy her? Yes. He'd
offer to pick something up for her, the next time that he was out.
The next time he came back from that place.

"Come in."

She didn't fly this time, but walked in quietly, on her toes. Why? Ah, yes, she was practicing walking softly, like a ballerina. He had forgotten.

"What delicate kitten feet," he said, and kissed her forehead. "What dainty, beautiful steps."

"Daddy, do you have to go out tonight?"

He paused. Quieted. His mustache remained completely still, not touched by his breath at all.

"Why do you ask?"

She looked up at him with her little girl eyes. Whore eyes. No, little girl eyes.

"Because I miss you, Daddy. We used to play games in the nursery. Mama says that you're sick and that's why you leave. Do you see doctors, Daddy? Is that why you go?"

He took off his spectacles, polished them.

"The whore tells you it's a sickness, does she? Some things aren't for little girls to know about."

His daughter blinked, too rapidly, and he realized that his voice had changed, that he wasn't her daddy, but something else. He tried to soften it.

"Would you like a necklace?"

"A... what?"

"Would you like a necklace? The next time I go out. To deal with my... sickness."

"A necklace?"

"A necklace! A necklace! Are you too stupid to understand what I'm saying?"

Her hands flew to her mouth, and she took a step back.

He ran his hands through his hair.

"Oh, my darling. Oh, my little girl. Forgive me. Forgive your tired, old father. Come here. Please."

He held his arms out to her, as he had done so many times, and she cautiously walked into them. He buried his face in her hair, smelling childhood and womanhood and rot. He pulled away.

"Go. Go from me."

She padded silently to the door, a princess in her nightdress.

"Darling, before you leave, I have a question for you."

"Yes, Daddy?"

"You're good at your studies. How do you spell the word 'kidney'?"

"Kidney?"

"Yes, like the one we had at dinner."

"It was very good. Why didn't you eat any?"

"Never mind that. Kidney. Spell it for me."

"K-I-D-N-E-Y. Kidney. I... I think."

He looked at his letter. Frowned.

"Did I... spell it right?"

Her eyes, so wide. Her face, so open. Perfect. In one piece, unseamed, seamless, without seams.

She wanted so badly to please him.

He smiled at her. "Beautiful job, my precious one. Dream sweet dreams tonight."

She scurried away, forgetting her ballet walk, and he heard her laughing as she ran to the nursery. His heart ached.

He turned back to his letter.

"Catch me when you can Mishter Lusk."

He stared at the page, the red ink. Felt the box under his desk with the toe of his fine shoe. Noticed the plain space on the upper right portion of the letter. Where was this written from?

He sighed, took out his pen again. His hand shook.

"From Hell."

Covered with blood, this time. There was no way around it. Not after what he had done. Hours. Hours and hours with this one. In a room with a window, even. Would somebody walk by? Wouldn't they *please* walk by? She had screamed "Murder!" and his soul had thrilled. Surely somebody would respond to that! To the cries of a beautiful woman begging for her life! But...no. Could any city really become so callous? So careless?

"I'm sorry, Polly," he had said.

"That... that's not my name, sir!"

He wept while he used his knife.

He could hardly find his ink pot. It had rolled on the floor. He scrabbled through flurries of papers, and finally decided on a creased envelope.

"Why, old boss?" he scrawled. He pressed so hard that the nib of his pen tore through the paper. He swore and tried again.

"You though your-self very clever I reckon. But you made a mistake. You'll never catch me. Clews and hints I gave you, and you still dident find me. I have you when you dont expect it and I keep my word as you soon see and rip you up. ha ha I love my work an I shant stop until I get buckled and even then watch out for your old pal Jacky.

Catch me if you Can

Jack the Ripper

Sorry about the blood still messy from the last one. What a pretty necklace I gave her."

He stood up, trembling. Wiped his red hand across his face, leaving streaks across his stubbled skin. He stuffed the letter into his pocket and reached down to pull the ribbon from Polly's beautiful hair. Patted her cheek, or what was left of it. He wrapped her ribbon around his fist, straightened, and closed the door behind him without a sound.

Termination Dust

Laird Barron

Let be be finale of seem.

—Wallace Stevens

Hunting in Alaska, especially as one who enjoys the intimacy of knives, bludgeons, and cords, is fraught with peril. Politically speaking, the difference between a conservative and a liberal in the forty-ninth state is the caliber of handgun one carries. Le sigh. Despite a couple of close calls, you've not been shot. Never been shot, never been caught, knock on wood.

That's what you used to say, in any event.

People look at you every day. People look at you every day, but they don't see you. People will ask why and you will reply, Why not?

Tyson Langtree's last words: "I tell you, man. Andy Kaufman is alive, man. He's alive, bigger than shit, and cuttin' throats. He's Elvis, man. He's the king of death." This was overheard at the packed Caribou Creek Tavern on a Friday night about thirty seconds before bartender Lonnie DeForrest tossed his sorry ass out onto a snowbank. Eighteen below zero Fahrenheit and a two and a half mile walk home. Dead drunk, wearing coveralls and a Miners Do It Deeper *ball cap.*

Nobody's seen the old boy since. Deputy Newcastle found a lot of blood in Langtree's bed, though. Splattered on the walls and ceiling of his shack on Midnight Road. Hell of a lot of blood. That much blood and no corpse, well, you got to wonder, right? Got to wonder why Langtree didn't just keep his mouth shut. Everybody knows Andy Kaufman is crazy as a motherfucker. He been whacking motormouth fools since '84.

You were in the bar that night and you followed Langtree back to his humble abode. Man, he was surprised to see you step from the shadows.

For the record, his last words were actually, "Please don't kill me, E!"

Jessica Mace lies in darkness, slightly drunk, wholly frustrated. Heavy bass thuds through the ceiling from Snodgrass' party. She'd left early and in a huff after locking horns with Julie Vellum, her honorable enemy since the hazy days of high school. Is hate too strong an emotion to describe how she feels about Julie? Nope, hatred seems quite perfect, although she's long since forgotten why they are at eternal war. Vellum—what kind of name is that, anyhow? It describes either ancient paper or a sheepskin condom. The bitch is ridiculous. Mobile home trash, bottom drawer sorority sister, tits sliding toward earth with a vengeful quickness. Easiest lay of the Last Frontier. A whore in name and deed.

JV called *her* a whore and splashed a glass of beer on her dress. Cliché, bitch, so very cliché. Obviously JV hadn't gotten the memo that Jessica and Nate were through as of an hour prior to the party. The evil slut had carried a torch for him since he cruised into town with his James Dean too-cool-for-school shtick and set all the girlies' hearts aflutter a few weeks before the Twin Towers crumbled a continent away.

Snodgrass, Wannamaker, and Ophelia, the beehive-hairdo lady from 510, jumped between them before the fur could fly. Snodgrass was an old hand at breaking up fistfights. Lucky for Julie, too. Jessica made up her mind to fix that girl's wagon once and for all, had broken a champagne glass for an impromptu weapon when

Snodgrass locked her in a bear hug. Meanwhile, Deputy Newcastle stood near the wet bar, grimly shaking his huge blond head. Or it might've been the deputy's evil twin, Elam. Hard to tell through the crush of the crowd, the smoke, and the din. If she'd seen him with his pants down, she'd have known with certainty.

Here she is after the fracas, sulking while the rest of town let down its hair and would continue to do so deep into the night. Gusts from the blizzard shake the building. Power comes from an emergency generator in the basement. However, cable is on the fritz. She would have another go at Nate, but Nate isn't around, he is gone-Johnson after she'd told him to hit the bricks and never come back no more, no more. Hasty words uttered in fury, a carbon copy of her own sweet ma who'd run through half the contractors and fishermen in the southeast during a thirty-year career of bar fights and flights from the law. Elizabeth Taylor of the Tundra, Ma. Nate, an even poorer man's Richard Burton. Her father, she thought of nevermore.

Why hadn't Nate been at the party? He *always* made an appearance. Could it be she's really and truly broken his icy heart? Good!

She fumbles in the bedside drawer, pushing aside the cell charger, Jack's photograph, the revolver her brother Elwood gave her before he got shredded by a claymore mine in Afghanistan, and locates the "personal massager" she ordered from Fredericks of Hollywood and has a go with that instead. Stalwart comrade, loyal stand-in when she's between boyfriends and lovers, Buzz hasn't let her down yet.

Jessica opens her eyes as the mattress sags. A shadow enters her blurry vision. She smells cologne or perfume or hairspray, very subtle and totally androgynous. Almost familiar. Breathless from the climax it takes her a moment to collect her wits.

She says, "Jack, is that you?" Which was a strange conclusion, since Jack presumably drifts along deep sea currents, his rugged redneck frame reduced to bones and sweet melancholy memories. All hands of the *Prince Valiant* lost to Davy Jones's locker, wasn't it? That makes three out of the four main men of her life dead. Only

Nate is still kicking. Does he count now that she's banished him to a purgatory absent her affection?

Fingers clamp her mouth and ram her head into the pillow hard enough that stars shoot everywhere. Her mind flashes to a vivid image: Gothic oil paintings of demons perched atop the bosoms of swooning women. So morbidly beautiful, those antique pictures. She thinks of the pistol in the dresser that she might've grabbed instead of the vibrator. Too late baby, too late now.

A knife glints as it arcs downward. Her attacker is dressed in black so the weapon appears to levitate under its own motive force. The figure slashes her throat with vicious inelegance. An untutored butcher. It is cold and she tastes the metal. But it doesn't hurt.

Problem is, constant reader, you can't believe a damned word of this story. The killer could be anyone. Cops recovered some bodies reduced to charcoal briquettes. Two of those charred corpses were never properly identified, and what with all the folks who went missing prior to the Christmas party...

My life flashed before my eyes as I died of a slashed throat and a dozen other terrible injuries. My life, the life of countless others who were in proximity. Wasn't pretty, wasn't neat or orderly, or linear. I experienced the fugue as an exploding kaleidoscope of imagery. Those images replay at different velocities, over and over in a film spliced together out of sequence. My hell is to watch a bad horror movie until the stars burn out.

I get the gist of the plot, but the nuances escape into the vacuum. The upshot being that I know hella lot about my friends and neighbors; just not everything. Many of the juiciest details elude me as I wander Purgatory, reliving a life of sin. Semi-omniscience is a drag.

In recent years, some pundits have theorized I was the Eagle Talon Ripper. Others have raised the possibility it was Jackson Bane, that he'd been spotted in San Francisco months after the *Prince Valiant* went down, that he'd been overheard plotting bloody revenge against me, Jessica, a dozen others. Laughable, isn't it? The majority of retired FBI profilers agree.

Nah, I'm the hot pick these days. Experts say the trauma I underwent in Moose Valley twisted my mind. Getting shot in the head did something to my brain. Gave me a lobotomy of sorts. Except instead of going passive, I turned into a monster, waited twenty-plus years, and went on a killing spree.

It's a sexy theory what with the destroyed and missing bodies, mine included. The killer could've been a man or woman, but the authorities bet on a man. Simple probability and the fact some of the murders required a great deal of physical strength and a working knowledge of knots and knives. I fit the bill on all counts. There's also the matter of my journal. Fragments of it were pieced together by a forensics team and the shit in there could be misconstrued. What nobody knows is that after the earlier event in Moose Valley, I read a few psychology textbooks. The journal was just therapy, not some veiled admission of guilt. Unfortunately, I was also self-medicating with booze and that muddied the waters even more.

Oh, well. What the hell am I going to do about it now?

If you ask me, Final Girl herownself massacred all those people. What's my proof? Nothing except instinct. Call me a cynic—it doesn't seem plausible a person can survive a gashed throat and still possess the presence to retrieve a pistol, in the dark, no less, and plug the alleged killer to save the day. How convenient that she couldn't testify to the killer's identity on account of the poor lighting. Even more convenient how that fire erased all the evidence. In the end, it's her word, her version of events.

Yeah, it's a regular cluster. Take the wrong peg from this creaky narrative and the whole log pile falls on you. Nonetheless, you know. You know.

What if…What if they were in it together?

Nights grow long in the tooth. A light veil of snow descends the peaks. Termination dust, the sourdoughs call it. You wait and watch for signs. Geese fly backwards in honking droves, south. Sunsets flare crimson, then fade to black as fog rolls over the beach. People leave the village and do not return. A few others never left but are gone just the same. They won't be returning either.

The last of the cruise ships migrated from Eagle Talon on Saturday. The Princess Wing *blared klaxons and horns and sloshed up the channel in a shower of streamers and confetti, its running lights blazing holes through the mist. A few hardy passengers in red and yellow slickers braved the drizzle to perch along the rails. Some waved to the dockworkers. Others cheered over the rumble of the diesels. Seagulls bobbed aloft, dark scraps and tatters against the low clouds that always curtain this place.*

You mingled with the people on the dock and smiled at the birds, enjoying their faint screams. Only animals seem to recognize what you are. You hate them too. That's why you smile, really. Hate keeps you warm come the freeze.

Ice will soon clog the harbor. Jagged mountains encircle the village on three sides in a slack-jawed Ouroboros. The other route out of town is a two-mile tunnel that opens onto the Seward Highway. This tunnel is known as the Throat. Anchorage lies eighty miles north, as the gull flies. Might as well be the moon when winter storms come crashing in on you. Long-range forecasts call for heavy snow and lots of wind. There will come a day when all roads and ways shall be impassable.

You've watched. You've waited. Salivated.

You'll retreat into the Estate with the sheep. It's a dirty white concrete superstructure plonked in the shadow of a glacier. Bailey Frazier & Sons built the Frazier Estate Apartments in 1952 along with the Frazier Tower that same year. History books claim these were the largest buildings in Alaska for nearly three decades, and outside of the post office, cop shop, library, little red schoolhouse, the Caribou Tavern, and a few warehouses, that's it for the village proper. Both were heavily damaged by the '64 quake and subsequent tsunami. Thirteen villagers were swept away on the wave. Four more got crushed in falling debris. The Tower stands empty and ruined to this day, but the Estate is mostly functional; a secure, if decrepit, bulwark against the wilderness.

You are an earthquake, a tidal wave, a mountain of collapsing stone, waiting to happen. You are the implacable wilderness personified. What is in you is ancient as the black tar between stars. A void that howls in hunger and mindless antipathy against the heat of the living.

Meanwhile, this winter will be business as usual. Snowbirds flee south to California and Florida while the hardcore few hunker in dim apartments like animals in burrows and play cribbage or video games, or gnaw yourselves bloody with regret. You'll read, and drink, and fuck. Emmitt Snodgrass will throw his annual winter gala. More drinking and even more fucking, but with the sanction of costume and that soul-warping hash Bobby Aickman passes around. By spring, the survivors will emerge, pale as moles, voracious for light as you are for the dark.

With the official close of tourist season, Eagle Talon population stands at one hundred and eighty-nine full-time residents. Three may be subtracted from that number, subtracted from the face of the earth, in fact, although nobody besides the unlucky trio and you know anything about that.

Dolly Sammerdyke. Regis and Thora Lugar. And the Lugars' cat, Frenchy. The cat died hardest of them all. Nearly took out your eye. Maybe that will come back to haunt you. The devil's in the...

Elam Newcastle is interviewed by the FBI at Providence Hospital. He has survived the Frazier Estate inferno with second degree burns and frostbite of his left hand. Two fingers may have to be amputated and the flesh of his neck and back possess the texture of melted wax. In total, a small price to pay considering the hell-on-Earth-scenario he's escaped. His New Year's vow is to find a better trade than digging ditches.

He tells the suit what he knows as the King of Pop hovers in the background, partially hidden by curtains and shadows. This phantom, or figment, has shown up regularly since the evening of the massacre at the Estate. Elam is not a fan and doesn't understand why he's having this hallucination of the singer grinning and gesticulating with that infamous rhinestone-studded glove. It is rather disturbing. Doubly disturbing since it's impossible to attribute it to the codeine.

The investigator blandly reveals how the local authorities have recently found Elam's twin brother deceased in the Frazier Tower. It was, according to the account, a gruesome spectacle, even by police standards. The investigator describes the scene in brief, albeit vivid, detail.

Elam takes in this information, one eye on the moonwalking apparition behind the FBI agent. Finally, he says, "Whaddaya mean they stole his hat?"

Scenes from an apocalypse:

Viewed from the harbor, Eagle Talon is an inkblot with a steadily brightening dot of flame at its heart. The Frazier Estate Apartments have been set ablaze. Meanwhile, the worst blizzard to hit Alaska since 1947 rages on. Flames leap from the upper stories, whipped by the wind. Window glass shatters. Fire, smoke, and driving snow boil off into outer darkness. That faint keening is either the shrieks of the damned as they roast in the penthouse, or metal dissolving like Styrofoam as the inferno licks it to ash. Or both.

Men and women in capes and masks, gossamer wings and top hats, mill in the icy courtyard. Their shadows caper in the bloody glare. They are the congregants of a frigid circle of Hell, summoned to the Wendigo's altar. They join hands and begin to waltz. Flakes of snow and ash cover them, bury them.

The angry fire is snapping yellow. Pull farther out into the cold and the dark and fire becomes red through the filter of the blizzard, then shivers to black. Keep pulling back until there are no stars, no fire, no light of any kind. Only the snow sifting upward from the void to fill the world with silence and sleep.

We make love with the lights off. The last time, I figure. She calls me Jack when she comes and probably has no idea. Jackson Bane died on the Bering Sea two winters gone. His ghost makes itself known. He knocks stuff over to demonstrate he's unhappy, like when I'm fucking his former girlfriend. Not hard to imagine him raving impotently behind the wall of sleep, working himself toward a splendorous vengeance. Perhaps that makes him more of a revenant.

My name is Nathan Custer. I fear the sea. Summertime sees me guiding tours on the glacier for Emmitt Snodgrass. Winter, I lie low and collect unemployment. Cash most of those checks down at the Caribou. Laphroaig is my scotch of choice and it's a choice I make every livelong day, and twice a day once snow flies. Hell of an existence. I fought with Jack at Emmitt Snodgrass' annual winter party in '07. Blacked his eye and demolished a coffee table. Don't even recall what precipitated the brawl. I only recall Jessica in a white tee and cotton shorts standing there with a bottle of Lowenbrau in her hand. Snodgrass forgave me the mess. We never patched it up, Jack and I.

Too late, now. Baby, it's too late.

While Jessica showers, I prowl her apartment naked, peering into cupboards and out the window at snowflakes reflected in a shaft of illumination pitched by the twin lamps over the lobby foyer. Ten feet beyond the Estate wall lies a slate of nothingness. Depending on the direction, it's either sea ice and, eventually, open black water, or mountains. This is five-oh-something in the P.M., December. Sun has been down for half an hour.

"What are you doing?" Jessica, head wrapped in a towel, strikes a Venus pose in the bathroom doorway. The back-lighting lends her a halo. She's probably concerned about the butcher knife I pulled from the cutlery block. Wasn't quick enough to hide it behind my leg. Naked guy with a knife presents an environmental hazard even if you don't suspect him of being a homicidal maniac, which she might.

"Getting ready for the party," I say, disingenuous as ever.

"Yeah, you look ready." She folds her arms. She thinks I've been using again; it's in her posture. "What the hell, Nate?"

Unfortunately for everyone, I'm not an outwardly articulate man. I'm my father's son. Mom didn't hate his guts because he slapped her at the '88 Alaska State Fair; she hated him because he refused to argue. When the going got shouty, Dad was a walker-awayer. I realize, here in my incipient middle age, that his tendency to clam up under stress wasn't from disrespect. He simply lost his ability to address the women in his life coherently.

"Uh," is what I come up with. Instead of, *Baby, I heard a noise. Somebody was trying the door. Swear to God, I saw the knob jiggle.* I don't have the facility to ask her, *If I was jacked up, wouldn't you have noticed it while we were in bed?* More than anything, I want to tell her of my suspicions. Something is terribly wrong in our enclave. People are missing. Strange shadows are on the move and I have a feeling the end is near for some of us.

"Jesus. Cal's right. He's right. The bastard is right. My god."

"Cal's right? He's not right. What did he say?" Add Building Superintendent Calvin Wannamaker to my little black book of hate. I grip the knife harder, am conscious of my oversized knuckles and their immediate ache. Arthritis, that harbinger of old age and death, nips at me.

"Hit the road, Jack." She points the Finger of Doom, illustrating where I should go. Presumably Hell lies in that general direction.

Maybe I can bulldoze through this scene. "That makes twice you called me Jack today. We have to get ready for the party. Where the hell are my pants?" I look everywhere but directly into the sun that is her gaze.

"You've lost your damned mind," she says in a tone of wonderment, as if waking from a long, violent dream and seeing everything for how it really is. "You need to leave."

"The party. My pants."

"Find another pair. Goodbye. And put that back. It was a present. From Jack!" She's hollering now.

"Wait a second… Are you and Cal—"

"Shut your mouth and go."

I put the cleaver in the block, mightily struggling to conjure the magic words to reverse the course of this shipwreck. This isn't love, but it's the best thing I've had in recent memory. No dice. Naked guy hurled from the nest by his naked girlfriend. This is trailer park drama. Julie Vellum will cream over the details once the gossip train gets chugging. Maybe, just maybe, I'll throw a fuck into her. Ah, sweet revenge, hey? The prospect doesn't thrill me, for some reason. I walk into the hall and lurk there awhile, completely at a loss. I press the buzzer twice. Give up when there's no answer, and start the long, shameful trudge to my apartment.

The corridors of the Estate are gloomy. Tan-paneled walls and muddy recessed lights spaced far enough apart it feels like you're walking along the bottom of a lake. The effect is heightened due to the tears in my eyes. By the time I get to the elevator, I'm freezing. The super keeps this joint about three degrees above an ice-locker.

"Nate!" The whisper is muted and sexless. A shadow materializes from behind the wooden statue of McKinley Frazier that haunts this end of the fifth floor. It's particularly murky here because the overhead has been busted. A splinter of glass stabs my bare foot. I'm hopping around, trying to cover my balls and also act naturally.

"Nate, hold still, pal." Still whispering. Whoever it is, they're in all black and they've got a hammer.

Oh, wait, I recognize this person. I'm convinced it's impossible that this could be happening to me for the second time in twenty years. This isn't even connected to that infamous Moose Valley slaughter. It's like winning top prize in a sweepstakes twice in one's lifetime. Why me, oh gods above and below? I'm such a likeable guy. Kurt Russell wishes he was as handsome as I am. So much to live for. Living looks to be all done for me.

The hammer catches the faint light. It gleams and levitates.

"What are you going to do with that?" I say. It's a rhetorical question.

Jessica Mace can't actually speak when the feds interview her. She's still eating through tubes. The wound at her neck missed severing the carotid by a millimeter. She scribbles curt responses to their interrogation on a portable whiteboard. Her rage is palpable, scarcely blunted by exhaustion and painkillers.

Ma'am, after this individual assaulted you in bed, what happened?

Came to. Choking on blood. Alive. Grabbed gun. Heard noises from living room. The killer had someone in a chair and was torturing them.

Who was in the chair?

Nate Custer.

Nathan Custer?

I think so. Yes.

Did you see the suspect's face?

No.

Approximately how tall was the suspect?

I don't know. Was dark. Was bleeding out. Confused.

Right. But you saw something. And you discharged your firearm.

Yes. It was him. I'm sure.

Him?

Him, her. The killer. My vision was blurry. They were a big, fuzzy shadow.

Are you admitting that you fired your weapon multiple times at… at a shadow?

No. I shot a goddamned psycho five times and killed him dead. You're welcome.

How can you be certain, Ms. Mace?

Maybe I can't. Killer could've been anyone. Could *be* anyone. The doctor. The nurse. Maybe it was you. YOU look fucking suspicious.

Calvin Wannamaker and his major domo Hendricks are bellied up to the bar at the Caribou Tavern for their weekly confab. They've already downed several rounds.

DeForrest is polishing glasses and watching the new waitress's skirt cling in exactly the right places as she leans over table No. 9 to flirt with big Luke Tucker. Tucker is a longshoreman married to a cute young stay-at-home mom named Gladys. Morphine is playing "Thursday" on the jukebox while the village's resident Hell's Angel, Vince Diamond, shoots pool against himself. VD got paroled from Goose Bay Correctional Facility last month. He has spent nineteen of his forty-eight years in various prisons. His is the face of an axe murderer. His left cheek is marred by a savage gash, freshly scabbed. Claims he got the wound in a fight with his newest old lady. Deputy Newcastle has been over to their apartment three times to make peace.

The bar is otherwise unoccupied.

"Found a dead cat in the bin." Wannamaker lights a cigarette. A Winston. It's the brand that he thinks best suits his Alaska image. He prefers Kools, alas. "Neck was broke, eyes buggin' out. Gruesome." The super loves cats. He keeps three Persians in his suite on the first floor. He's short and thin and wears a round bushy beard and plaid sweaters, or if it's a special occasion, black turtlenecks. Hendricks started calling him "Cat Piss Man" behind his back and the name kind of stuck. Neither man was born in Alaska. Wannamaker comes from New York, Hendricks from Illinois. They've never adjusted to life on the frontier. They behave like uneasy foreigners in their own land.

"Oh, yeah?" Hendricks says with a patent couldn't-give-a-shit less tone. No cat lover, Hendricks. *Don't like cats, love pussy,* he's been quoted time and again. He's taller than Wannamaker, and broad-shouldered. Legend says he worked for the Chicago Outfit before he got exiled to Alaska. Everyone considers him a goon and that's a fairly accurate assessment.

"Floyd found it, I guess is what I mean," Wannamaker says.

Floyd is the chief custodian and handyman for the Estate. He was also a train-hopping hobo for three decades prior to landing the Estate gig.

"The hell was Floyd doing in the bin?"

"Makin' a nest. Divin' for pearls. I dunno. He found a dead cat is all I know. Thinks it belonged to the Lugars. They split ten days ago. Must a been in a rush, cause they locked their doors and dropped the keys in my box without so much as a by your leave. Earlier and earlier every year, you know that? I don't get why they even make the trip anymore. I get three or four calls a day, people looking for an apartment. At least."

Hendricks sips his beer. He doesn't say anything. He too is checking out the posterior of Tammy, the new girl.

"Yeah, exactly." Wannamaker nods wisely in response to some ghost of a comment. "I hate snowbirds. Hate. Too cheap to pack their old cat and ship him to Florida. What's Lugar do? Snaps the poor critter's neck and dumps him in the garbage. Bah. Tell you what I'm gonna do, I'm gonna file a report with Newcastle. Sic the ever lovin' law on that sick jerk. Shouldn't have a cat. If he didn't own his apartment I'd yank his lease faster than you can spit."

Hendricks pushes his bottle aside. "That's a weird story."

"Lugar's a weird dude. He sells inflatable dolls and whatcha call 'em, body pillows."

"Is that what he does?"

"Oh, yeah, man. He flies to Japan every so often and wines and dines a bunch of CEOs in Tokyo. They're nuts for that stuff over there."

"Huh. I figured he'd retired. Guy's gotta be pushing seventy."

"I guess when you love what you do it ain't work."

Words to live by.

Last words of Mark Ferro, aged thirty-three as he is executed by lethal injection for a homicide unrelated to the Frazier Estate Massacre: "It was meeeeeee!"

You've exercised a certain amount of restraint prior to the blizzard. That's over. Now, matters will escalate. While everybody else has gathered upstairs for Snodgrass' annual bash, you sneak away to share a special moment with Nathan Custer.

Does it hurt when I do this? *It's a rhetorical question.*

You don't expect Custer can hear you after you popped his eardrums with a slot screwdriver. Can't see you either. Blood pumps from the crack in his skull. Smack from a ball peen hammer took the starch right out of our hero. He coughs bubbles. Don't need tongue or teeth to blow bubbles, though it helps.

It may not even be Custer under that mask of gore. Could be Deputy Newcastle or Hendricks. Shit, could be that arrogant little prick Wannamaker at this rate. True story, you've fantasized about killing each of them so often that the lines might well be erased.

Except, haven't you wanted to end your existence? Sure you have. You'd love nothing more than to take your own miserable head off with a cleaver, string your own guts over the tree the way those cheap Victorian saps strung popcorn before Christmas went electric.

This is where it gets very, very confusing.

For a lunatic moment you're convinced it's you, slumped there, mewling like a kitten, soul floating free and formless while an angel of vengeance goes to work on your body with hammer and tongs. Yeah, maybe it's you in the chair and Custer, or Newcastle, or Wannamaker, has been the killer all along. It ain't pretty, having one's mind blown like this.

You were certain it was Custer when you put him in the chair, but that was a long time ago. So much has changed since then. The continents have drifted closer together, the geography of his features has altered for the worse. It's gotten dark. There's the storm and your sabotage of the reserve generator to thank. You've gathered wool and lost the plot. Can't even remember why you'd reserve special tortures for this one.

Why are your hands so fascinating all of the sudden?

Oh, Jesus, what if Snodgrass spiked the punch? He'd once threatened to dose his party-goers with LSD. Nobody took him seriously. But, what if? That would explain why the darkness itself has begun to shine, why your nipples are hard as nail-heads, why you've suddenly developed spidey-sense. Oh, Emmitt Snodgrass, that silly bastard; his guts are going to get extracted through his nose, and soon.

You detect the creak of a loose board and turn in time to see a snub-nosed revolver extending from a crouched silhouette. A lady's gun, so sleek and petite. Here's a flash of fire from the barrel that reveals the bruised face of the final girl. Don't she know you're invulnerable to lead? Didn't she read the rules inside the box top? Problem is, it's another sign that your version of reality is shaky, because you are sure as hell that you killed her already. Sliced her throat, ear to lovely ear. Yet, here she is, blasting you into Kingdom Come with her itty bitty toy pistol. What the fuck is up with that?

Double tap. Triple, dipple, quadruple tap. Bitch ain't taking any chances, is she? You're down, sprawled next to your beloved victim, whoever he is. Your last. The final girl done seen to that, hasn't she?

Custer, is that you? you ask the body in the chair. He don't give anything away, only grins at you through the blood. Luckily you're made of sterner stuff. Four bullets isn't the end. You manage to get your knees and elbows underneath you for a lethal spring in the penultimate frame of the flick of your life, the lunge where you take the girl into your arms and squeeze until her bones crack and her tongue protrudes. When you're done, you'll crawl away to lick your wounds and plot the sequel. Four shots ain't enough to kill the very beating heart of evil.

Turns out, funny thing, the final girl has one more bullet. She

hobbles over and puts it in your head.
Well, shit—

"Christ on a pony, what are you *dooo-ing*?" This plaintive utterance issues from Eliza Overstreet's ripe mouth. She's dressed as a cabaret dancer or Liza Minnelli, or some such bullshit. White, white makeup and sequins and tights. A tight, tight wig cropped as a Coptic monk's skullcap. All *sparkly.*

Emmitt Snodgrass cackles, and pops another tab of acid. The rest of the batch he crushes into the rich red clot of punch in a crystal bowl shaped as a furious eagle. The furious eagle punch bowl is courtesy of Luke Tucker, collector of guns, motorcycles, and fine crystal. The suite is prepared—big Christmas tree, wall-to-wall tinsel, stockings and disco balls hung with care. Yeah, Snodgrass is ready for action, Jackson.

Eliza gives him a look. "Everybody is going to drink that!"

He grabs her ass and gives it a comforting squeeze. "Hey, hey, baby. Don't worry. This shit is perfectly safe to fry."

"But it's all we've got, you crazy sonofabitch!"

The doorbell goes ding-dong and the first guests come piling in from the hallway. It will be Bob Aickman, bare-assed and goggle-eyed on acid, who will eventually trip over the wires that cause the electrical short that starts the tragic fire that consumes the top three floors of the Estate.

Deputy Newcastle operates two official vehicles: an eleven-year-old police cruiser with spider web cracks in the windshield and a bashed in passenger side door, and an Alpine snowmobile that, by his best estimate, was likely manufactured during the 1980s. Currently, he's parked in the cruiser on Main Street across from the condemned hulk that is the Frazier Tower. The sun won't set for another forty-five minutes, give or take, but already the shadows are thick as his wife's blueberry cobbler. It's snowing and blowing. Gusts rock the car. He listens to the weather forecast. Going to be cold as hell, as usual. Twenty-seven degrees Fahrenheit and sinking fast. He unscrews the thermos and has a sip of cocoa Hannah packed in his lunchbox. Cocoa, macaroni salad and a tuna sandwich on white bread. He loathes macaroni and tuna, loves cocoa, and adores dear Hannah, so it's a wash.

His beat is usually quiet. The geographic jurisdiction extends from the village of Eagle Talon to a fourteen-mile stretch north and south along the Seward Highway. Normally, he deals with drunks and domestic arguments, tourists with flat tires and the occasional car accident.

Then along came this business with Langtree and the slaughterhouse scene at his shack on Midnight Road. A forensics team flew in from Anchorage and did their thing, and left again. Deputy Newcastle still hasn't heard anything from headquarters. Nobody's taking it seriously. Langtree was a nut. Loons like him are a dime a dozen in Alaska. Violence is part of the warp and woof of everyday existence here. Takes a hell of a lot to raise eyebrows among the locals. The deputy is worried, and with good reason. The angel on his shoulder keeps whispering in his ear. The angel warns him a blood moon is on the rise.

Despite the fact his shift ended at three o'clock, Deputy Newcastle has spent the better part of an hour staring at the entrance of the abandoned Frazier Tower. Should have gotten leveled long ago, replaced by a hotel or a community center, or any old thing. Lord knows the village could use some recreational facilities. Instead, the building festers like a rotten tooth. It's a nest for vermin—animals and otherwise—and a magnet for thrill-seeking kids and ne'er-do-wells on the lam.

Custodian Floyd is supposed to keep the front door covered in plywood. The plywood is torn loose and lying in the bushes and a hole led into gloom. This actually happens frequently. The aforementioned kids and ne'er-do-wells habitually break into the tower to seek their fun. Deputy Newcastle's cop intuition tells him the usual suspects aren't to blame.

"I'm going in," he says.

"You better not," says MJ. The King of Pop inhabits the back seat, his scrawny form crosshatched by the grilled partition between them. His pale features are obscured in the shade of a slouch hat. He is the metaphorical shoulder-sitting angel.

"Got to. It's my job."

"You're a swell guy, deputy. Don't do it."

"Who then?"

"You're gonna die if you go in there alone."

"I can call someone. Hendricks will back my play."

"Can't trust him."

"Elam."

"Your brother is a psychopath."

"Hmm. Fair enough. I could ring Custer or Pearson. Heck, I could deputize both of them for the day."

"Look, you can't trust anyone."

"I don't." Newcastle stows the thermos and slides on his wool gloves. He unclips the twelve gauge pump action from its rack and shoulders his way out of the cruiser. The road is slick beneath the tread of his boots, the breeze searing cold against his cheek. Snowflakes stick to his eyelashes. He takes a deep breath and trudges toward the entrance of the Frazier Tower. The dark gap recedes and blurs like a mirage.

True Romance isn't Deputy Newcastle's favorite movie. Too much blood and thunder for his taste. Nonetheless, he identifies with the protagonist, Clarence. In times of doubt Elvis Presley manifests and advises Clarence as a ghostly mentor.

The deputy adores the incomparable E, so he's doubly disconcerted regarding his own hallucinations. Why in the heck does he receive visions of MJ, a pop icon who fills him with dread and loathing?

MJ visited him for the first time the previous spring and has appeared with increasing frequency. The deputy wonders if he's gestating a brain tumor or if he's slowly going mad like his grandfather allegedly did after Korea. He wonders if he's got extra sensory powers or powers from God, although he hasn't been exposed to toxic waste or radiation, nor is he particularly devout. Church for Christmas and Easter potluck basically does it for him. Normally a brave man, he's too chicken to take himself into Anchorage for a CAT scan to settle the issue. He's also afraid to mention his invisible friend to anyone for fear of enforced medical leave and/or reassignment to a desk in the city.

In the beginning, Deputy Newcastle protested to his phantom partner: "You aren't real!" and "Leave me alone! You're a figment!" and so on. MJ had smiled ghoulishly and said, "I wanna be your friend, Deputy. I've come to lend you a hand. Hee-hee!"

Deputy Newcastle steps through the doorway into a decrepit foyer. Icicle stalactites descend in glistening clusters. The carpet has eroded to bare concrete. Cracks run through the concrete to the subflooring. It is a wasteland of fallen ceiling tiles, squirrel nests, and collapsed wiring. He creeps through the debris, shotgun clutched to his waist.

What does he find? An escaped convict, dirty and hypothermic, like in the fall of 2006? Kids smoking dope and spraying slogans of rebellion on the walls? A salmon-fattened black bear hibernating beneath a berm of dirt and leaves? No, he does not find a derelict, or children, or a snoozing ursine.

The Killer is waiting for him, as the King of Pop predicted.

Deputy Newcastle sees shadow bloom within shadow, yet barely feels the blade that opens him from stem to stern. It is happening to someone else. The razor-sharp tip punches through layers of insulating fabric, enters his navel, and rips upward. The sound of his undoing resonates in the small bones of his ears. He experiences an inexplicable rush of euphoria that is frightening in its intensity, then he is on his knees, bowed as if in prayer. His mind has become so disoriented he is beyond awareness of confusion. His parka is heavy, dragged low by the sheer volume of blood pouring from him. He laughs and groans as steam fills his throat.

The Killer takes the trooper hat from where it has rolled across the ground, dusts away snow and dirt, and puts it on as a souvenir. The Killer smiles in the fuzzy gloom, watching the deputy bleed and bleed.

Deputy Newcastle has dropped the shotgun somewhere along the way. Not that it matters—he has no recollection of the service pistol in his belt, much less the knowledge of how to work such a complicated mechanism. The most he can manage at this point is a dumb, meaningless smile that doesn't even reflect upon the presence of his murderer.

His final thought isn't of Hannah, or of the King of Pop standing at his side and mouthing the words to "Smooth Criminal," eyes shining golden. No, the deputy's final thought isn't a thought, it's inchoate awe at the leading edge of darkness rushing toward him like the crown of a tidal wave.

A storm rolls in off the sea on the morning of the big Estate Christmas party. Nobody stirs anywhere outdoors except for Duke Pearson's two-ton snow plow with its twinkling amber beacon, and a police cruiser as the deputy makes his rounds. Both vehicles have been swallowed by swirls of white.

Tammy Ferro's fourteen-year-old son Mark is perched at the table like a raven. Clad in a black trenchcoat and exceptionally tall for his tender age, he's picking at a bowl of cereal and doing homework he shirked the previous evening. His mother is reading a back issue of the *Journal of the American Medical Association*. The cover illustration is of a mechanical heart cross-sectioned by a scalpel.

Tammy divorced her husband and moved into the village in September, having inherited apartment 202 from her Aunt Millicent. Tammy is thirty-three but can pass for twenty-five. Lonnie DeForrest's appreciation of her ass aided her in snagging a job at the Caribou Tavern waiting tables. She earned a degree in psychology from the University of Washington, fat lot of good that's done her. Pole dancing in her youth continues to pay infinitely greater dividends than the college education it financed.

She and Mark haven't spoken much since they came to Eagle Talon. She tells herself it's a natural byproduct of teenage reticence, adapting to a radically new environment, and less to do with resentment over the big blowup of his parents' marriage. They are not exactly in hiding. It is also safe to say her former husband, Matt, doesn't know anything about Aunt Millicent or the apartment in Alaska.

Out of the blue, Mark says, "I found out something really cool about Nate Custer."

Tammy has seen Custer around. Impossible not to when everyone occupies the village's only residence. Nice looking guy in his late forties. Devilish smile, carefree. Heavy drinker, not that that is so unusual in the Land of the Midnight Sun, but he wears it well. Definitely a Trouble with a capital T sort. He goes with that marine biologist Jessica Mace who lives on the fifth. Mace is kind of a cold fish, which seems apropos, considering her profession.

She says, "The glacier tour guide. Sure." She affects casualness by not glancing up from her magazine. She dislikes the fascination in her son's tone. Dislikes it on an instinctual level. It's the kind of tone a kid uses when he's going to show you a nasty wound, or some gross thing he's discovered in the woods.

"He survived the Moose Valley Slaughter. Got shot in the head, but he made it. Isn't that crazy? Man, I never met anybody that got shot before."

"That sounds dire." Guns and gun violence frighten Tammy. She doesn't know if she'll ever acclimate to Alaska gun culture. However, she is quite certain that she prefers grown men leave her impressionable teen son out of such morbid conversations, much less parade their scars for his delectation. Barbarians aren't at the gate; they are running the village.

"It happened twenty years ago. Moose Valley's a small town, even smaller than Eagle Talon. Only thirty people live there. It's

in the interior… You got to fly supplies in or take a river barge."
Mark isn't looking at her directly, either. He studies his black nails,
idly flicking the chipped polish.

"Gee, that's definitely remote. What do people do there?" Besides shoot each other, obviously.

"Yeah, lame. They had *Pong*, maybe, and that's it. Nate says everybody was into gold mining and junk."

"Nate says?"

Mark blushes. "He was a little older than me when it all went
down. This ex-Army guy moved in from the Lower Forty-Eight to
look for gold, or whatever. Everybody thought he was okay. Turns
out he was a psycho. He snapped and went around shooting everybody in town one night. Him and Nate were playing dominoes
and the dude pulled a gun out of his pocket. Shot Nate right in
the head and left him on the floor of his cabin. Nate didn't die.
Heh. The psycho murdered eleven people before the state troopers
bagged him as he was floating downriver on a raft."

"Honey!"

"Sorry, sorry. The cops *apprehended* him. With a sniper rifle."

"Did Nate tell you this?"

"I heard it around. It's common knowledge, Mom. I was helping Tucker and Hendricks get an acetylene bottle into the back of
his rig."

She hasn't heard this tale of massacre. Of course, she hasn't made
many friends in town. At least Mark is coming out of his shell.
Despite the black duds and surly demeanor, he enjoys company,
especially that of adults. Good thing since there are only half a
dozen kids his age in the area. She's noticed him mooning after a
girl named Lilly. It seems pretty certain the pair are carrying on a
rich, extracurricular social life via Skype and text…

"Working on English?" She sets aside her magazine and nods at
his pile of textbooks and papers. "Need any help?"

He shrugs.

"C'mon. Watch ya got?"

"An essay," he says. "Mrs. Chandler asked us to write five hundred words on what historical figure we'd invite to dinner."

"Who'd you pick? Me, I'd go with Cervantes, or Freud. Or Vivien Leigh. She was dreamy."

"Jack the Ripper."

"Oh… That's nice."

A young, famous journalist drives to a rural home in Upstate New York. The house rests alone near the end of a lane. A simple rambler painted red with white trim. Hills and woods begin at the backyard. This is late autumn and the sun is red and gold as it comes through the trees. Just cool enough that folks have begun to put the occasional log into the fireplace, so the crisp air smells of applewood and maple.

He and the woman who is the subject of his latest literary endeavor sip lemonade and regard the sky and exchange pleasantries. An enormous pit bull suns itself on the porch a few feet from where the interview occurs. Allegedly, the dog is attack-trained. It yawns and farts.

The journalist finds it difficult not to stare at the old lady's throat where a scar cuts, so vivid and white, through the dewlapped flesh. He is aware that in days gone by his subject used to camouflage the wound with gypsy scarves and collared shirts. Hundreds of photographs and she's always covered up.

Mrs. Jessica Mace Goldwood knows the score. She drags on her Camel No. 9 and winks at him, says once her tits started hitting her in the knees she gave up vanity as a bad business. Her voice is harsh, only partially restored after a series of operations. According to the data, she recently retired from training security dogs. Her husband, Gerry Goldwood, passed away the previous year. There are no children or surviving relatives on record.

"Been a while since anybody bothered to track me down," she says. "Why the sudden interest? You writing a book?"

"Yeah," the journalist says. "I'm writing a book."

"Huh. I kinda thought there might be a movie about what happened at the Estate. A producer called me every now and again, kept saying the studio was 'this close' to green-lighting the project. I was gonna make a boatload of cash, and blah, blah, blah. That was, Jesus, twenty years ago." She exhales a stream of smoke and studies him with a shrewd glint in her eyes. "Maybe I shoulda written a book."

"Maybe so," says the journalist. He notices, at last, a pistol nestled under a pillow on the porch swing. It is within easy reach of her left hand. His research indicates she is a competent shot. The presence of the gun doesn't make him nervous—he has, in his decade of international correspondence, sat among war chiefs in Northern Pakistan, and ridden alongside Taliban fighters in ancient half-tracks seized from Russian armored cavalry divisions. He has visited Palestine and Georgia and seen the streets burn. He thinks this woman would be right at home with the hardest of the hard-bitten warriors he's interviewed.

"Life is one freaky coincidence, ain't it though?" She stares into the woods. Her expression is mysterious. "Julie Vellum died last week. Ticker finally crapped out."

"Julie Vellum…" He scans his notes. "Right. She cashed in big time. Author of how many bestselling New Age tracts? Friend of yours?"

"Nah, I despised the bitch. She's the last, that's all. Well, there's that guy who did psychedelic music for a while. He's in prison for aggravated homicide. Got involved with a cult and did in some college kids over in Greece. Can't really count him, huh? I'm getting sentimental in my dotage. Lonely."

"Lavender McGee. He's not in prison. They transferred him to an institution for the criminally insane. He gets day passes if you can believe it."

"The fuck is this world coming to? What is it you wanna ask me?"

"I have one question for you."

"Just one?" Her smile is amused, but sharp. It has been honed by a grief that has persisted for more than the latter half of her long life.

"Just one." He takes the small recorder from his shirt pocket, clicks a button, and sets it on the table between them. "More than one, of course. But this one is the biggie. Are you ready?"

"Sure, yeah. I'm ready."

"Mrs. Goldwood, why are you alive?"

Wind moves the trees behind the house. A flurry of red and brown leaves funnel across the yard, smack against the cute skirting. A black cloud covers the sun and hangs there. The temperature plummets. Gravel crunches in the lane.

The dog growls, and is on its feet, head low, mouth open to bare many, many teeth. The fur on its back is standing in a ridge. It is Cerberus's very own pup.

"Oh, motherfucker," says Jessica Mace Goldwood. She's got the revolver in her hand, hammer cocked. Her eyes blaze with a gunfighter's fire as she half crouches, elbows in tight, knees wide. "It's never over with these sonsofbitches."

"What's happening?" The journalist has ducked for cover, hands upraised in the universal sign of surrender. "Jesus H., lady! Don't shoot me!" He glances over his shoulder and sees a man in the uniform of a popular parcel delivery service slamming the door of a van and roaring away in a cloud of smoking rubber.

"Aw, don't fret. Me and Atticus just don't appreciate those delivery guys comin' around," she says. The pit bull snarls and throws himself down at her feet. She uncocks the revolver and tucks it into the waistband of her track pants. "So, young man. Where were we?"

He wipes his face and composes himself. In a hoarse voice he says, "I guess what happened in Alaska doesn't let go."

"Huh? Don't be silly—I smoked that psycho. Nah, I hate visitors. You're kinda cute, so I made an exception. Besides, you're gonna pay me for this story, kiddo."

He tries for a sip of lemonade and ice rattles in the empty glass.

His hand trembles. She pats his arm and takes the glass inside for a refill. Atticus follows on her heel. The journalist draws a breath to steady himself. He switches off the recorder. A ray of sun burns through the clouds and spotlights him while the rest of the world blurs into an impressionistic watercolor. A snowflake drifts down from outer space and freezes to his cheek.

She returns with a fresh glass of lemonade to find the journalist slumped in the lawn chair. Someone has placed an ancient state trooper's hat on his head and tilted it so that the man's face is partially covered. The crown of the hat is matted with dried gore that has, with the passing decades, indelibly stained the fabric. A smooth, vertical slice begins at the hollow of his throat and continues to belt level. His intestines are piled beneath his trendy hiking shoes. His ears lie upon the table. Steam rises from the corpse.

Atticus growls at the odors of shit and blood.

Jessica gazes at him in amazement. "Goddamnit, dog. *Now* you growl. Thanks a heap." She notices a wet crimson thumbprint on the recorder. She sighs and lights another cigarette and presses PLAY. Comes the static-inflected sound of wind rushing across ice, of snow shushing against tin, of arctic darkness and slow, sliding fog. Fire crackles in the background. These sounds have crept across the span of forty years.

A voice, garbled and muted by interference, whispers, "Jessica, we need to know. Why are you alive?" Snow and wind fill a long gap. Then, "Did you cut your own throat? Did you? Are you dead, Jessica? Are you dead, or are you playing? How much longer do you think you have?" Nothing but static after that, and the tape ends.

Intuition tells her that the journalist didn't file a plan with his network, that he rolled into the boondocks alone, that when he doesn't arrive at the office on Monday morning it will be a fulfillment of the same pattern he's followed countless times previously. The universe won't skip a beat. A man such as he has enemies waiting in the woodwork, ready to wrap him in a carpet and take him far away. It will be a minor unsolved mystery that his colleagues have awaited since his first jaunt into a war torn region in the Middle East.

She can't decide whether to call the cops or hide the body, roll the rental car into a ditch somewhere and torch it. *Why, yes, Officer, the young fellow was here for a while the other day. Missing? Oh, dear, that's terrible…*

"Jack?" she says to the hissing leaves. Her hand is at her neck, caressing the scar that defines her existence. "Nate? Are you out there?"

The sun sets and night is with her again.

Three years, six months, and fifteen days before Dolly Sammerdyke is eviscerated and dropped down a mineshaft, where her bones rest to this very day, she tells her brother Tom she's moving from Fairbanks to Eagle Talon. She's got an in with a woman who keeps the books at a shipping company and there's an opening for an onsite clerk. Tom doesn't like it. He lived in the village during a stretch in the 1980s when his luck was running bad.

"Listen, kid. It's a bum deal."

"Not as if I have a better option," she says.

"Bad place, sis."

"Yeah? What's bad about it? The people?"

"Bad people, sure. Bad neighborhood, bad history. Only one place to live in Eagle Talon. Six-floor apartment building. Ginormus old tenement. Dark, drafty, creepy as shit. It's a culture thing. People there are weird and clannish. You'll hate it."

"I'll call you every week."

Dolly calls Tom every week until her death. He doesn't miss her calls at first because he's landed a gig as a luthier in Nashville and his new girlfriend, an aspiring country and western musician, commands all of his attention these days.

Did the Final Girl do it? Was it this person or that? You can only laugh at the preposterousness of such conceits. You can only weep. As

the omniscient narrator of some antique fairy tale once declaimed:
Fool! Rub your eyes and look again!
*   You will never die—nothing does.*

From the journal of Nathan E. Custer as transcribed from the original
text by the Federal Bureau of Investigation, Anchorage:

I've never told anyone the whole truth about Moose Valley, or this recurring dream I've suffered in the following years. Probably not a dream; more of a vision. Nonetheless, for clarity's sake, we'll go with it being a dream. The dream has two parts. The first part is true to life, a memory of events with the tedious details edited from the narrative.

In the true to life part of the dream, Michael Allen and I are playing dominoes in the dim kitchen of my old place in Moose Valley. I'd seen him standing in the yard, a ghostly shape in the darkness, and had invited him to come out of the weather without thinking to ask why he was lurking.

It's fall of '93, around four in the morning. He's winning, he always wins at these games—pool, checkers, cards, dominoes—although everybody likes him anyway.

Allen has only been in town for a few months. An ex-Army guy, so he's capable, with an easy smile and a wry wit. Long hair, but kempt. Keeps to himself for the most part in a one-room cottage by the river. He's passionate about Golden Age comic books and the poetry of James Dickey. I was in the cottage for maybe five minutes once. Dude kept it to a minimum and neat as you please. Gun oil scent, although no guns in view. Yeah.

He pockets my last eleven dollars with a shrug and an apologetic grin. Says, Thanks for the game, and pulls on his orange sock cap and stands. I turn away to grab a beer from the icebox, hair of the dog that bit me, and the bullet passes through my skull above my ear and I'm on the floor, facedown. He squeezes the trigger again and I hear the hammer snap, a dud in the chamber. Or he hadn't reloaded from slaughtering the Haden family across the street. We'll never know.

Anyway, I'm unblinking, unresponsive, paralyzed, so he leaves me for dead. The front door slams and sunlight creeps across the tiles and makes the spreading blood shiny.

The second part of the dream is a fantasy cobbled and spliced from real events. I have a disembodied view of everything that happens next.

Allen slips down to the launch and steals a rubber raft. He lets the flow carry him downstream. He's packed sandwiches and beer, and has a small picnic. God, it's a beautiful day. The mountain peaks are white with fresh snow, but the lower elevations are yet green and gold. The air is brisk, only hinting at the bitter chill to come. A beaver circles the raft, occasionally slapping the water with its tail. The crack is like a gunshot. Allen chuckles and scans the eggshell-blue sky from behind a pair of tinted aviator glasses.

The current gradually picks up as it approaches a stretch of falls and rapids. A black dot detaches from the sun and drops toward the earth. Allen unlimbers the 30.06 bolt action rifle he's stowed under a blanket. His balance is uncertain and the first round pings harmlessly through the fuselage of the police chopper. He ejects the shell and sights again, cool as the ice on the mountains, and this will be a kill shot. The SWAT sniper is a hair quicker and Allen is knocked from the raft. He plunges into the water and sinks instantly. The raft zips over the falls and is demolished.

A sad, tragic case closes.

The fact is, Allen survives for a few minutes. He is a tough, passionless piece of work, a few cells short of Homo sapiens status, and that helps him experience a brutal and agonizing last few moments on the mortal plane. He is sucked into a vortex and wedged under and between some rocks where he eventually suffocates and drowns. This is a remote and dangerous area. The cops never recover the body.

Small fish nibble away his fingers, then his face, then the rest of it.

Once November

E. Catherine Tobler

Ghosts appear most often between October and February.

Only one woman was claimed within these months, and she at the beginning of November. She never appears in November—no one can say why—nor why those who always accompany her are pulled from their own months to join her. None, in point of fact, have appeared on the days they were taken; for this I cannot blame them—would you revisit the day you were murdered?

It is now January. It was once November.

Polly kisses what little remains of my mouth, her own soft and fragrant. In the right air, she still smells like her soap, like you've run your hand up the length of a bristling branch of rosemary and have burst enough leaves to get their oil on you. You would think she'd stink of wine or gin, but these scents are long fled. Some things vanish, some yet remain.

Elizabeth, whose gray eyes have rested long upon me, looks away. Her mouth settles into its disfigured slant. She is upset that he loved me best, that he ruined me most, that he abandoned her mid-cut and later unleashed his anger on Catherine. Catherine whom he wrote about, Catherine whom he ate. Elizabeth is forever unfinished, nearly perfect in her coat, rose and maiden hair fern still firmly pinned. Blood yet saturates the silk handkerchief 'round her neck.

The sliver of mirror is sharp in my hand as Polly offers it to me. It is still her prized possession; Elizabeth never wants to see it or herself within. Dark Annie was slow to come around but when she looked to see what he had made of her, she wept. I look into the mirror and cannot breathe—

(of course ye canna breathe, ye glock, ye are long-since in lavender, aren't ye? There is no breath to be had under this dirt)

—for all the glory his shiv has made of my face, my body. An awful sound pours from me, the mewling of some alley cat looking for something it will never find, and Polly pats my shoulder.

"Will be fine and dross," she tells me.

With her missing teeth, the words slur in her mouth. She doesn't know or care that these words are wrong. One cannot be both—but then how else can we be dead and yet alive, walking these streets without care, ever looking for the fall of his shadow, the bite of his blade?

Polly's hands remain unmarred; she slides one down the length of my hair, a tangle of colors, wet with blood. He loved me best and so does Polly, wanting to take care of me the way she can't her five chavies. Were they little, I asked her once. She could not answer, only stroked the slit he had carved in her tongue and rocked back and forth, back and forth. I lean into her hand now and she calms.

"Such a good ladybird," she whispers. "Keeper of me own name. Would that he had loved me so well."

Polly was first, but first was not best. Last was best. Elizabeth never let me forget.

Ghosts may be seen wandering the entire Chapel—they do not gravitate to the places of their deaths or their lives. I cannot blame them for this peculiarity, either, for who would want to revisit happier days to look upon the stones where their life's blood spilled? These streets have changed, the worst slums cleared away, yet lookers come even so. I came.

I wanted an experience, didn't I? I wanted to see the place she died; I wanted to see if the crack remained in the window glass.

Annie loves roses. Her gaze often lingers on the rose Elizabeth wears. It remains red, as fresh as the night he pinned it on her, the maiden hair fern like a cloud of angel wings around it. Annie has tried on occasion to claim the rose for her own, but it will not come unpinned from Elizabeth's coat no matter how she pulls. Elizabeth laughs now, but the first time, they ended in a dewskitch, Elizabeth shrieking that Annie was a roller as she smashed her fist over and over into Annie's face. It didn't leave a mark on her. We were dead. What else could be done to us?

We spend the day walking. The quartet behind me grumbles, more loudly depending on the shadowed streets we cross. We are deeply sensitive to the places we died, the places we lived. The latter is less familiar—death ever closer than life now—but we remember them even so. The four others find more comfort indoors than out whereas I take comfort under open sky—

(no ceilings, ye wee toffer—far too long have ye gazed upon such, spread wide upon your back)

The place I died is also the place I lived, if two floors down. This is what pulls me now, though never in a straight line. If the streets have changed, new vendors and shop fronts, my memory still takes the paths it knew, be it through those vendors or walls. We have no worry of such things. Stone and glass do not forestall.

The others do not want to go, but I am going and Polly insists they follow. If they don't, the ache of separation will only be worse. The knowledge that one of their own is roaming untethered is so painful as to be almost unbearable.

This is how we came together, five pieces of a whole, following a transcendent ache until we reached its end. Where did it flow and ebb—where was its pull strongest? I did not understand it until I was faced with the four of them. I follow a similar ache now, but it makes no sense—there are no others.

"Do ye feel that, then?"

It's Catherine who asks. She pulls herself past Elizabeth, Annie, and Polly, to curl around the wreck of my shoulders as I stand staring. I can almost hear the drip of her blood, can feel its warmth around my feet as it pools. We should be bled dry by now, bodies drained to husks, but no. Our blood still runs the cobbles of these streets, the tatters of our flesh.

Outside the building where I once lived stands a woman. She is Polly's age at most, time gently lining her face the way it never would mine. She is now the age of all them who had gone before—but for me. I was youngest, made prettiest for always.

Elizabeth sobs; it is a strange sound, sudden and unexpected and she tries to break free from our group, but Annie holds her firm. Elizabeth crushes herself into Annie, buries her face; the rose at Elizabeth's breast shatters fresh scent through our huddle.

Ghosts are best seen when you stand still. If you move they flicker like a lamp when the gas is turned down. Flicker, flicker, gone.

They still call this the worst street in London, and people are fools for coming. Without revolver or knife, visitors are sure to find a poor end in this alleyway. They warn of coming here. They always have, they almost always certainly will. You don't want to see the ghost of a dead girl, you don't want to hear the cries of "murder!" in the depth of night.

Oh—But you do.

'Tis only a room, let to someone else who never knew the horrors it contained.

This is the lie I tell myself as I move across the cobbled street, toward the building that has gone blue in the gloaming light—

(they know, because there's push to be made, living in the room where the young dollymop was nobbled—dismembered—oh girl, did he drink ye? They say he couldn't help himself, having tasted Catherine. How long did your heart's blood mark his mouth after he kissed

that warm flesh? No one would believe the truth—he never buried you under floorboards. The thought of concealing your beauty was intolerable.)

—toward the girl who lingers at windows. She peers inside and I do not dare. 'Tis but a deadlurk. Yet, there are walls and a ceiling yet, which define a space that beats with a heart that was once my own. My hand seeks the hollow of my chest, empty and tattered all these years, dripping scarlet to the stones. He took my breasts, my heart, and these he placed under my head as if to make a prayer of them. As if some fairy would come and collect them in the night. There were no fairies that night, nor any other.

The glass beside the door has been fixed. Still, I slip my hand through and make as if to unlatch the door as I always had—

She's humming. The girl has a song in her mouth and it's a song I know and once heard in this very doorway. *Scenes of my childhood arise before my gaze, bringing recollections of bygone happy days…*

How can she know—

Despite the closeness of the other women, these women who have raised me all these years and taught me to not be afraid of the beautiful thing he made me, I feel that familiar ache, a pull toward someplace else. A need to go even though I cannot.

"Who are ye?" I whisper.

And she hears me, for her gaze turns from the window and falls upon me. Plain as day and twice as fair. I know her eyes.

Should you see a ghost, the worst course of action is panic or flight.

Do not fear them—this is not common advice, but if you go looking for a thing, you should not show aversion if you truly find it.

Ghosts cannot harm the living—this is common advice and poorly given, because it's the worst kind of falsehood. This fragment of a woman before me did not flicker mercifully into the shadows. She had no face, nothing the living might recognize as a body, he had mutilated her so. She was forever the wreck he made of her, her chemise ever torn and bloodied.

Her chest is hollowed, as empty as a nest in winter but for the blood that trickles from her. It is this which makes me cry, stumble, flee.

Nose and fingerprints smear the window glass. I can see the ghosts of lookers lined up, some only children, pressing up on their toes to see the room.

"Come away with me."

He never spoke those words to Elizabeth, though Elizabeth swears over and over he did, oh he did bid her come away. She knew him best, she whispers, and twirls in her black coat. The scent of her rose spreads but cannot completely obliterate the damp stench of the street. She refuses to look at any of us, spinning until the world blurs. This fantasy is better than the reality of the woman who runs.

"Come away with me… come, come."

He wasn't so tall, the cove. I invited him inside and latched the door behind as best I could. The room was still finer than I could afford, and I wanted a fine room for him. He wanted to take time in his pleasure, he said. Would make it worth my while and the rent was needed. He seemed eager; I remember the way he surveyed the room, the way he seemed pleased with its walls, its privacy. Often such a thing was done in alleys, with haste.

The collar of his ebon overcoat was velvet—

(watch for the blade he carries up his sleeve, you gulpy haybag—ye always lose yerself in the collar, that fucking collar)

—and it still feels like a whisper between my thumb and forefinger. I couldn't stop touching it once I'd drawn the overcoat from his shoulders.

When he cut me—

(when he killed ye)

—I would remember the feel of the velvet,

—and when they all turn their dead eyes on me,

—and when Polly reaches a shaking hand for me—

There is only the feel of the ebon velvet.

"Keeper of me own name," Polly whispers. Her arm encircles the ruin of my waist and there is no longer rosemary, but the stench of rot that rises from her. She lifts a hand to my face and does not touch me. "Who are ye, then?"

She asks the same question I asked of the woman at the door, and while I know the answer to these riddles, Polly does not. Can not.

Should you flee a ghost, they will not follow. This is another falsehood, made to comfort the children we once were.

'Tis but a deadlurk, child, an empty room without so much as a shadow. No ghost may hide here.

As adults, we know that ghosts can never be escaped. They may stand in brightest daylight and look you dead in the eye. I crossed an ocean and still this one drew me back, to look upon that room, to admit what had been done. It was a simple thing—no one could have known or should be blamed.

Everyone says these words, but in this case, they are true: it should have been me. This ghost should have been me.

They wrench me through the bloodied streets, careless of where we go. Their hands are as merciless as his own were, but they leave no mark. They strike me, pull my hair, push me down into the sodden trash.

It is Polly who cries most, she who loves me best. Elizabeth only says that she knew I was ever amiss, could not be who I was. Catherine holds me after and Annie presses her hands around mine. They are cold against my feverish skin. A ghost should not feel this warm—'tis only a deadlurk.

Ye blower.

You Judy.

Ye filth.

Only the feel of the ebony velvet.

Softly, Catherine's voice.

"Does it matter her name? He had her, no mistake."

Polly and Elizabeth shriek and flee down the alley. Their distance makes we three cringe. Five pieces of a whole. Did it matter, my name? To them, it did. Catherine kisses my sunken forehead, and I close my eyes (though I cannot, ever, ever), and I think I have for so very long been someone I am not—

It did not matter to him; he had no personal claim on any of us. We were but whores, flesh for cutting. He held each of us close only to draw his shiv across our throats—Elizabeth says he danced her, slid a warm hand 'round her waist and rocked her as if there were a band playing—but he cared not who we were, who we might yet be.

And Mary? Oh Mary, what you must have thought.

Returning to the place you saw a ghost may often disappoint; sometimes they linger, sometimes they are well and truly fled, never to be seen again. In the end, one must acknowledge that the behavior of ghosts is less predictable than that of swallows in their movements against spring skies.

Should you return—

Of course I return. That alley and those windows draw me as if on a tether. I press my nose to the glass and peer in, much like the morning after. The morning I returned home and found her in bloody tatters. My room was a ruin and she—

And she—

She asked to use my room, for it was far more fair than her own. My rent was overdue and she said she had a toff cove, someone who wanted a quiet place. A place he might take a drink—

—from her heart.

A place he might undress her slow—

—with the length of his blade.

Of course I return—these rooms were my own—and so too does she.

It should have been her. They all say it, until it transforms to a litany. The words have a presence and weight, a heat that coils like blood. The words carry me back to the alley, only Catherine at my side. The others would rather endure the pain of our parting than come with me, me who they thought they knew.

It doesn't matter who I am, Catherine whispers—like him, she says it doesn't matter, because we are all the same, nameless, possessing nothing so distinctive to set us apart. One whore is like another, isn't it so? We all spread open so easily, our bodies coming apart in the same fashion under his shiv. This curve is like that curve, this flesh bleeds as that does. No matter that we dreamed, that we birthed children who yet roam this world, that we ached to learn what we never would (why *are* skies so blue in the autumn?). It did not matter who occupied the room. But it does matter, Elizabeth says, and stares at me as if she can dismember me all over again.

Catherine pulls me down streets and smells like lilies and daisies that have soaked in the rot of the streets we move through. That scent is enough to choke me, though I've no throat, no nose. This body yet remembers, though, and there is a small and distant sob the closer we come to the room.

Catherine releases me when we near and I drift, letting myself become untethered for once. Mary Kelly lingers in the shadowed doorway and her eyes find mine as soon as I reach for the gutter spout. I cannot feel the metal under my hand, my thumb yet bleeds.

"Who are ye?" I ask even though I know.

Her chin lifts—oh she is scared, because we both know why she's come at all, and it—It—

"It should hae been me."

Her voice breaks on that word—have. I move through the window glass, into the room which is cold as a grave. Here, my tattered skin rolls with a shudder and the blood flows more certainly than ever to flood the floor. I will flood this room if we stay overlong. *'Tis but a deadlurk, child—*

The door latch has been repaired, but for me it moves as if still broken, the door creaking inward so that I may look upon Mary

Kelly again. She stares and I wonder what she sees. Does she see me as I was that morning? Shuttering images fill this empty room: the blood, the ruin, the neatly folded clothes upon the chair. Barnett cried—oh he cried over the loss of you, Mary. How far away were you then?

She kicks off her shoes, steps over the threshold, into my pooling blood.

Ghosts cannot harm the living—they will tell you this over and over as they smooth the hair from your feverish head, and they will be wrong.

This room is ever as it was; my feet don't trod upon the bare floor, but sink rather into the blood of that morning. They thought she was me—they all did. Maybe it did not matter—did Barnett pay the rent or were such trivial concerns forgot in the wake of the blood?

I reach a hand for the figure of the girl—the girl who is ever twenty and five, flayed open and bleeding still. I have grown to forty-three and miss the girl I was. The girl I should have been. She is cold, as cold as this room in the winter—it is now January—and she latches the door behind me.

There were clothes upon a chair. Though there is no chair now, I fold my clothes into a neat pile, every corner just so. They will think it a dare, someone at play. They will never understand the absolution.

I have brought a blade with me—her eyes widen. How like his? Blood cascades out of her in a sob. The bite against my throat—

It was once November.

Silver Kisses

(for Mary Jane Kelly, Whitechapel 1888)

Ann K. Schwader

To know his best-beloved one completely
Must be each lover's prayer; yet how absurd
That I must woo by night, & most discreetly
For taking such fond wishes at their word.
No scarlet sorrow of my lady's heart,
No mystery murmured vital in the vein
Escapes my longing as a charm apart—
So jealousy must judge such love insane.
Four fairest friends before thee, sweet street sparrow,
Have called my keen attentions all their own
For too brief moments… thus my hungering
Which ever sharper grows until its sting
Wins through at last to know thee to the bone,
Thy crimson whispers, & thy very marrow.

Thank You!

The following people helped to make the book you hold in your hands possible. I owe them a colossal debt of thanks.

Jill Frost Henderson
James and Virginia Lockhart
Jennifer Lockhart
Marty Halpern
Claudia Noble
Arnaud de Vallois
Mike Roth
Rand Burgess
Andrew S. Fuller
Michael Lee
Jubela, Jubelo, & Jubelum
The Bizarro Family
Ripperologists everywhere
The Authors
...and most of all, you, the reader.

Copyright Acknowledgments

ROSS E. LOCKHART is an author, anthologist, and freelance editor, as well as the Publisher/Editor in Chief of Word Horde, a genre publishing company launched in 2013. A lifelong fan of supernatural, fantastic, speculative, and weird fiction, Lockhart holds degrees in English from Sonoma State University (BA) and SFSU (MA). He is a veteran of small-press publishing, having edited scores of well-regarded novels of horror, fantasy, and science fiction.

In 2011, Lockhart edited the acclaimed Lovecraftian anthology *The Book of Cthulhu*. In 2012, a follow-up, *The Book of Cthulhu II,* was published by Night Shade Books, and his rock-and-roll novel, *Chick Bassist*, was published by Lazy Fascist Press. Lockhart lives in an old church in Petaluma, California, with his wife Jennifer, hundreds of books, and Elinor Phantom, a Shih Tzu moonlighting as his editorial assistant.

Find Ross online at http://www.haresrocklots.com.

Lightning Source UK Ltd.
Milton Keynes UK
UKOW02f2158200716

278883UK00004B/240/P